I0583776

DIM GLOWS THE HORIZON

DIM GLOWS THE HORIZON

WAR OF THE DAMNED™ BOOK FOUR

MICHAEL TODD   MICHAEL ANDERLE
LAURIE STARKEY

DISRUPTIVE IMAGINATION

Dim Glows The Horizon (this book) is a work of fiction.
All of the characters, organizations, and events portrayed in this novel
are either products of the author's imagination or are used fictitiously.
Sometimes both.

Copyright © 2021 Michael Todd, Michael Anderle, and Laurie Starkey
Cover by Ryn Katryn Digital Art
Cover copyright © LMBPN Publishing

LMBPN Publishing supports the right to free expression and the value of
copyright. The purpose of copyright is to encourage writers and artists
to produce the creative works that enrich our culture.

The distribution of this book without permission is a theft of the
author's intellectual property. If you would like permission to use
material from the book (other than for review purposes), please contact
support@lmbpn.com. Thank you for your support of the author's rights.

LMBPN Publishing
PMB 196, 2540 South Maryland Pkwy
Las Vegas, NV 89109

First US edition, August 2018
Version 1.01, December 2020

DIM GLOWS THE HORIZON TEAM

Beta Readers

Dorothy Lloyd
Tom Dickerson
Dorene Johnson
Diane Velasquez
Timothy Cox
Sarah Weir

JIT Readers

Tim Bischoff
Mary Morris
James Caplan
John Ashmore
Peter Manis
Daniel Weigert
Micky Cocker

If we missed anyone, please let us know!

Weapons Consultant
John Kern
Proprietor
Spurlock's - Henderson NV

Editor
Lynne Stiegler

DEDICATION

*To Family, Friends and
Those Who Love
to Read.
May We All Enjoy Grace
to Live the Life We Are
Called.*

M oloch took a sip from the ornate chalice and
grimaced at the unexpected texture. He ran the tip
of his claw over the top of the liquid within to remove the
offending strand of hair, then snapped his fingers to
summon the servant.

"Send this back to the kitchen, and tell them if they
don't strain the hair out of the next one, they won't live
long enough to regret being lax a third time."

"Of course, Master." The bound soul shook as he
bowed, causing his chains to rattle.

Moloch rolled his eyes at Baal. "I swear, finding good
help even in a sea of souls is like finding fried rabbit on
Easter."

Baal looked at Moloch quizzically.

"Everyone is always sold out, thanks to the humans and
their ridiculous whims. Why they choose to make our food
their pets, I don't know."

Baal groaned. "I heard some of them keep chickens as
pets. They don't eat them."

Moloch shrugged. "Personally, I was never fond of the feathers. They always get stuck in my teeth. I did love chasing them when I was just a spawn. It was a very good time, and Lucifer always laughed at the game when he passed."

"I forgot your father worked for Lucifer before you. It feels as if you have been with us forever."

Moloch chuckled. "Centuries pass, and we don't notice. When I came of age, I just sent my father to the deep recesses and locked him away. It was his time."

Baal laughed. "Is that why you haven't claimed any of your snot-nosed bastards as your own? Don't want to take your place next to your father when the time comes?"

Moloch inclined his head with a wry smile. "That...and I just hate children. I would end up eating any I claimed before it had a chance to grow up."

Baal raised his chalice to Moloch. "Eat them while they're young. That way they're at least a *little* tender."

The demons laughed loudly, spilling blood on the already red tablecloth as they tapped their chalices together. Moloch put his down, his humor fading in an instant.

Baal swallowed hard.

Moloch sat straight and steepled his claws on the table in front of him. "Baal, I asked you to take care of Lilith and her meatsack, but yet again she has thwarted my plans. You are dear to me, which is why I have not summoned you until I could be certain of keeping my cool. However, it is time to answer for your failures in France."

Baal held his head in his claws. "I know I failed," he admitted. "My apologies, Moloch. Things didn't quite go as I had planned. The IRS was supposed to have detained Katie before she got wind of the incursion, but they failed to cover their tracks. My contact had her served but didn't change the file to reflect why. One quick search by one of her minions and the general was all over them like flies on shit. The IRS never even had a chance to get close to her."

Moloch pursed his lips. "And Mexico?"

"They didn't even have to fight." Baal scoffed. "It was pathetic."

"What? I thought that the drug lord was a sure thing. He'd had that demon in him for close to a decade!"

"Yes, well, he apparently liked to relax as well. They snuck right through the grounds and into his house and yanked the demon right out of him. They didn't even kill anyone."

Moloch slammed his hand on the table and shook his head. "You didn't heed my warning about her, Baal."

"You are right. I have to admit, I underestimated the human...and Lilith. She is much more powerful than I imagined. I wasn't prepared for her. I honestly figured the other two demons would be better than her."

"Well, it's done with now," Moloch growled. "We will have to come up with some new angle. Something creative, since our simpler efforts have failed."

"I agree," Baal replied as the servant set down a bowl of fried hairy gerbils and chocolate-covered human heads.

Moloch reached over and grabbed a human head by a small tuft of hair sticking through the chocolate. He popped it in his mouth and crunched down, then wiped the blood and chocolate from the corner of his mouth. Baal hovered over the bowl for a moment before he selected a gerbil and bit down a little halfheartedly.

Moloch raised an eyebrow. "You aren't eating like you usually do."

Baal shrugged and rubbed his slightly diminished stomach with his free hand. "All the stress is getting to me."

"Understandable," Moloch replied.

"Oh, I did hear some encouraging news from above."

"Oh, yes? Do tell."

"When what the humans call Incursion Day hit, those loyal to the cause went into hiding. Most of the demons that spawned were from you and the portals. However, there has been a rise in random demon spawning on Earth. In fact, it has gone up about fifty percent since the dip."

"Yesss," Moloch hissed and rubbed his hands together. "That means the infected are starting to come out of the woodwork. I thought it would take some time. I didn't assume it would happen so soon after the failure in France."

"The cities are crawling again, and we are getting numerous requests for larger, more powerful demons. The infected are getting a little wild with their ideas." Baal grinned, thinking of the chaos that granting some of those requests was going to cause.

Moloch chuckled darkly. "That's good. *Very* good. They will begin wreaking havoc on Earth—stealing, murdering, and fighting for the cause like our own little group of rebels. I like it. The more we have, the better, and those with a little more human sense are ten times more useful than the idiot demons we send in during wars." He tapped his claws on the table as he turned over the possibilities presented by the new information. "We need to up that number. Get those requests filled as fast as possible. We need the distraction as much for Lilith as the human armies. I want them to be too absorbed with the chaos among their people to pay attention as we continue to create a new plan of attack."

Baal smiled and grabbed a handful of gerbils, popping them in his mouth. "And look at that...my appetite is suddenly back."

Moloch grinned. "Mine too, Baal. My appetite for *blood*."

Katie smoothed her hair back into a ponytail and removed a smudge of eyeliner under her right eye. She pulled her tight black t-shirt down and looked at herself in the mirror. She figured she looked good enough to go get her next assignment. After all, it was her work that spoke for her. The outfit was just window dressing. She went to her closet and pushed the built-in drawer with her French lace bras closed.

Pandora sighed. *That drawer is far too empty.*

I know, I know. I've had other things on my mind, is all. Besides, half of what we have is at the cleaners. I'm just trying to get caught up on everything now that I'm back in New York.

Well, taking on more side jobs isn't going to help you find that time.

Katie rolled her eyes. *We've talked about this. We need untraceable money. I'm tired of the government watching my every move. We'll use the money in the accounts they're monitoring for the everyday purchases.*

Like condos and furniture? Pandora snarked.

Exactly like that, though I think everything here is about complete.

Too bad. I liked having hot men bring furniture in on a regular basis. Reminded me of when I was in Rome during the heyday. Caesar had hot men attend me with large fans and hand-feed me with peeled grapes during my visits. She sighed wistfully. *Don't even get me started about the time I was there for Bacchanalia...*

I'm not even going to ask.

To be honest, I see that a lot of the less-attractive Roman attitudes made it through to modern times. People have a hard time stepping back and looking at history. Civilizations rise and fall, and there have been no exceptions so far.

Hopefully, we will be sitting on a beach in the tropics sipping Mai Tais when that happens.

Preach it, sister.

Katie smiled, slipped a weapon into the holster on her hip, and pulled her lightweight jacket on. She headed out of the condo and grabbed a cab to take her over to speak to Mason about her next assignment.

When she arrived, his men walked her back to his office and nodded as they closed the door behind them.

The bookie stood up behind his desk and held out a hand for her to shake. "Katie, it's good to see you back."

She shook the outstretched hand and took the seat he indicated. "Thank you, it's good to be back. So, what do you have for me?"

Mason made a face and shook his head. "Unfortunately,

finding you a gig has been more than a little challenging since you went public with your wings. The mobs and such don't want to touch you, and our infected clients want nothing to do with you after the stunt you pulled on the last job."

Katie rolled her eyes. "Of course, that would have gotten out."

Mason shrugged, his face making it clear that he'd warned her about the consequences of not following instructions. "However, I do know there is a consignment of high-value goods being moved between New York and Washington, DC. There are no ethical issues connected to this one, so your wings will not be a problem."

Katie nodded. She had started to think she should lean toward gigs that didn't make her skin crawl, anyway. Besides, she had a public presence now, and a duty to live up to the image of hope she presented to the world. Or some shit like that.

Either way, she wasn't going to take the shadier jobs.

Good grief, get off *of it,* Pandora grumbled.

What? I told you that things would be different, and this is a good change.

Whatever. You are harshing my sugar buzz with all this bull-shit over ethics. Just do the jobs and take the money.

How about you leave the logistics to me?

Fine, fine, but don't come crying to me when all you get are jobs babysitting preschoolers.

"So, what would my role be?" Katie asked the bookie.

"Simple stuff. You would join the existing security team. You will be their go-to if anything happens. You make sure the load gets from New York to DC without any problems. Once the valuables are secured in the vault, you get paid and come home."

Katie nodded. "That seems simple enough."

"Yes, and paid very well, though I have to warn you that these valuables aren't just Grandma's china. They are historical artifacts, paintings, sculptures; things people would be interested in stealing and selling to make a pretty penny. You are probably looking at human thieves rather than your normal demon foes."

"I wouldn't say that too soon." Katie chuckled. "You would be surprised how many major criminals throughout history were demon-powered."

Mason's eyes widened when the sense of Katie's revelation sank in. "Well, let's just hope you don't have to deal with any of them on this job."

Katie lifted an unconcerned shoulder. "It would just be a standard day for me if I did. When is this happening?"

"The transport will leave tonight, so you have a few hours to take care of anything personal. The file in front of you has the address and information to memorize as usual. The details are in there as well. Report in, report out, and we will be all set."

"That is perfect," Katie replied. "I'll make sure to let my contacts know I will be out of touch for a while."

She stood up and shook the bookie's hand, then grabbed the file and opened it. She read through the details and repeated the address aloud for Pandora to remember, then shut the file and slid it over to him, nodding before walking from the room.

It was about time she had an easy job. She was starting to think she would never have something simple to take care of. She loved action, but after France, she wouldn't mind a simple open-and-shut gig.

I know a simple open-and-shut gig you could have...

Katie groaned internally. *Not now, Pandora.*

"You would think that after all this preparation the others would at least *attempt* to be on time," a short man wearing long black robes grumbled.

"They are kidnapping someone. I'd rather they be thorough than lead the cops back here."

Just then the door flew open and six people in similar black robes, their hoods over their heads, walked in, carrying a bound and gagged man. The guy was terrified, and blood was coming from his nose. His eyes were wide with fear. They set him down in the middle of a chalk circle in the center of the room, which was ringed by arcane symbols and surrounded by dozens of wildly-flickering candles. The wax dripped and created a puddle on the floor, but the abandoned apartment complex was dank enough for no one to ever notice.

"It would have been so much easier to knock him out," a woman complained. "He was a fucking fighter."

The leader dismissed her complaints. "The first rule of summoning is that the vessel has to be awake. I haven't spent my whole adult life preparing to summon this demon only for us to screw this up because the sacrifice was unconscious. Now, circle around the altar. We need to get this going."

Everyone joined hands around the altar. The leader

walked around the outside, holding a small dagger aloft as he chanted. He reached the end of the incantation and sliced his palm. He allowed the blood to pool and smeared a little of it on each acolyte's lips as he passed.

The acolytes swayed, losing themselves to the rhythm of their chant as the leader intoned the Latin incantation.

"Lucifer *invocaverimus te.* Moloch *invocaverimus te. Tui pessimi mitte nos, mitte nos in* Judas Maccabeus, *et Dominus faciet in nomine eius heros.*"

Thunder echoed outside and the walls shook, sending plumes of dust down over them. They continued to chant, their eyes closed and the blood on their mouths. The leader put both hands in the air and rolled his head on his neck.

"*Principum mortuorum patrocinium nobis miseris. Ut faciam super te vocamus in tremore vestram demonly operis hic in terris.*"

Thunder clapped again, and the altar in front of them was replaced by a swirling black portal. The acolytes' hoods were blown back from by hot wind that emerged from the opening. Many opened their eyes, reveling in the spiritual ritual they had been preparing for since Incursion Day.

The leader took a step back, and the others opened their circle wider as a large insubstantial demon hand grasped the edge of the portal. They heard heavy breathing as it lifted its head out, then pulled itself from the portal. It growled and snarled, weak from being on Earth without a vessel. It wasn't ready to fulfill its purpose yet. It needed to incubate inside the human long enough to gather its strength.

The group dropped their hands and moved back, giving the demon room. It looked at the man, who was whimpering and struggling on the floor. A dark grin moved over the huge demon's lips as it headed toward the sacrifice, cracking the floor beneath it with its mass.

The man on the floor struggled wildly against his bonds. When he saw the demon, his mouth opened in a silent scream and he worked his legs frantically to push himself away until his back hit the wall.

The demon roared and twisted its body, diving through the chest of the human.

The leader ran over, pulling a syringe from the pocket of his robes before the demon took hold completely. He pushed the needle into the vessel's neck and administered the drugs. Almost instantly, the man fell unconscious and slumped to his side. The leader tossed the syringe to the floor. "That should hold the demon until we are ready for him to emerge."

"Why not let the demon feed off the man's waking fears?"

"The demon is strong; stronger than any of ours. The damn thing will burst out of that human as soon as it smells a tasty treat. We want to make sure it's the right time and place for that to happen. We don't want to become collateral damage. The whole point of this is to have the demon take care of the ones we need gone. We are strong, but not strong enough to handle so many men while we're in a moving vehicle. Besides, this demon will make headlines and garner even more fear of the demon crisis. We'll kill two birds with one stone."

The woman inclined her head. "Understood."

"Now, go get the van ready." He handed her a small wallet. "Here is a supply of the drug that will keep the demon sedated. It is to be administered every two hours until we are ready to release him. Make sure you don't screw this up. It cannot be fixed once the demon has been released."

She pocketed the wallet. "Then what?"

"Then we wait until we are given the call to move out."

The others nodded in understanding and moved to complete the task at hand. Several of the stronger men lifted the human and carried him to the underground parking area. The truck was parked and ready. They threw the guy into the back of the van and strapped him in, wrapping cuffs around his arms and ankles. They knew that if the demon awoke they could not hold him for long, but they were the best they had.

"Remember—every two hours," one of the guys told the other inside the van.

He nodded. "I got it."

They shut the van doors and tapped the back. The driver took the van to a spot in the shadows, just in case anyone wandered into the parking garage unexpectedly. The man laid inside the van, his breathing shallow from the effect of the drugs on his respiratory system. The human who kept watch inside was not infected, but she had no fear. She wore a pentagram dangling from a rope over her robes and held tightly to a syringe, ready if the man were to unexpectedly stir.

They had planned for months, and she wouldn't be the one to fail.

2

Katie strutted into the police station. She nodded at the cop at the front as she passed him and pulled open the door to the back. It was especially loud in the bullpen that day, with the usual contingent of red-eyed infected handcuffed to the benches to be processed. The cops had really stepped up their game recently. They no longer relied on Katie for every single arrest. That was the whole point of her being there—to teach them how to handle the demon infestation. She wasn't the least bit worried about running out of work.

There were plenty of demons to go around.

Detective Schultz was standing over one of the desks and Travers was on the phone in his office. Katie milled about, waiting for one of them to be free. The precinct was so used to her being there by that point that no one paid her much notice, which of course pricked Pandora's vanity no end. Katie liked it. She felt like she was part of something, something she'd lacked since Calvin went on vacation.

After about five minutes Schultz looked up and nodded at Katie. He finished what he was doing and waved for her to follow him into Travers' office.

She shut the door behind her as Travers hung up the phone. "You would think we were the only precinct in the city. I can't get a minute to myself with these phone calls about demons."

Katie snickered. "Yeah, I see you guys have stepped up your game. Before you know it there won't be any left, and you'll be back to boredom and donuts."

Cops eat donuts?

They aren't aliens, Pandora. And yes, they eat donuts, it's kind of a running joke.

Oh, hell no, that has to end. Donuts are for the Queen of the Damned, not the fucking Thin Blue Line.

I don't really think you are going to be able to take that one on and win. Just think of it as a positive thing. You have a connection over fried dough.

Pandora scoffed and grumbled quietly, but Katie went back to her conversation. Travers chuckled and patted a huge stack of papers on his desk.

"I don't think it's quite as heroic as you believe. We have been forced to up our game. I don't know; it's like they are all congregating out here. Either New York is some sort of demon magnet, or more are coming out of the fiery woodwork."

Katie frowned. "Connected to the bigger demons?"

Travers shook his head. "Actually, no, or at least not that we can tell. What we're coming up against out there mostly are the cults of infected demon worshippers.

They're summoning demons and infecting innocent people. None of the incidents appear to be connected."

A shiver went down Katie's spine at the memory of her own cult experience. Schultz noticed her discomfort but didn't say a word.

"So," Travers pressed, "what can I do for you?"

Katie dragged herself back from the past. "Oh, I wanted to let you know I'll be out of town on one of my other assignments. Should be gone for about a day, but no more than that."

"A day? I thought those things were quick and done."

"Normally they are, but since I made headlines, I'm limited to a certain type of gig. It would usually only take about four hours, but because of the security on this one it's estimated to take about twelve hours on the outside and then I'll hitch a ride back on a train."

"A train? Why not a plane? Don't you have your own?" Schultz asked.

Katie shook her head. "I can't fly commercial because I make everyone nervous, and I don't want to use my company jet for this. It's not a demon issue that I know of."

"I know I shouldn't ask, but..."

Katie smiled and shrugged. "Nothing too crazy, and nothing illegal—that I know of. I'm acting as security for a truckload of historical artifacts and some rare documents being transported by some old really rich family. They have been passed down for generations. Apparently, they are not only business people, but also adventurous types. The file said they have collected these artifacts and papers from all around the world, and don't ever sell them or loan them to museums."

"What do they do with all of them?" Schultz asked.

"Play Scrooge McDuck, probably." Travers laughed. "Keep them all locked up in some vault where they go in to revel in their richness. I know these types. They'll throw a richest-family-in-the-world party and put them out on display. They'll say it's for charity, but it's really so they can get their ego massaged by showing off all their cool stuff."

"Ohhhh." Schultz nodded. "I went to one of those parties once—some family raising money for the commissioner when he was running for office. I rented my tux, and I am pretty sure I was the only one who didn't have a whole closet full of tuxes at my disposal. I didn't pay—the ticket was given to me—but if I had, it was ten thousand dollars a plate."

"Holy crap, I didn't spend ten grand on a car last year."

Katie just sat there chuckling as they talked back and forth. They always had this way of getting completely off topic, but she just let them do it. It was the best thing for her to do, and it was amusing.

"What kind of car did you buy, a tractor?"

"No, I bought my sixteen-year-old daughter a used car so when she backs into a light pole or hits the curb and scrapes the sides she isn't doing it to something that will cost me a ton of money to fix. She, of course, wanted one of those new Teslas, and although thirty grand isn't bad for a brand-new car these days, I can't work on an all-electric car. Hell, I can't even get my Facebook to stop converting to pirate mode."

"You have Facebook?"

"Yeah, but moving on…Katie, where were we?"

Katie smirked. "The job I have to do."

Travers nodded. "Oh yeah, rich family, lots of expensive stuff. So, were you just lucky to get the job or did they think there is some reason to be concerned about demons?"

"Well, there are demons out there, and because some of their historical pieces are from religious sources, they want to be careful. There are certain documents they didn't want to talk too much about. They have information about hunting demons or something along those lines. They don't know if they are accurate, but they are being transferred to DC for research. The family figured it was better to be safe than sorry."

Schultz rolled his eyes and threw up his hands in exasperation. "Uh, yeah. What took them so long? Incursion Day was months ago. Then France, not to mention all the smaller but just as destructive incursions since then. I mean, come *on*, people."

Katie shrugged. "I have no idea. To be honest, there might not be anything to what they found. At the same time, it might be the opposite of what you are thinking. It could be documents that would help the *demons*, not us."

Travers' expression was thoughtful. "Still, if there were documents out there that could hurt us, they should have been turned over immediately. But that's the problem with these super-richies—they cling onto their stuff like they can take it with them when they die. They would be real upset if those documents fell into the wrong hands and they ended up on the wrong side of history."

Schultz nodded in agreement.

Katie shrugged. "Well, let's just hope that doesn't

happen. I'm crossing my fingers for an easy-peasy night. Drop this stuff off and come home with nary a scratch."

Katie stood up and shook their hands, and Schultz walked her out to the front. She could tell she'd struck a nerve with him. She could only assume it had something to do with the pictures of his wife and college-age kids he kept on his desk. If Katie hadn't been infected, she could easily have been right beside his daughter in college.

"Take care of yourself tonight," Schultz told her as he opened the door to the lobby for her.

"You know I will." Katie smiled. "And you do the same."

Schultz nodded, and Katie waved at the cop at the desk and walked out of the building. She looked up at the hotel across the street and smiled. That was where it had all started—her new life in New York. It was still crazy to her how quickly things had changed. She'd come a long way from being just a simple mercenary. The transition from that to running what was left of the team, owning an empire, and starting fresh in life had passed too rapidly for her to even take in. Oh, and then there was the whole thing with angels and wings, but that was a completely different matter.

"Are we close?" one of the infected asked.

"We should be. They are scheduled to be driving this stretch of highway in about ten minutes," the leader of the cult replied. He glanced in his rearview mirror. "And at this time of night, there won't be a ton of cars on the road."

The first speaker laughed. "When did you start caring about the safety of others?"

The leader chuckled. "I don't. I just want to make sure that we get in and out with those documents. The more people there are, the more likely we are to have issues. You never know who could try to play Joe Save-a-Lot and start blasting at us with those damn demon-killer bullets. If it's all the same to you, I'd like to get out of here without any bullet holes in me, and I'm damn sure my demon feels the same."

"I second that," the guy in the back replied, holding a syringe ready just in case the drugs wore off too soon.

They had put the newly infected in the back seat of the car. He was shaking but out cold from the drugs they had given him. The woman who had been administering the sedative had two needles, one in case the guy woke too soon, and the other a drug that would counteract the sedative; something to give him right before the job had to be completed.

"How you doing back there?" the leader asked.

"So far so good, but I'll be glad to get this beast out of the car—I am not going to lie. I don't want to be the first thing it sees when it wakes up, and I *definitely* don't want to be a snack."

"You'll be fine. It should be any time now. Before you know it, we will have those artifacts, and we can get to work building an even larger gate to hell. They thought Incursion Day and France were huge, wait until they see the entirety of hell coming toward the city! Even those damn mercenaries won't be able to stop hundreds of thousands of these bad boys." He grinned. "And *we* will be at the back of it all, waiting for our well-deserved reward. They will see that we are worthy of running with the big dogs."

"I wonder if they even know we are planning this?" The woman sighed.

"Doesn't matter if they know. All that matters is that they know who was behind it all when the gates open."

"Very true," she replied, letting out a deep breath. "I can't even imagine what it will be like to bow to Him. Seriously, after all these years..."

"Don't count your chickens just yet. We have to get those artifacts first," the leader replied. He narrowed his eyes and looked at the approaching headlights. "Give me the binoculars."

He put them up to his face, easing off the gas. Up ahead he could see a truck and two blacked out SUVs, one in front and one in the back. He dropped the binoculars and smiled. "There they are."

He pushed the accelerator to the floor, going as fast as he could to get as close as possible. The guy in the back started to groan, and the cult member with the syringes jumped back against the window.

"Uh, he's waking up."

"Don't give him that sedative. They are right there."

The car sped forward a few moments longer, and then the leader slammed on the brakes; veering over to the side of the road, but still moving forward. "Okay, give him the counteragent and push him out."

The cult member stabbed the guy in the neck with the blue syringe as the woman turned around in the front and threw open the back passenger door. They grabbed the guy by his shoulders and threw him from the moving car, watching as he rolled into the road. The leader drove another hundred feet or so and spun the car around, stopping on the side of the road. They watched as the guy started to twitch and pull at the cuffs around his hands and ankles.

"Come on, come onnn, wakey wakey," the leader whispered, clutching the steering wheel.

Suddenly the guy's eyes opened wide, his pupils burning red. He arched his back and screamed as his body blew apart. Pieces of him shot in all directions, and a chunk hit the windshield of the car with a wet slap. The leader turned on the wipers and smeared the pieces of flesh and blood away, staring in awe at the giant demon who unfurled, stretching to his full height. They leaned forward to look out the top of the windshield, amazed by how strong and large the beast had gotten in a matter of hours.

The demon rolled his head from side-to-side, then stretched his arms wide. The beast's muscles bulged, and he clamped his fists shut and snarled. Hot saliva soaked the ground as he stomped forward, leaving a large indentation in the pavement with every step.

His eyes shifted in all directions, landing on the carload of cult members. They froze, feeling their oncoming death until the demon was distracted by an oncoming car. The beast roared loudly and swiped at the car.

The cultists continued to watch with wide eyes as the car somersaulted a couple of times before landing on its side. The demon stomped over and ripped the roof of the car off. It stuck a clawed hand in and fished out the driver, tossing him into his mouth.

The woman breathed her relief. "Well, at least we weren't a snack."

"Yet," the guy in the back replied.

"He knows what his job is," the leader replied calmly. "He will find them. Just give him one moment."

"And if he finds us first?"

"Then we watch from hell."

Katie rubbed her face and pressed the button to roll down the window. She let the cool night air brush her face, hoping it would wake her up. She was tired—too tired to be on a job—and Pandora wasn't any help at all.

You're the one who left without dinner. I am just conserving our energy in case anything... Wait, what's that?

What's what?

That surge of energy?

Probably indigestion from all the donuts you made me eat this morning.

No, no, I already processed them.

You are just paranoid.

The SUV began to slow down, and Katie looked out of the window. There was a mess; what looked to be some sort of accident. She squinted at the car, which was not only missing the roof but was also on fire. She put her hand to her chest and rubbed it, feeling that all-too-familiar sensation.

Told you.

The driver slammed on his brakes to avoid the disaster

ahead. The lights over the highway flickered, and Katie tilted her head to the side.

Standing in the center of the road was a huge-ass black-scaled demon, which looked to be finishing up the last few bites of a human body. His eyes glowed bright red, and his lips curled in pleasure as he swallowed the last bit. A tennis shoe fell to the ground, the victim's foot still inside.

Katie sighed and rolled her eyes. She knew that this was why she got paid the big bucks, but *damn*! She had really thought she was going to make it through the night without having to deal with any demons. She probably should have known better. At least then she wouldn't be disappointed.

Are you fucking serious? All I want to do is get to DC, hit up a donut shop, and get back home. But noooo, this fucking nutsack is going to try to stop me from doing that. Seriously, I can't believe your fucking luck! You are the world's unluckiest fucking human-angel-demon-infected hybrid bitch ever.

You need to put up or shut up. Either way, stop fucking complaining. What the hell did you think would happen after years now of hunting demons together?

Oh, I don't know, a fucking night off, maybe? Even Lucifer doesn't work his staff this hard. They get at least one day to bask in the lava pits of fucking hell.

I can send you back if that's what you want.

Calm down, sister. Even you can't exorcise yourself.

Yet...

What the hell does that mean?

"Looks like we got company," the voice on Katie's walkie shouted. "Katie, you want to take this, and we'll back you up?"

Katie rolled her eyes. "By all means. That's what I'm here for, right?"

"10-4. We got your flanks."

"Just hold tight." She sighed. "Let me have a go at this asshole first."

You ready?

Aren't I always?

3

K atie reached over and turned the volume up on the SUV's radio, blasting out a rock song by none other than her hot admirer Brock. She drew Harry to make sure she was fully locked and totally loaded. The driver of the SUV lifted an eyebrow and looked at the gun with wide eyes.

"What?" Katie raised an eyebrow. "Overkill?"

He smiled and winked. "Whatever it takes."

"My sentiments exactly." Katie smirked and opened the door.

Pandora's heeled boot hit the pavement. She was madder than hell and ready to get to her donuts. She slammed the door behind her and stalked toward the demon, putting the gun back into the holster.

Hey, that was my dramatic move, Katie complained.

You want drama or results? The nation's capital awaits us, and I am not spending any more time dealing with this idiot than we have to.

Fine, Katie grumbled.

People were jumping from their cars and running away as fast as they could. The demon picked up a Volkswagen Beetle and tossed it into some trees. Luckily it was empty; the driver had fled.

Pandora gave a running commentary with a bored look on her face. *Always throwing cars. They just don't appreciate the kind of craftsmanship that goes into making one of those things. And a classic, no less.*

I don't think he cares.

He should. Look, there's a Pinto, a piece-of-junk twenty-year-old Civic with stupid undercarriage lights, and even a fucking giant earth-killing diesel truck. And he has to toss the Beetle. What kind of monster is this thing?

The same kind as you...and since when did you care about cars?

I don't, just making conversation while I wait for an opening.

Katie sighed, waiting for Pandora to do something —anything—to get this clown out of the way. The demon growled hungrily, looking for another human snack, but everyone had taken off. He looked at Katie and smiled. The demon didn't know yet that it was actually Pandora—or Lilith, as he would know her. All the nutsack saw was a tasty morsel trotting down the middle of the dark highway.

The horn of the car next to the demon blared loudly, stuck from crashing into one in front of it. The demon didn't even look down, just slammed his fist like the Hulk into the hood. The horn stopped going off. Everyone stood silently on the side of the road watching the showdown. The only sounds came from Pandora's clicking heels and the demon's feet crunching through the asphalt.

Pandora immediately started maligning the demon,

taking whatever verbal jabs she could. "Holy fuck, it's a nutsack in name and actuality. Look at it, all wrinkled and lowering the tone of the place. Hey, Nutsack! Yeah, you! What's up, buttercup? Didn't mommy give you any pants to put on before she sent you out to play? Seriously, how rude is it to walk around with your balls all hanging out there for everyone to see? Don't you have any shame? Some of us were planning to eat, you know."

Pandora kicked a piece of debris out of the way and watched the demon sink into confusion as he tried to figure out who she was. She laughed, knowing the damn thing was nowhere near as powerful as his mighty size boasted. Someone down there had sent this thing just to ruffle some feathers.

She kicked a chunk of rubble in the demon's direction. "You aren't even a level-five, Nutsack. You probably got those big fucking gangly muscles because you've been shootin' up the juice, and you don't even have the brains to use them properly."

Pandora's gaze was suddenly captured by a hot guy in a Mustang a little way away. She smiled and blew him a kiss, snickering at the bewilderment on his face as he looked from her to the demon.

WATCH OUT!

Pandora looked back just in time to see a massive car flying her way. She dropped to her knees and bent all the way back, touching her head to the ground. The car flew right over her and crashed into a car behind her. She let out a deep breath and chuckled, getting back to her feet. "Whew, that was a close one."

You fucking think? You should be watching what you are

doing, not fucking staring at guys who will probably be another snack in about five minutes if you don't fucking get your head out of your ass and take care of this bastard.

Whoa, whoa, calm down there, angel. Don't want to twist up that halo.

I fucking hate you today, Pandora.

I know. It's wonderful to be on the other side of it for a change.

Please just do something. Anything, to kick this demon's ass before more innocent people die.

Pandora rolled her eyes and picked the car up. She held it over her head and turned around, winking at the guy again.

Katie sighed. *Oh, yeah, because that isn't going to clue anyone in that you are the one fighting, and not me.*

Pandora heaved the car at the demon's head, and the demon blinked stupidly at the car as it came at him. Pandora shook her head and rolled her eyes. The brainlessness of the creature almost hurt her feelings.

What I really want to know is whether demons have gotten dumber or if it's just because I have been up here so much?

The car slammed into the demon with enough force to knock him back a few steps. His huge foot caught in the broken window of the car behind him, and he tripped trying to dislodge it. His momentum caused him to bounce back for several feet. His cheek scraped the pavement, leaving a smear of blood in his wake.

Pandora laughed and used the hood of a car as a springboard to cover the distance between them, rolling to a stop and coming to her feet in one fluid movement. She wasn't going to waste any more time. She was hungry, and really tired of listening to Katie bitch.

Even though Pandora didn't want to admit it, she knew Katie was right. Too many innocent people had died already, and if she continued playing games, the death toll would quickly rise. She needed to get the demon off the highway and away from a populated area. As she ran, she assessed the trees to her left, where a thick forest went back for as far as she could sense.

Just as the demon pulled himself to his feet, she leapt, slamming into his chest and knocking him into the guardrail. She grabbed his face and punched him hard enough to send a sharp shiny tooth flying out of his mouth. It bounced across the ground as Pandora flipped the demon onto his back and wrapped her arms around his neck, pulling backward until her feet hit the ground.

"All right, Nutsack, you are coming with me. You want to fight? Fine. Let's fight, but not in the middle of the fucking street. Didn't your mother ever tell you not to play in traffic? You could get hurt."

The demon growled and tried to slap her off, but was unable to reach that far behind him due to the overabundance of muscle in his upper body. His heels cut furrows through the mud as Pandora dragged him, lecturing him on the virtues of manners. Katie just sat inside her body, trying not to laugh at the level of sarcasm that Pandora was putting out there. She was on a roll, as was to be expected when her daily sugar requirement hadn't been satisfied.

"And do you know what *really* pisses me off?" She growled and threw the demon through an opening. The demon sailed across the clearing and crashed face-first into a tree. "The fact that *I* was supposed to be an hour closer to my donuts. But nooo, *you* had to roll up and ruin my fucking night!"

That's right, channel your inner donut anger.

Damn straight!

The demon groaned and pushed himself up on his hands, then slowly picked himself up off the ground. A branch above him cracked and fell, knocking him in the head. He shook the pieces off and blinked at Pandora. A look of recognition crossed his face, and for a moment he looked afraid.

"Oh, so *now* you realize who the fuck you are fighting? No one had a problem recognizing me when I was down below as your fucking *Queen*!"

The demon shook off the look on his face and growled, not willing to give up. Pandora stood up tall and cracked her knuckles. A smirk moved across her lips, and she shrugged.

"Looks like someone wants to play."

The thuds of boots hitting the pavement and the clicking of weapons echoed across the highway. Several of the security guards ran toward the people huddled on the side of the road. They pushed them back as far as they could to prevent anything else from happening to them. Once the civilians were secured, the guards fanned out and stood with their weapons pointed at the woods.

"If the thing comes out—the demon, the big one—aim

for the head and shoot it," the lead guard said into the walkie.

The guards stood there for several moments, hearing nothing but silence. Suddenly the trees began to shudder. Screams and roars echoed, along with crunching and breaking branches. There was a loud *boom,* and the ground shook, and a few of the men put their arms out to stabilize themselves. The silence after that last only a few seconds before the demon roared in a squeaky voice, making the guards wince. They looked at each other, wondering but not really wanting to know what the hell was going on in the woods.

There was one more low growl, which could have been from Katie or the demon, then absolute quiet.

"Uh, what do we do?" one asked.

The leader really didn't know what to say.

Pandora coughed and wheezed, waving her hand in front of her to clear the dust blowing all around her.

"Told you, taking the nut sack gets them *every fucking time.*"

If I wasn't inside my body, I might throw up. Katie grimaced.

Pandora laughed and stepped back for Katie to take back over, ready to lounge like a lioness after a good kill.

Katie shook her head and started back out of the woods, brushing the dust off as she walked. When she reached the edge, the guards put down their weapons, and she smiled. The squealing of tires drew her attention, and she turned just in time to see the group that had let the demon out in the first place speed off. She sighed and jogged to the road, nodding to the guards.

They nodded back and put up their weapons, now that the demon was taken care of.

Katie walked back over to the SUV and jumped in the passenger seat, taking a rest as the guards called in the attack and began organizing somewhere for the survivors to wait for the authorities. She pulled out her phone and dialed the general, knowing something had to be done. It was late, but he picked up his cell phone. He didn't sound like he had been asleep.

"I didn't wake you, did I?" Katie asked.

"Wake me? No. I don't think I've slept more than four hours in a *very* long time. What's going on?"

"I was on a side job, transporting some artifacts to DC."

"For the rich family out in New York? Yeah, I knew they were coming in."

"Yeah, well, apparently so did others. They set loose a big-ass demon in the middle of the highway. Pretty sure he ate a guy, and probably killed a couple more tossing cars all over the place. We took the demon down, but the people responsible got away. I wondered if you could get some of your guys to see if they can find the assholes who did this. I can't stop and chase them right now, and I think intel might be more helpful in this situation."

The general sighed. "Well, I'll be honest with you…with all of the recent incursions and instances like you just ran into, we're pretty tapped out. We brought in a lot of men with these new units, but all of a sudden the infected started bringing in demons again. They all came out of hiding. Fucking cults, abducting people and turning them. It's a mess."

"Right, the cops in New York were talking about that when I left. Okay, well, we could use Timothy, my IT guy. That would be for a fee, of course."

The general chuckled gruffly. "Katie, you are becoming more mercenary every day."

"That's probably a good thing, since I *am* a mercenary," she replied sweetly.

His chuckle deepened. "That you are, and a damn good one. All right, go ahead and put Timothy on the case, but I want you to consider this a job for me. I want to know all the information as it comes in."

"I can do that," Katie replied.

"Good. Now I'm going to drink some whiskey and pass out. I have a big day of meetings tomorrow."

Katie laughed as he hung up and shook her head. What she wouldn't do to have a day full of meetings, and not the kind that meant she had to watch Pandora rip the balls off some huge demon. She dialed Timothy, wanting to get him on the case right away.

"Hey, boss. What's up?"

"There has been an attack on a load of artifacts that I was hired to get safely to DC. I am on a stretch of 95 about two hours outside of the city. Can you use the cameras to watch the situation, and then try to ID the assholes who were responsible for this? They got away while we were kicking demon ass."

"Sure thing."

"They were driving what looked to be a red BMW, but I can't be sure since they sped off pretty fast. You'll see. It's all kind of a clusterfuck."

"No problem, I have direct access to the traffic cams right now."

"I won't ask how you got that."

Timothy snickered. "Probably better that way."

"Oh, and Timothy? We are working for the general on this one, so make it good."

Timothy sniffed. "Don't I always?"

Katie got back into the SUV, and they finally headed for DC. She pulled Tom out, put her boots up on the dash, and retrieved a rag from her bag to give the gun a thorough cleaning. It had gotten a serious workout in France, and deserved a little love.

"That's a big-ass gun," the driver remarked, glancing over.

"Mmmhmm," she purred. "I have two, Tom *and* Harry."

The driver nodded, and she could see him thinking about it. "Ha! I get it. Tom, Dick, and Harry. But you don't have a... Well, I just assume you don't..."

Pandora cackled as the guy fell over his words. Katie smirked and shook her head. "No. Instead of a dick, there's a bitch."

"Oh," he replied with a nervous chuckle. "Creative. I like it. And by the way, that was some damn awesome work back there."

Katie inclined her head slightly. "Thank you."

Thank you, Pandora grumbled.

"Do you get that strength from your demon?'

"Most of the time, yeah. I don't really have the upper body strength to lift a Cadillac as a normal human."

Just then Katie's phone dinged in her pocket. Pandora squealed when she saw Brock's name on the screen, and Katie lifted an eyebrow when she read the message.

Our leave starts in three days. We are not sure what's up, though. We might be stuck in France for a few days waiting for a flight. We will definitely get to New York in between if there's a chance. I'd really like a break, and of course to hang out with you.

That's right, Pandora chuckled. *He wants to hang out...with his wang out. He wants to receiver...your beaver. He wants to be smashin' that...that... Oh, fuck it. He wants that booty, girl.*

Katie rolled her eyes. *You are worse than a fifteen-year-old boy. Maybe he actually wants to hang out.*

Yeah, okay, you just keep on saying that...all the way up to the moment he sticks it in.

Katie had no comeback since the idea wasn't entirely unappetizing.

Figure out exactly what date and time you will be off the military clock and send me a text. How many do you have?

Four plus me, and cool on the date and time. Should have that in a few.

Perfect. I'll send over my jet to pick you guys up.

France owes me a favor anyway, so there shouldn't be any customs bullshit.

You just texted me that a country owed you a favor?

Katie smiled and ran her fingers over the keyboard as she thought of the perfect response. She smiled and started typing.

It's good to be me xo

4

Timothy hung up the phone and cracked his knuckles. He leaned back in his chair and swiveled it back and forth. Finally, he had a task that had some *oomph* to it. He had been bored ever since he'd played detective with the IRS agent, which was funny enough to keep him going—especially since he'd received a check and a note from George a couple of days before telling him it was payment toward the total due. He hadn't actually expected him to pay. It had been a scare tactic. Old George wasn't getting off the hook that easy, though.

He put his fingers on the keyboard and started hacking into the traffic cams. He scanned the stretch of 95 in real time, looking for the aftermath of the battle. He figured it would be easier if he started at the current time and worked his way back. As he tapped through the camera footage, he yawned, picking up his coffee and taking a long sip. Finally, after about twenty minutes of scanning the highways, he found the scene. Luckily there was footage of the exact place. There were cop cars everywhere, and a ton of smashed cars.

"Pandora's handiwork, no doubt." He chuckled.

She's scary, his demon whispered.

Well, you're safe for now. She's nowhere near here.

Yeah, you say that and then BAM—bitch jumps out of nowhere and rips your soul out with her teeth.

Timothy grimaced with how loud he yelled *'bam'* and shook his head. *You act all big and bad talking all the time about banging bitches and such nonsense, but when it comes down to it, the main bitch makes you wet your panties. I find that curiously poetic.*

I find it disturbing.

Good, remember that next time you try to lift a boner for a chick in short shorts.

His demon grumbled and settled inside of him, tired of the conversation. Timothy went back to work, rewinding the footage until there was nothing but passing cars. He stopped and pressed Play, leaning back to watch the scene unfold. Just as Katie had told him, a red BMW came barreling down the road, pulled over to the side, and kicked some random human out of the car. Timothy scrunched his nose in disgust at both the human's exploding body, and the munch fest the demon had afterward.

He smiled as he watched Pandora strut out of the SUV stopped just down the road. It was like watching an action movie, only he was cheering for a demon in a human body that might have angel antecedents. All he was missing was the popcorn. The plot thickened at every turn. He watched through the time period where they disappeared into the woods and zoomed in on the license on the back of the BMW as it squealed toward DC.

"There you are, my pretties. Where are you going in such a hurry?"

He turned to his right and pulled up another screen, typing the car's information into the system. He tapped his finger on the desk, then reached over to grab his pizza. As he ate the pizza, he wiped the grease on his napkin, careful not to get anything on the Dior button-up he'd spent way too much money on to wear in an underground bunker.

After a few minutes, the name of the owner of the car came up on the screen. He wrote down the information and opened a new window, putting the name into the search function. Almost instantly five people with the same surname popped up. He tilted his head and narrowed his eyes, looking at the family on the screen. They were all related in some way and had priors in several states, including Nevada. The computer said they had lived in Las Vegas for twenty years before starting their crime spree.

What do you want to bet that they all became infected about that time?

Probably. They look like an All-American family, and that boy doesn't look much older than Katie.

Timothy went through their information, reading about their life before the arrests. The patriarch of the family had managed a hotel in Vegas, the wife was a nurse at the local hospital, and the four kids were all off at college. They didn't look like the kind of family that would be involved with demons, but Timothy knew the weak were always susceptible to being conned.

"Martin and Lacy Flannigan and their four little beauties. Trevor, a former slacker at the University of Nevada, Las Vegas, and his three sisters, Emily, Rachel, and Cecily. Aw, isn't that just the cutest. It's the demon version of the Manson family. Oh, wait, it says here Trevor is deceased. Hmmm, too bad."

He wrote down the information and picked up his cell phone to call Katie.

"That was pretty fast. I'm not even to my drop yet."

"Yeah, it wasn't that hard to track these people. They obviously aren't pros."

"Who are they?"

"They are a family, actually. A mom and a dad, and their three daughters. There might have been someone else in the car, especially if it was a cult situation, but Flannigan was the name registered. It was actually their son's name on the registration, but the records say he is deceased."

"Great—a grieving mother, just what the demons love. Does it say where they are now?'

"Well, they hailed from right here in Las Vegas. Their son even went to University of Nevada, but then one day they started to get nailed with little misdemeanor charges, and that was when they started to move around."

"Ha! I went to UNLV. Looks like all the creeps come out of there."

"Small world." Timothy laughed. "You probably even ran into little Trevor a couple of times."

Katie paused, tilting her head to the side. "I'm sorry, what did you say?"

"Trevor Flannigan, their son. I was just saying you might even have run into him before you became the big badass mercenary."

"Uh...yeah." She shook her head. She wasn't sure how, but she had just managed to run into the family of the guy who'd gotten her infected. Of course, he was dead. Korbin shot his fucking head off his shoulders right in front of her.

"You want me to call the general?"

"No, I got this one. Just forward him the intel you have. I'll call him now. Thanks."

She hung up the phone and stared out the front window for a moment, unsure how she felt about it all. Either Trevor had followed in his parents' footsteps or them in his. Or maybe he was the one who got them infected. She dialed the general, keeping her emotions in check.

"That was fast."

"I employ the best."

The general paused. "I just got the file, and the name rang a bell..."

"Yeah, me too."

"You want to handle this?" The general knew who this was, but he wasn't going to get her all riled up.

"Nope."

"Okay, then I will have a team take care of it. Thanks for the speedy work. We'll deposit the money."

"Thanks."

Well, this is fucking awkward.

Katie was more than happy to get out of the SUV when they finally pulled up to the government building. She was feeling claustrophobic, and just wanted to get back to New

York and reality. The last few hours had seemed like the Twilight Zone.

They backed the truck up to the loading dock, and she stood watch with the rest of the guards to make sure the artifacts made it the last few feet into the well-fortified vault. When the offload was complete Katie shut the truck's doors and hopped down, grabbing her bag out of the SUV.

The leader of the guards walked over and handed her an overly thick envelope. "Thanks for everything you did. When the family found out, they asked me to add a bonus. Something to show their appreciation."

"That was nice. Tell them thank you." Katie smiled and stowed the envelope in her bag.

The guard nodded. "You want to ride back with us?"

"No, I think I'm going to wander DC for a while and then take a train back to the city. Have me some downtime where no one can make me take on a demon."

"Don't jinx yourself." He chuckled, handing her a card. "And if you are ever looking for something on a more regular basis, give me a call. We can always use good men and women on our team."

"I appreciate it." She smiled and took the card, nodding as she slipped it into her pocket. "You guys be safe."

"You too." He climbed into the SUV.

Katie stood back as they took off out of the short drive and pulled onto Washington Avenue. She slung her bag over her shoulder and walked back to the door of the federal building where they had just unloaded.

The same guard came to the door. "Did we forget something?"

Katie smiled and shook her head. "No, I was just wondering if you had a bathroom I could change in. I don't really want to walk around the streets of DC with my weapons out."

"Yeah, come on in. It's down the hall, third door on your right."

Katie nodded and headed there, going into the single-stall bathroom. She locked the door and pulled out a pair of jeans, a black t-shirt, and a jacket. She changed her clothes and pulled on her sneakers, then folded the ones she'd taken off and placed them on top of the weapons and ammunition in her bag. She was about to close the bag when Trevor's face fluttered through her mind. She pulled one of her knives back out, sticking it in her back pocket.

"Better safe than sorry," she muttered.

She looked in the mirror for a moment, taking in the news. She couldn't believe that out of all the people in the world she could have been dealing with, she was fighting the fucking Flannigans. Their son had changed her entire life, but she doubted they even knew—or cared for that matter. They were on a mission; one that she and the demon their son had put into her had thwarted without even breaking a sweat.

Let it go, Pandora told her soothingly. *We got them, and the general will take care of it. The asshole is dead. Has been for a while. Don't let this affect you.*

I'm not, Katie replied, taking a deep breath as she slung her bag over her shoulder. *In fact, even if I didn't know it at the time, he did me a favor. He opened my eyes and forced me to see the world for what it really was.*

No, I think I did that.

Katie chuckled. *True, but you were his parting gift to me.*

I am definitely a gift.

Yep, like herpes. The gift that keeps on giving.

She left the bathroom and waved at the guard as she let herself out. She pulled out her phone and looked up the closest donut shop since she knew Pandora would not accept getting on the train to New York without a donut or five. She skimmed through the recommendations and settled on Astro Donuts and Fried Chicken.

Donuts and fried chicken? Humans are weird, but hell, I'm not going to argue.

They walked the four blocks to Northwest and went inside. Katie's mouth was watering, and it had nothing to do with Pandora. The donuts were arranged in a display case, fresh and some even still hot.

Katie gawked. *I think we should move here! I can make a honey chicken sandwich on a fucking Savory Donut. This is amazing.*

Fine, but no hot sauce. I know how your stomach gets, and I am not *taking a train with you like that.*

No problem, planned on leaving it off anyway.

Katie went up to the counter and ordered her doughnut, chicken, and honey butter sandwich as well as a dozen donuts. She ended up getting the assorted dozen because between the PB&J donut and the maple bacon, she just couldn't make up her mind, and neither could Pandora. Fifty dollars later they headed out of the donut shop with a bag full of goodies and hailed a cab. The driver quickly pulled up, not used to people needing a ride in that area.

"Where to?" he asked, swallowing hard as she looked at him with red-ringed eyes.

Katie slipped on her sunglasses, noticing his stare, and smiled. "Union station, please."

You are going to make me wait until we are on the train?

Yes. We aren't heathens, or at least I'm not.

Ha-ha. Very funny, Pandora said dryly.

When they arrived, Katie tipped the driver extra to make up for scaring the hell out of him and hurried inside. She bought a ticket to New York City, got through security by using the military ID the general had given her so she could carry her weapons on public transportation, and took her time walking through the station toward her train.

Katie stopped at a newsstand when one of the magazines on display caught her eye. She lowered her glasses and stared at the magazine that was front and center. Slowly she moved forward and picked it up. On the front was an obviously Photoshopped image of Katie from the fight in France.

Katie quietly read, *"Special Issue: The Demons Inside Us."*

Oh. My. God. That says there is an authentic recreation of what you would look like as a pin-up model. Are you fucking kidding me? There is no way...you can't not buy this. We have a long train ride ahead of us, and I need some serious entertainment.

Katie sighed and handed the guy a ten, shoving the change into her pocket. She shifted the bag to her other shoulder and walked toward her train platform, staring down at the front cover. Part of her didn't even want to look, but the other part felt the same way it did whenever a demon crunched into a person. It was insane and disgusting, but damned if you weren't curious enough to watch.

Katie kept her head down as she showed her ticket and boarded the train. She went to find the private room she had paid extra for. She didn't feel like being stared at by everybody on the train while she ate her way through a dozen donuts, or while trying to figure out how she felt about being turned into material for the spank-bank of any guy who bought the rag. Once inside, she threw her bag into the overhead compartment and put her bag of food next to her.

She waited patiently until the train started to pull out of the station before she opened the box of donuts and selected a crème brûlée. She put her feet up on the empty bench across from her and opened the magazine, flipping through the pages until she found the pull-out section with her picture.

She cracked up completely when she saw the spread. "Oh my God! What the hell is *that*?"

Wow, talk about missing the fucking mark. They made your waist smaller than mine, your hips are jutting out like they are made of clay, and what fucking look is that on your face? You look like you're having the big O.

I think they took my face from that shot where I was falling and blasting demons at the same time. But you're right, my fighting face is a whole lot like my fucking one. I'll have to remember that next time.

Look at how big they made your feet.

They would have to be that big to support the fucking watermelons attached to my chest. Seriously, I'd fucking fall over if my tits were double Gs!

Pandora couldn't stop laughing. The magazine had completely ruined any opportunity they'd had to be taken seriously. Anyone who looked at that spread would know there was no way Katie could humanly or demonly contort her body to look like that. It wasn't even attractive. It was like they took her perfect body and tried to make it even better, but instead she looked like she had been poorly molded from some high school kid's weird-ass fantasy.

What the fuck have they done to your legs?

It's called a thigh gap.

That doesn't explain that enormous camel toe they gave you. That shit looks painful. After all the effort I put into making sure that any man who saw your thighs immediately started to wonder if he could learn to breathe through his ears... Pandora sniffed indignantly, completely affronted. *I really hope that was part of the edit. Whoever did this shit must never have seen a woman in the flesh.*

Like one of those greasy slimeballs no woman would touch even with somebody else's hooha? Oh my God, there's text. I can't even look!

Pandora giggled, making her read through every single sentence that was printed with the picture. She couldn't believe the writer actually thought she would be happy with long walks on the beach and quiet nights reading a book. Maybe her old self, but she had morphed into one badass bitch.

I feel like you should like call Playboy *or something and offer to do a real shoot and answer all of these questions truthfully. It would be a jab to get back at whoever created this monstrosity.*

You mean do a shoot where it doesn't look like a swarm of bees have gone to town on my vagina?

Yes, exactly that.

Yeah, not happening, P.

She closed the magazine and tossed it into the other seat. It was definitely not coming back with her. If Calvin ever got his hands on it, he would never let her live it down. It was bad enough that the rest of the world was staring at it. She didn't need to keep finding printouts of it taped to every surface.

5

The golden morning light poured through the windows of the condo and pooled on the hardwood floors. Angie was awake, reading the newspaper as she drank her coffee and scrambled up some eggs with bacon. Katie had gotten home the evening before and gone straight to bed, exhausted from her job. Angie wasn't even sure what job she'd been doing, but then again she never knew unless she happened to catch her boss on the news.

She plated her eggs and grabbed the remote to the television, seeing a large multi-car accident on the news. She wondered why they would put something like that from Maryland on the New York station, but she figured it included someone important or something. She clicked it off and walked over into the dining room, sitting down just as Katie walked in.

"Good morning, you want some coffee?"

Katie waved her off. "I can get it. You do work for me, but you aren't my servant. I do have to admit, you make some of the best coffee that I've ever had."

"I order it online. I love it. It's from this little coffee farm in Columbia."

Katie grabbed a cup and went into the dining room, sitting down across from Angie, holding the cup with both hands and taking a sip. Angie flipped through the paper, pausing only to read the obituaries, and then closed it and slid it down the table.

Katie raised an eyebrow. "I'm just wondering why you always read the obits?"

Angie looked up and smiled. "I'm watching for the day my ex gets it from one of his druggie friends. It's only a matter of time."

"You know you're free now, right? His death is not the only way out anymore."

"I know." Angie smiled. "Old habits, I suppose. You just never know which way your luck will turn."

Katie grinned. "Well, yours turned to the positive. Don't forget how lucky you are to have a second chance at life. Don't get stuck in the past. I know it's hard, I had to tell myself that yesterday, but it's what is best."

Angie nodded and took a bite of bacon. She reached over and pulled her black scheduling book over to her and opened it. Inside was everything that she had to remember, from dry cleaning to appointments, and reminders for Katie.

"Do you have anything going on this week I should know about?"

"Oh, damn, yes, thank you for reminding me. I need you to figure out the logistics of getting my jet over to France to pick up Brock and his four friends and bring them back here to New York. I promised them a good break while they were on leave and he texted me the day and time this morning. I'll forward the text to you."

"Okay..."

"I want you to make sure they are treated very well. They really put their asses on the line in France and lost one of their guys. It was really sad. They deserve to lay in the lap of luxury while they are here."

"Will you be hanging out with them?"

"Yeah, but I won't be there to pick them up. Just make sure there is food on the plane, alcohol, whatever young soldiers on leave would want."

Angie snickered. "Strippers?"

"Okay, no strippers." Katie laughed.

Boring, Pandora interjected.

Katie ignored her. She was not about to get into why it was not a good idea to have those men on a plane high in the air with strippers and alcohol. "I also need you to find the best place to put them up, but make sure it is near us. I don't want to have to trek all over the city to get them."

"Right. Plane to France, and nice hotel for five guys. Budget?"

Katie got up from the table and snatched a piece of bacon from Angie's plate. She took a bite and walked toward her room, waving her hand in the air. "No budget that isn't absolutely ridiculous of course!"

Angie took in a deep breath and wrote that exact sentence down, just to make sure she had a record when the bill came in. It was going to be a wild ride for those boys, and Angie was stoked to be the one to get to plan it.

Calvin brought Sofia's hand to his lips, staring up at the television in the living area. Timothy was lounging in the overstuffed armchair, his feet hanging over the side, kicking back and forth. On the television were their soaps, a woman with angel wings on the screen staring at a large demon portal in the center of Central Park.

"Man, I love this storyline, but it feels weird."

"What does?" Sofia asked.

"Watching it without Katie and Pandora. When they first came here, before we knew Pandora at all, she became obsessed with three things, donuts, game shows, and soap operas. At first, it was just Katie in here watching them, but slowly she managed to get everyone involved. Even Damian, the priest we had, the one I came onto the team with; and he was *not* the kind of guy to like soaps. He was more of a local pub going, book reading, whiskey drinking intellectual."

"I thought he was a priest."

"He is, an infected one."

"Are all those people gone now?"

"Yeah." Calvin sighed. "Not all dead though. Korbin and Stephanie live in happy bliss, having been exorcised by Katie. Damian is off with his church helping other churches deal with their demon problems, and I think almost everyone else is... well you know."

"It sucks they couldn't be here to see the world as it is now." Sofia smiled, rubbing his shoulder.

"Yeah, it is. But we had a hell of a time while we were here. Katie would make this sugared popcorn and make it all kinds of crazy colors. It was like food coloring and melted sugar poured over popped corn. It was amazing.

Everyone would gather around and watch the soaps, with plenty of commentary of course."

Sofia laughed. "I didn't know anyone could get *that* into these shows."

Calvin shrugged easily. "I don't think it was the show as much as it was the time together. We were always like a big family. I mean, if you think about it, we only had each other. We weren't allowed to contact anyone from the past, so our families thought we were dead and we couldn't really have a normal relationship. We had each other, and it was nice to do things together. Things that didn't involve demon slaying or going to funerals."

Timothy laughed. "I like that bar you guys took me to. The one with the duct-taped furniture."

Sofia raised an eyebrow, and Calvin laughed. "We had this bar we went to all the time, and there were always fights so they would just kind of patch the furniture back together and wait until another person landed on it. It was a fun place. We met up with the other local teams there, celebrated those we had lost, and just enjoyed the only people we had in our lives."

"Why don't you still do that?" Sofia asked.

"Most of the merc teams have broken up. Here it's just me, Timothy, Katie, and the people out at the armory, but they aren't fighters. When the rules were lifted a lot of the teams went their own ways. Some gave up the life for a normal one, others headed off on their own. In fact, I haven't talked to any other team in a long time."

Sofia's nose crinkled prettily. "It's a good thing though, right? You get to have a life now."

"Yeah, but we're still infected." Timothy sighed. "It's hard for the red-eyed to have any kind of actual life."

Sofia shook her head. "It cannot be so bad, surely?"

Calvin made a face. "I would have to agree to a certain extent. You are different, the demon in me doesn't bother you. Most people are freaked out, and it's understandable. People see the infected on the news, they don't see the people who have the demons but fight them back. Except for Katie, she's become somewhat of a legend, helped people to see that the Damned aren't all bad. We live in a world where demons have become a commonplace thing, and there are too many battles for the everyday person to take in."

Timothy stood up. "Yeah, well, humans have a tendency to ignore what it is that scares them," he replied. "I may not have been infected my whole life, but I tell you what, people were more worried about catching the gay than they are of my demon."

Calvin burst out laughing and held a hand to his chest. "You mean it's *contagious?*"

Timothy waved him off. "Yep, I cough and before you know it you got dicks coming at you from all angles. It's crazy, and there's no cure for it."

They all laughed as Timothy walked across the room. "I'm gonna go attempt to make some of this deliciousness that Katie makes. I mean, if I can highlight hair, do a mani-cure, and a wax all at the same time, I think I can manage some sugar-coated popcorn."

"I won't stop you," Calvin shouted.

Timothy walked out of the living area and into the kitchen. He pulled a bottle of riesling from the fridge and uncorked it. He went to get a glass but shrugged, figuring he was the only one who drank the stuff anyway.

"Why the hell not? You earned it, princess," he told himself, tipping back the bottle.

Timothy went through the cabinets to find the popcorn maker, a bag of kernels, and the oil he remembered Katie using. He looked at the popcorn maker and raised an eyebrow, not exactly sure how to operate it. He poured the oil into the little area marked oil and then opened the kernels, spilling some onto the counter and floor. He put the rest in the hole in the center and plugged in the machine.

"Well, here's hoping!"

When the corn started to pop, he clapped his hands. He pulled out a saucepan and grabbed the food coloring and sugar from the cabinet. He knew the ingredients, he just wasn't exactly sure how to make it. He started out with a half a stick of butter, several sloppily poured cups of sugar, and then took the blue food coloring and squeezed it in there.

He reached over and grabbed a spoon with one hand, taking a swig of the wine with the other and turned up the heat, watching the butter quickly melt into the bottom of the pan. He stirred it, looking over to see popcorn spilling out of the popper onto the counter.

"Shit." He dropped the spoon in the pot and ran over, grabbed a big bowl and put it under the spout. "Use your brain, sweetheart, use your brain."

When he walked back over to the pot, he lifted an eyebrow. He grabbed the spoon. The entirety of the butter and sugar mixture was clumped together and rock solid, the color of a Smurf. He tried to bang it off back into the pan, but it was stuck on the spoon. He grimaced and walked over to the trashcan, just throwing the whole spoon away.

"If at first you don't succeed...?"

He went through the motions again, this time using equal parts butter to sugar and using the yellow food coloring. He stirred and stirred the mixture, pulling out the spoon and splattering a line of melted sugar across the top of his hand. He jumped, dropping the spoon in the pot and racing over to the sink to run cold water over his hand.

This is funnier to watch than anything I've seen in ages, his demon cackled.

Just shut it.

I think your sugar is burning.

" Huh? Oh shit!"

He ran over and pulled the pot off the stove, looking in at the burnt mixture in the bottom of the pan. He set the pan in the sink and filled it with water, pulling out a new one. He shook his head and turned the heat down from high and set the pot on the burner.

"Okay, last try. If I don't get it, it wasn't meant to be."

On the third try he made sure to focus, kept his digits away from the molten sugar mixture, and just kind of threw some colors in there. When it was done, he had found that he had succeeded. He lifted the spoon and watched the mixture run back down into the pot.

"Perfecto. Top Chef all the way."

He mixed it all in with the corn and stood back, tilting his head to the side. He grabbed a piece and tried it, closing his eyes and smiling. The only issue was the color. He picked up the bottle of food coloring he'd used last, the label read 'black.'

"Whatever." He grabbed the bowl. "Beggars can't be choosers."

Angie sat at the dining room table, liking the view better from there than the office in the spare bedroom. She had several sheets of paper spread out in front of her, trying to get the details for the weekend all sewn up. She had figured out the plane situation after making a couple of calls and finding out that France really didn't want to tell Katie no on anything. In fact, they made sure to accommodate her in every way. Angie could tell it was all out of fear, but she didn't care, she was just glad that part was done and done.

Angie had called the jet staffing service and hired a few extra flight attendants for the flight. She figured that if there weren't strippers, there might as well be beautiful women serving their drinks.

On the phone with the company, she had hesitated to ask, having a hard time finding the courage to speak so plainly. About fifteen minutes of waffling, she finally bit the bullet and asked the company to staff attractive young girls. The guy just laughed, telling her that was a normal request in their line of work. After that, she booked a caterer to travel with them and moved on to the nearby accommodations. There were a ton of hotels in the general vicinity, but after looking at them all her head was starting to swim and they were all fading together into one. She took a break and walked over to the floor to ceiling windows, looking out over Central Park. It was a beautiful day, but she didn't have time to go out there and play around. Katie expected this visit for Brock and the others to be absolutely perfect.

She walked over to the phone and called down to the front.

"I was wondering, we have some guests coming in and I am trying to find the best hotel near us to house them all in individual rooms. What would be your suggestion?"

"How many are there?" the concierge asked.

"Five, and they are servicemen coming back from France. We want to make sure they are more than comfortable."

"Actually, I do have a suggestion. If you go to our site and click on the amenities section, you will see a place at the bottom referring to rentals. Click that, and it will give you prices and layouts of the condos that we have. They are pre-furnished and available for short-term stays."

Angie could have hugged the person on the other end of the line. "Oh, that sounds *great*, just perfect! Thank you, I'll look that up right away."

The concierge chuckled. "Of course, and if you choose to go with that option, you can call me back and I will put it all together for you."

"Thank you."

She got off the phone and went back to the computer to look up the condos. They were really nice, just like their condo but smaller. They were furnished to the hilt and even included a stocked bar and fridge at no extra cost. She skimmed down to the prices, and her eyes got big. They were more expensive than anything she had ever bought.

Then again, Katie was the one who said there was no budget and only the best.

She flipped through the pictures again and realized they were only a few hundred more a night than the next nicest hotel room near them, and it would put them just a few floors above them. Katie wouldn't even have to take a cab to get to them. On top of that, they might just be able to feel at home for once, instead of feeling like they were in a hotel room. The beds were of the best quality, the linens far superior to those in the hotel, and there were huge-ass 4k flat screen televisions in two of the rooms of each condo.

Angie grinned and reached for the phone to call the concierge back. "These guys are going to live like kings while they are here."

She looked around her remembering just how far she had come since Katie rescued her. She smiled and let go of the price realizing that she too lived in the lap of luxury, but she didn't even have to go out there and fight demons to protect her and the rest of the country. These boys really did deserve everything she could come up with.

6

B rock and the guys walked to the entrance of the base after being released to begin their leave. Sitting out front was a stretch Hummer limo, all lit up, the driver holding the door open for them. The guys gawked at the ride. They'd been expecting to have to take a cab to the airport.

Brock's buddy patted him on the shoulder and walked past, laughing.

"This is definitely not a military-grade Humvee." The guy kept laughing as he climbed inside.

Brock smiled and shrugged, looking back at the Eiffel tower before climbing in with the others. They threw their bags into a pile and sat back, looking around at the fancy interior of the limo. There were neon lights all along the ceiling, leather seats, plush carpet on the floor, and small televisions playing American football.

The driver rolled the tinted window down and grinned at them through the rearview mirror. "The bar is fully stocked for you."

He rolled the window back up, hearing the cheers from the guys. As they drove to the airport, the guys enjoyed some cold beers. Brock passed on the alcohol and watched out the window as they drove through the city. When they arrived at the airport, he expected to be dropped off at the front. He hadn't been told the airline they were booked on, but he knew Katie and figured the driver would let them know. However, as they approached the driver took a turn down a service road and entered the airfield. They pulled up to a large hangar and stopped to wait for the doors to slide open.

He parked the limo and got out to open the door for the guys. They all climbed out with their gear on their backs and stared, wide-eyed at the private jet in front of them. The door opened, and three ground staff secured the stairs for them. None of them took a step, still not believing that the beautiful plane was for them. A stunning brunette woman in a short skirt, heels and button-up white blouse walked out. She gave the guys a red-lipsticked smile and waved for them to go up.

Before they could move a muscle, a long-haired redhead walked up behind the brunette and put her hands on her hips. "Well, come on boys, we have a long flight home."

All of the guys laughed and hurried toward the stairs, not believing their luck. Brock chuckled, seeing what Katie meant by a good time, and followed along behind them. The women took their bags and had them stowed below before showing them around the plane.

"This is the service bar," one of the flight attendants explained, indicating the large oval bar at the front. "We have beer, wine, alcohol, soda, coffee, and water. When we get in the air, a catered buffet will be served up here as well. Ms. Maddison had us make sure to have everything you might want to eat, so feel free to take whatever you like. Straight to the back of the cabin is the bathroom and to the right is the bedroom. If anyone wants to take a nap, you are more than welcome to. There are over fifteen hundred movies on our onboard movie system, and we have Wi-Fi connected to the laptops in the back of each seat. We ask that you stay buckled in until the pilot tells us its safe and then let us know what we can do to make your flight memorable."

The guys all stared at her and then looked at Brock. "Is this like a part of your entourage?"

"No." Brock laughed. "I have to admit, I've never ridden in anything this nice before. This is all Katie."

"Man." His teammate chuckled. "Being a merc has definitely got its perks."

All the guys took seats relatively close to one another, not used to having so much room to spread out. They buckled in and sat back to wait for the plane to take off. The ladies hurried around the plane, taking care of everything they needed to be prepared for takeoff and then took their seats in the back.

Brock heard them giggling to each other.

"Maybe joining the service was the wrong choice," one of the guys joked. "If I had known mercenaries live like this, well shit, I'd give up three hots and a cot any day."

"Three hots? Try maybe some warm coffee and an MRE from three decades ago to last you two days."

All the guys laughed, but they knew that when they

were out there in a battle that wasn't too far from the truth. You never had time to really eat chow, even when the military cordoned off an area in the safe zone to serve it. Brock's team were special forces, and they were the ones responsible for stopping the battle, especially if the mercs weren't there. That meant they saw the most action, killed the most demons, and got the least sleep or food out of everyone. Sure, the pay was more, but not that much more.

In reality, though, none of the guys on that plane did it for the recognition or the money, they did it because that was what they knew they had to do. They were called to fight for their country, and now for their planet. To protect the land and the people from this unbelievable threat that if left unchecked would easily swallow them all whole. At the end of the day, even sitting in that jet, none of them thought they would actually ever be able to walk away from the lives they lived, it was too rewarding for them.

Brock looked out the window and watched the ground fall away beneath them as the plane took to the sky, reaching the end and soaring effortlessly into the sky. He was shocked when he couldn't even feel the landing gear retract, not like the military planes they had to take. He was lucky on one of those to have even a seatbelt, much less a smooth ride to wherever they were going. Brock, like the others, loved the jet, but mostly they were all just happy to be heading to New York and getting out from under the shadow of the events in France. They had just buried their teammate there.

They'd all wanted more for him than that.

France was more than happy to oblige, and the guys had left from the funeral to get on the plane. It had been a trying day, full of anger, grief, and stress, and Katie had gone above and beyond to ensure the guys were taken care of and worry-free, at least while their vacation lasted. He wasn't sure why she was doing it for them, whether it was personal toward him like he hoped, or just because she knew they needed it, but either way he was more than thankful to see his teammates smiling for the first time in a very long time.

The sun rose into the Nevada morning sky, casting spikes of blue and pink into the hazy horizon. Sofia had gotten up early, unable to sleep. Instead, she'd made some coffee and gone up top to take in the scenery before it got too hot. It was really beautiful here, she couldn't deny it, although she definitely missed the sound of the waves and that refreshing California air. But now that she had Calvin, she couldn't imagine being anywhere that he was not.

She took in a deep breath and closed her eyes, letting the light sun warm her already bronzed skin. She lifted the cup of coffee to her lips and took a long sip. As she swallowed, she felt her phone buzzing in her pocket. She smiled and pulled it out, expecting it to be Calvin wondering where she had gone. However, as she pulled it out, she saw her mother's name on the screen.

She answered with a grin. "*Hola, Mami. ¡Es bueno escucharte!*"

"Hello, my princess," her mother responded in English.

"I feel like I haven't talked to you in forever."

"Well technically, it's been forever and a day," her

mother teased. "We figured you were face-deep in your books, so we didn't want to disturb you."

"I'm never too busy for the two of you."

"Good," her mother replied and then paused. "We are going to be flying to San Diego in the morning to see you."

"Really?" Sofia half-laughed. "Why? I mean yay! But why so quick?"

"I don't know. We had a little time off, and we miss you. You *are* our baby, after all. Hold on, your father is talking in the background."

Sofia stood up and looked at the military vehicles making their rounds. She could hear her mother talking to her father in Spanish. Her heart started to beat wildly in her chest, and she stood frozen, not sure what to say. She couldn't put them off; they wouldn't understand why she wouldn't be home. They knew nothing about Manuel, and she couldn't tell them. It would break their heart to know she had gotten caught up in something like that. She had always been a good girl, wanting to make them proud, always making good decisions—until him.

"Okay, he needs food. He is grumpy." Her mother laughed. "We will see you tomorrow. Kisses, *mijita*."

"Kisses, *Mami*," Sofia replied nervously.

As soon as she hung up the phone, she took off across the sand, ran over to the elevator and pounded on the button a hundred times until it finally opened. She stood in the elevator freaking out, bouncing up and down, waiting for it to hit the right floor. When the doors opened, she ran through the halls to Calvin's room.

She jumped on the bed and shook Calvin roughly. "Calvin, wake up."

His eyes flew open. "What, what? What's wrong? Is it a demon?"

"She shook her head. "No, worse! My parents, they are coming to San Diego in the morning, and I'm not there. That is not okay."

She sat down on the edge of the bed and put her face in her hands, mumbling to herself. *"Oh, estoy tan muerto, tan muerto. Mis padres me van a matar. Voy a tener que decirles, y luego me negarán, me arrojarán a las gallinas. Le dirán a mi abuela y ella me sentenciará a una vida de vergüenza. Ni siquiera saben que no soy virgen."*

She sobbed into her hands. Calvin sat up and placed his hand on her shoulder. It was obvious that she had to get back to San Diego and fast, but there was no way that he could let her go back without some sort of protection. Sure, they had gotten the head guy, taken his demon out, but they hadn't been back to see if that had fixed the problem or not. There could very well be people still hunting her down, and he was not going to throw her back into that situation without someone there to make sure she was safe. The problem was, his vacation ended in three days, and he had to get back to work. Katie was counting on him.

"I need to find someone to be there with you, someone I can trust, and someone who will protect you if anyone comes after you, or even you and your family."

She looked at him with wet eyes. "But I thought it was over."

Calvin shrugged. "And it probably is, but we haven't been there to make sure. These were not just run-of-the-mill drug lords. The one we took care of, he had been infected for almost ten years. We pulled his demon out, but that doesn't mean that he is magically a good person. I can't send you home alone, and I have to get back to work."

Sofia was pale but adamant. "I have to be there, though. My parents will take me back to Mexico in the blink of an eye if they think I am unsafe or caught up in anything like that. My family is very strict and very old-school Mexican when it comes to those things. They expect me to be where I need to be at all times which does not include being shacked up with you in Nevada in an underground bunker."

Calvin chuckled. "I know, I know you need to get back. Just let me think for a minute. If you want, go ahead and start packing. One way or another we will get you home for your parents. Did they say how long they were staying?"

She shook her head. "No, just that they were flying to San Diego in the morning to see me."

She got up from the bed and opened up her suitcase, pulling clothes out of the drawers and tucking them in neatly. She had done some shopping with Timothy online while she had been there, collecting a new wardrobe since the old one was left in her old prison where it should be. She was really glad she had bought those clothes, though, her mother would have died if she showed up and Sofia was scantily clad looking like one of the women from the soap operas. She was a young single girl, and though they tried to understand the times, that didn't mean they didn't expect modesty and good behavior. She was over eighteen, so she was an adult, but that wasn't how things in their family worked.

"What about Timothy? Could he come with me? It would be very easy to explain his presence, a roommate or friend that went to school with me. And he is gay, so my father will not have concerns about him sleeping under the same roof as me."

"He really isn't combat-trained, so he wouldn't be prepared for these men. Besides, we need him here. He is the only person that can work intel for us. He is our IT guy and set up the whole system. None of us know how to work the thing, and we struggle if he leaves the base for just a few hours while he runs an errand or something."

"Ugh." She threw her head back in exasperation. "I can't seem to keep myself out of trouble."

Calvin got up and walked over rubbing his hands up and down her arms. "Heeey, it's going to be just fine. Everything is going to be okay, I promise. We are going to fix this. I am going to go topside and make a phone call, okay? I will be back in a few. Just keep packing and getting ready to go."

She nodded, and he leaned down and kissed her on the nose. He grabbed his phone from the dresser and made his way to the surface, walking over behind the armory where the wind would be blocked. He shook his head and dialed Katie's number.

"It's a bit early for you," she answered.

"I'm assuming Pandora woke you up?"

"Of course, if she can't sleep no one can. What's up? Everything okay?"

"Not really," he replied.

"Why? What's wrong? Is everyone safe?"

"Sorry, yes, everyone is safe. It's Sofia. She got a call

from her mother this morning. Her parents will be arriving in San Diego to see her tomorrow morning. She is freaking out, and I can't go to protect her because I only have three days left on my vacation."

"Why doesn't she tell them she's out of town?"

"Her family doesn't work that way. They are very old-school Mexican. They expect her to toe the line with them until she finds a husband, and do the same when she marries."

Katie rolled her eyes. Sofia was nice and all, but she couldn't imagine just handing the reins over to some man. "Right, I get it. I went to college with a girl like that. So, what's your plan?"

"I wanted to know what you would think about asking Korbin and Stephanie for help?"

"Korbin and Stephanie? But they won't even know who you are, and they are living a happy life on their little farm."

"They have a life, yes, but it isn't real. They have to know something is up by now, with all the demons coming out. And we need them, no matter what we want for them. I'm not saying we have to go and infect them, just ask them for their help. Think about what Korbin would say if he were in this situation with any of us."

Katie sighed not wanting to say yes but not seeing any way around it. He was right, they not only needed Stephanie and Korbin, but the world also needed them. Things were much worse than they were when she sent them off in a blissful haze. However, now that their team was split up, Katie didn't have backup anymore.

"All right, fine. There is enough known about demons

now to fully explain to the two of them what happened. I don't want to come with you though."

"Why? I thought you missed them like I do."

"Of course, I do. But remember, I took their demons, I exorcised them, and to do it, I tricked them into telling me yes. I basically forced a life of happiness on the two of them."

Calvin gasped and chuckled. "How dare you."

"It's not funny, you know how Korbin can be, and that was not his demon being stubborn. You have to go on your own and explain to Korbin, what I did and why I did it. If I am there, he will just start blaming me and getting upset. He won't truly understand it, because he doesn't remember any of it. I think you should do it alone. You know him better than any of us besides Damian ever did."

"Maybe you're right, but you can't hide from them forever. You know once they know they won't be able to stand by and let it happen."

"I know," Katie sighed. "And that's what I'm afraid of."

7

Calvin stood on the top of the hill, looking down at the quaint farmhouse. He hesitated, wanting to delay a moment before he made his way down the long dirt drive, which led past a beautifully manicured lawn with bright blue and pink flowers planted close to the wrap-around porch. To the right, a white picket fence surrounded a patch of garden where tomatoes, corn, and several different herbs grew.

Calvin swallowed, the guilt of interrupting that perfect existence weighing heavily on his mind. He took a step forward and stopped when the front door opened. Korbin stepped out carrying a cup of coffee and smiling back at Stephanie, who bounced out of the house behind him.

Calvin thought about all the conversations over the years he had with Korbin, and how pissed he was going to be when he realized the truth. Not angry, but pissed because Calvin and Katie had been kicking ass and taking down demons while Korbin had been sowing the seeds of his little private heaven.

Calvin chuckled and headed down the hill and up the driveway. As he got closer Korbin and Stephanie stopped, Stephanie moved to Korbin's side and took his hand. They smiled kindly at Calvin as he approached and for just a moment he thought maybe they knew who he was.

Korbin wiped his hands on a towel hanging from his belt loop and walked over, extending his hand to Calvin. "Welcome."

"I hope you don't mind the intrusion," Calvin replied.

Korbin's eyes crinkled at the corners. "Not at all, we don't get too many visitors out here these days."

"Or any days," Stephanie added. She laughed and came over to shake Calvin's hand.

Korbin tilted his head. "What can we do for you?"

"I... um..." Calvin wasn't sure how to start the conversation. He couldn't just blurt it out.

Korbin narrowed his eyes. "Wait, I know who you are."

Calvin's eyebrows shot up. "You do?"

Korbin grinned and shook his finger. "Sure. You're one of the mercenaries who battled those demons in France. We watched the live feed of the whole thing. You were definitely kicking ass out there."

Calvin smiled ruefully as he realized it wasn't the past they remembered, it was the media. "Thank you. We train hard every single day."

Stephanie nodded. "Your skills are amazing. I could see martial arts, weaponry skills, and of course the power from your demon. It was a terrible situation, sure, but I have to admit you and Katie are fascinating to watch."

"Oh sure," Korbin nodded. "I imagine you have to, there are so many threats out there now, not just human on human anymore. The evil sometimes feels like it has taken over this world. So many attacks, especially since Incursion Day, but I have a feeling they were going on a lot longer than that."

Calvin laughed. "Yeah, things don't just pop up out of nowhere like that, that's for sure."

Korbin scrutinized Calvin's face. "We even went out and drove two hours and got us some of the special bullets and such. Out here it's quiet but you never know, you want to be prepared."

"That's smart. I've learned that these demons don't always have rhyme or reason for what they do. It's not a normal war situation." Calvin looked at Korbin and back to Stephanie. "How are you guys doing out here? You like the area? Are you happy?"

It was an odd question, but Calvin didn't know quite how else to ask.

Korbin looked at Stephanie. "It's beautiful out here, just how we always wanted things. But I have to admit, we enjoyed it a lot more before we really understood what the demons had been up to." He pulled Stephanie close. "When Incursion Day happened I thought it was a fluke, a bad day. But as time has passed, we see that it is more than that. We see that they are looking at bigger things, making bigger plans, attacking cities overseas, going after people who are just innocent bystanders, you know? Like us, I suppose."

Korbin and Stephanie exchanged a firm glance. Calvin smiled and nodded, seeing the fight still in their eyes. He knew he couldn't leave there without asking for their help, it was too important.

"We've been talking about coming to help since we saw it on the television," Stephanie told Calvin.

Korbin nodded with enthusiasm. "That's right. I am ex-military, combat-related, and Stephanie is trained in martial arts. We may not be infected, but I think we have a lot to offer."

"That's actually refreshing to hear." Calvin smiled. "I came here today with a specific purpose, I wanted to find out if the two of you would like to help me."

Korbin furrowed his brow, still smiling kindly. "That's an interesting request, but let me ask you, why us? How did you even know about us to come out here?"

Calvin chuckled, pushing his boot through the dirt. "You may not remember it, but I do actually know you. Much better than you realize. The thing is because of the way the story played out, you just might have a really hard time believing the stories."

Korbin looked down at Stephanie, and she smiled at him, nodding. "Actually, with everything going on in the world, you might be surprised what we believe and what actually starts to make sense."

"Then you will hear me out?"

"Of course, we will," Stephanie replied. "Why don't you come on in. I'll pour us some iced tea, and we can sit in the air-conditioning and talk."

"You all right with that, Korbin?" Calvin found it strange to say his name again.

Korbin was equally surprised. "I sure am. Life is funny that way, you never know what will come walking down that old dirt road."

"Or who you'll find standing up on the hill in the distance," Stephanie added with a wink.

Calvin smiled and followed them into the house, hoping what he was about to say would be received as well as he was at their front gate.

As it had been for the past couple of weeks, the police station was loud and boisterous. There was a steady stream of arrests coming in and out of the office as well as a plethora of calls and 911 dispatches connected to the demon activity throughout the area. The city was barely even focused on the normal crime, and in fact, it had gone down quite a bit. The normal criminals were too afraid to run into demons to be out ruining lives.

Travers sat behind his desk, scrolling through the numbers as Schultz flipped through the enormous file of the day's arrests. "Arrests are up sixty percent since this time just a month ago. Just today I would say ninety-five percent of the arrests were demon related. Some are just petty crimes, general mischief, but there are murders, cultist weirdness, and violent crimes all over the place."

"I know." Travers sighed and ran a hand over his hair. "We even got a call from one of the heads of the crime families out here asking for some assistance with a demon issue. Their activity has been pretty much non-existent for the first time since the twenties, the 1920's. Can you believe that?"

Schultz rolled his eyes. "I think I would rather deal with

the mob than with all of this. How do you do detective work on a dismemberment and portal opening?"

"That's the thing," Travers explained when Katie made a face. "They all seem to be green. They stay at the scene or very close by and are caught almost immediately. We are shipping these infected out left and right. It's a good thing we aren't housing them, we would have to build ten new facilities just to keep up with this year's catches."

Schultz sighed and rubbed his face. "My daughter is coming home from college early. She says the campuses just aren't safe right now. She said she can't even walk home at night. It's no longer if you will be attacked but when and by how many red-eyes waiting in the shadows. The campus police just aren't enough to keep them safe."

"Hell, I'm starting to think the regular police aren't enough to keep everyone safe. We just don't have the training, the gear, or the know how to keep this up. The military is stretched stupid thin, and from what I've been told the governor is being pressed hard to bring a military presence into the city. He thinks it would only make things worse, push the city to riots and looting."

"He may be right." Schultz sighed. "If we are understaffed now, think of what we would be like when on top of everything people are rioting and looting in the streets. We already have a group of nutbags chilling in Central Park waving their This is the Rapture signs, throwing their religious tracts in everyone's faces. All of the nutbags would come out of the woodwork, and we would have cults summoning demons in the middle of Times freaking Square."

Travers nodded in agreement. "The thing is, this all

seems a little *too* coincidental to me. Every day it seems to get worse. The guys are pulling twenty-four-hour shifts and still can't keep up with it. They are leaving one arrest midway with rookies just to chase down another perp right in the middle of it all. One thing I learned really fast with this demon shit is that coincidences are rarely that."

"You think there's something bigger on the horizon, don't you?'

Travers pressed his lips together. "How can I not? Between the surges of attacks, the fact that none of them seem planned or orchestrated by any larger entity, and the quietness of the large incursions, it feels like something is in the wings. The main demons, this Moloch character and his minions, they don't seem like the kind that would just give up. They hit France with force, but we all saw a quiet period beforehand and knew something big was coming."

Schultz scratched his head confused. "Then wouldn't that mean it should be quiet right now."

"Yeah, if we were dealing with beings that didn't learn from past mistakes, but I think we've come to learn through our allies and enemies that these demons aren't unintelligent beings, at least not the high-level ones. They saw that staying quiet, keeping the calm alerted us to bigger things. What if their plan now is to allow this all to continue to build? Maybe they are helping these cults, and these idiots cause a ruckus as a distraction of sorts. Keep pushing us to our limits until we're worn to the bone, and then come out of nowhere with something we don't expect."

Schultz nodded. "That makes perfect sense, actually.

There's a rumbling of something going on, all connected to these small arrests, this unrest within the city."

"And it's not just here. I've talked to buddies of mine in California, Kentucky, and Iowa. They all say the same thing about the amount of unrest there is."

"Okay, so we feel the attack coming, we see the signs, but we have no idea where it could take place, how big it will be. We don't even know if it will be through infected humans, a portal or both. How do we prepare for something, short of sending someone to hell as a spy, which we know won't work?'

"We don't," Travers replied. "We pull off of the knowns. We look at everything we know about the demons: their powers, how they attack, and what their track record indicates. Then we start moving to be prepared for it. We don't put all our eggs in one basket like France did with the portals. We spread out and be ready to move at a moment's notice. We don't assume that if one incursion breaks out that will be the only one. We have to plan ahead on this, it's the only way we can really see to survive it. With the lack of men and the way we are stretched so thin, this place is going to start looking like Gotham City, only we don't have a Batman."

Shultz snickered. "No, but we have an angel..."

"Katie can't take them all on at once. She is tough, but not that tough. The mercenaries have all but disbanded. The days of teams rolling out to take down a whole incursion singlehandedly are over. We have to pull together using the forces we have developed, and continue to strengthen those. In the meantime the little guys—that's us, in case that wasn't clear—keep it together on the streets."

Schultz walked over to the bookshelf and pulled down a book on preventative measures in case of a threat of mass proportions. He opened up the chapter on early warnings and slid it across the desk to Travers. "At least we have the latest procedure, as much use as it is since it's geared toward a human threat." He squared his shoulders. "Still, we can use the knowledge we've gained from working with Katie to figure it out. We implement what we can from where we are and then start moving up the chain of command, getting the go-ahead to implement the bigger things."

"Shit. I'm impressed, Schultz. You still got a little fire in you yet." Travers chuckled. "From here I can get the chief to get a meeting with the commissioner. In the meantime, we start bringing in some of our part-timers. The weekend warriors, the ones who are on the brink of retirement but can fill the streets. We give our younger guys a little time to rest and take care of the families, and get us back on twelve-hour shifts to start with. No one is going to be any good if they haven't slept in three days." He shook his head. "It all starts to blur after that."

"I'll go see if the captain has a minute."

"I'll write down a list of all the things we need to have happen to prepare for whatever is coming. Let me know if he is down for it."

Schultz nodded his head and left the room, heading over to the captain's office. He walked in to find the captain with one hand on the desk, rubbing his tired face. Schultz knocked on the doorframe.

"Captain, do you have time to speak to Travers and me? We had some ideas we would like to run past you."

The captain looked up and nodded. "No better time than the present."

Schultz grabbed Travers, and they both went into the captain's office, shutting the door behind them. They sat down in front of his desk, which was covered in stacks and stacks of paperwork. He had been there for three days straight, taking a rest in one of the holding cells here and there, but mostly just plowing through.

The captain leaned forward over the desk and stared at both of them, a look of concern in his eye. "You guys are seeing what I'm seeing, aren't you?"

"Sir?" Travers replied.

"There is something big coming, something rumbling right below us and it's about to explode."

Brock's team rowdily exited the jet, a couple of the guys slipping the flight attendants their numbers as they thanked them. They'd had a blast on the plane ride to New York, thanks to the stellar efforts of the ladies. So far, the trip had been a welcome pampering after everything they had been through.

A certain sadness tinged Brock's enjoyment of the experience. Lamb had been laid to rest in France, and his sacrifice still had a rawness Brock couldn't bring himself to examine too closely. He knew it was a risk that they all agreed to take on from the beginning, but that didn't make his death any easier.

When the plane landed, they went to catch a breath of

fresh air and straighten out a little after the excess during the flight while the crew unloaded their gear.

A man in a suit with an airport badge walked out the door and put his hands in front of him. "Gentlemen, if you would follow me right this way, your car is waiting."

"Yes, *gentlemen*," one of the guys joked, ramming his shoulder into the guy next to him.

The guys situated their bags on their shoulders and followed him out through the private side of the airport. The people on the main concourse looked up as the men passed by on the other side of the rope.

"Oh my God, it's Brock!"

"Brock! *Brock*! We love you!"

He smiled and waved, remembering the days when groupies like them were a part of daily life. However, this time it was different.

Other people started to line up at the rope, and they were clapping for the whole team. His teammates walked a little taller when they got their first taste of a crowd calling their names. They all took a few minutes to greet the crowd, at Brock's urging. He knew exactly what a boost to morale it would be, both for his team and for the people who now had an outlet for the relief they'd felt when they saw the demon hordes defeated.

Brock grinned when he saw a pretty redhead press her number on one of the guys. Another was signing a newspaper for an elderly gentleman in a USMC cap.

Wow, this is pretty different from the tour, his demon remarked. *Feels kind of...I don't know, wholesome? I felt better about the orgies.*

It isn't the Brock Show anymore. Brock smiled. It was

about all of them; all of the soldiers, all the heroes who had saved the day in France. The people had seen the television coverage and recognized their efforts. It made all of the guys feel good about themselves, proud of what they were doing. It was the kind of rejuvenation that they all really needed after months of nothing but fighting.

How do you feel about that? I mean, you got all the attention back then. Now you're just a poster boy for something much bigger.

Brock loved it. For once he wasn't being singled out for his singing or his looks, but instead for something much more important—his effort to *protect*. It was a small contribution, but nevertheless, it felt good and right to serve the people of the world. Sure, he could have been living the high life, but it wouldn't have sat right with him in the end. Making the decision to dedicate himself to service had been the right thing to do. It had been a tough call after living as a pampered rock star, but he felt more than satisfied with his life as it was now.

The guys looked at each other with huge smiles on their faces. The man at the front opened the door to the outside and revealed a limousine just for them. The guys laughed and patted Brock on the back.

Brock grinned and followed them out, appreciating Katie's effort to show his team her thanks. Even if he didn't get anywhere near Katie that week, it would be worth it just to see their spirits lifted.

His demon snorted. *You keep telling yourself that. You might even convince yourself it's true. You've got it baaaad...*

8

Calvin followed Korbin and Stephanie into the living room. Stephanie excused herself to the kitchen. Calvin looked around at the evidence of their all too brief utopia, the keepsakes placed here and there, the photos of the two of them doing ordinary everyday things together. They really did look happier than he had ever seen either one of them before Katie had exorcised them.

Stephanie returned a moment later. "Thought maybe something a little stronger than tea was in order." She smiled, holding up three beers.

Calvin grinned. "Oh, thank you, that is definitely right up my alley."

Korbin indicated a chair. "Please, have a seat."

Calvin nodded and all three sat down, Stephanie and Korbin on the couch across from him. Calvin set his beer down on a coaster on the coffee table and put his hands together, trying to figure out where to start. He figured he should start with the basics.

"You were both infected, but Katie pulled your demons from you to give you a chance at a happy life together.."

"Katie is the woman on the television, the one with the wings, right?" Korbin asked.

"Yeah, that's her." Calvin chuckled. Stephanie nodded. "Even without the wings, she is just...spectacular. I *love* her!" She held a finger up to Calvin. "In a platonic way, of course. Everything that woman has done? I expect we don't know even half of it, but it would be hard not to love her."

Korbin rescued Stephanie from her fangirl moment. "We both very much admire her. She does so much for the world, and has no fear. It's really amazing, especially for a woman that young."

Calvin cleared his throat and smiled. "Katie is pretty special. She cares about other people. She wants the ones she loves to have amazing lives and be anything they want. That's why she did what she did to the two of you."

"What did you mean by that?" Stephanie looked at him in confusion. "I don't understand. Neither of us has ever met Katie, but you've mentioned her twice now. I mean, that would be really awesome. She looks like a fun person, but we spend most of our time right here at the house."

Calvin shook his head. "Not recently. Before all this. Before you got married and had the house and the garden. We were all really good friends, in fact."

Korbin chuckled and then furrowed his brow, just like he used to do. Calvin held back a smile, not ready to go into their history together. Slowly the smile slid off Korbin's face as he thought about what had been said.

"You're saying we knew Katie?"

"Yeah." Calvin chuckled. "Let me give you some background. My name is Calvin, and you brought me into the mercenaries along with Damian, a priest, who is now serving his church by traveling around the world. Katie came much later. She was a college volleyball player who was drugged by a cult and infected. Now, when she was infected, we didn't know, but her demon was very powerful. In fact, her demon is Lilith, the wife of Lucifer."

Korbin's eyes widened in shock. "Whoa."

"Yeah, well, she turned out to not be so bad, and never took Katie over fully. They work as a team, kicking demon ass."

Stephanie frowned. "What about the wings?"

"That's something that has just developed lately, brought to her via Gabriel, the angel. Apparently, she is somehow part angel as well. We haven't gotten to the bottom of that one quite yet. Anyway, there have been a lot of us coming and going, some dying, and some exorcised, going back to lead semi-normal lives. Before then, it wasn't Katie's Killers. It was Korbin's Killers."

Korbin's face dropped, and he looked at Stephanie in complete shock. She reached over and took his hand, her face both shocked and comforting at the same time. He stood up and walked over to the window, putting his hands on his hips and staring out at his garden.

"You okay?" Calvin asked. "I know it's a lot to take in all at once."

"Uh, yeah." He laughed. "I mean, I guess it makes sense. I *am* in much better shape than I should be at my age."

Stephanie chuckled. "I have to admit, I have skills that are a little too good for a madam."

"Well, that's because you were kicking demon ass with Katie all over the West Coast. The two of you were like this crazy team, researching powerful Damned and either taking them down or ripping the demons right out of them. I guess the incursions weren't enough to keep your attention. That, and the ammo business you helped run. To be honest, without you, the whole thing might have been a flop."

"Ammo business?" she asked.

"You heard me right. Katie is part owner of the company that makes the demon-killing ammunition. And you too, Korbin; you are part owner. That's where the monthly deposit in your bank account comes from."

Korbin turned around. "I thought I struck it lucky with the military, but I wasn't about to question it."

"That would have been some fucking luck." Calvin laughed. "Of course, we kept part of your share in an account for you. It would have been too big of a deposit to explain away with the military."

"Well, that makes sense. And Katie and I—we ran this business and were mercenaries?"

"Yep, with the help of Stephanie, and the one who makes the metal, Joshua. There are also the former brothel workers. You gave them all jobs there when you closed down the business. Most of them stayed, even after you were exorcised."

Korbin walked back over and sat down on the couch, clutching his hands together and leaning forward. "And Katie, she is the one who did this to us?"

"You make it sound like a bad thing, but if you could remember, you'd know merc life was hard. She loved you both so much, and she wanted your love for each other to have a chance to grow without demons butting in. She wanted you to have a chance at a real life."

"And you?"

"I still work with the mercs. I turned down the top position and offered up Katie for it. She didn't want to take it at first, but she is doing a good job. It's only three of us at this point, since most of the merc teams have gone their own way since Incursion Day. It's a lucrative business, demon-killing, if you can stay alive long enough to see the deposits."

Stephanie smiled. "I guess in a way we should be thankful to Katie. We are married, happy, and alive. We got a chance that apparently not everyone gets."

"True." Calvin smiled.

"So why do you want us to come back?"

"Well, I need a couple of badass humans to help me watch over someone I love very much. She has been through a hell of a lot, and though Katie and I took care of the main threat, I have a feeling that there are more people out there trying to get to her. I guess I was hoping the two of you could maybe help me out for a few days. I wouldn't have broken into your happiness, but you are literally the only normal humans that I trust."

Korbin chuckled. "I don't know about normal, but we are pretty trustworthy."

"To be honest, I don't even know what normal is anymore." Stephanie laughed. "Especially not after this conversation. Now, I just want to make sure—we aren't infected anymore, right?"

"No," Calvin replied. "You aren't. Katie took care of

that, and I promise, if you were, you would know about it. Demons tend to talk more than most people would really like."

If you fed a brother some tacos every once in a while, maybe we could have normal conversations. Calvin was almost surprised to hear his demon. He had been silent for a couple of weeks.

I was starting to think you weren't there anymore.

In your dreams, pal. I just figured you would want some privacy with your little girlfriend for a bit.

Appreciate it.

Hey, it's Korbin. He coming back?

That's what I'm hoping.

"As far as Sofia is concerned, I really have no idea if anyone will actually attack her, but I don't want to take any chances. She was mixed up with some really bad demon drug lords. After saving her from that, I don't want to take even the slightest chance if I have any doubts. It's one of those things, you know? Do what you can to protect the people you love."

Korbin looked at Stephanie and she smiled, stretching up and kissing his cheek. She gave him a slight nod. Korbin looked at Calvin with a grin.

"We will do it, on one condition."

"Okay, what's that?"

"We get to meet Katie and have a chance to talk about everything."

Calvin gritted his teeth and sighed, knowing that Katie wasn't going to be happy. Not because she didn't want to see Korbin and Stephanie—she loved them, after all—but because she knew that there was a possibility they would be angry with her for exorcising them without talking to them about it first. He pulled his phone out of his pocket and held it up to Korbin and Stephanie.

"Let me just make sure she will be in the area. She's kind of been all over lately. I'll just step outside, if you don't mind."

"Sure, take your time," Stephanie smiled.

Calvin stepped outside and took a deep breath before dialing Katie's number.

"How did it go?" she answered.

"Welllllll...."

"Uh oh. What?"

"They said they will agree to do it on one condition: they get to sit down and talk with you about everything that happened."

"Of course, they would want that." Katie laughed. "With everything so open now it's the least I can do, but it will be a while before everyone is out of town and I can come over."

"That's fine. We will be in San Diego for a little while handling Sofia's parents, so I will call you when it's all done and dusted."

"All right. Keep me in the loop, and please remind them I did it out of love."

"Nope, throwing you to the wolves."

Katie chuckled. "I will sic Pandora on you."

"That is enough to scare anyone." Calvin laughed. "I'll tell them."

They hung up and Calvin headed back inside, nodding at them and smiling as they looked up at him. "She will meet with you once we are done, and she takes care of what she has to do."

"Perfect." Korbin smiled. "Now what?"

"Now you hurry and pack a bag. This is time-sensitive, so we need to get to the base and then to San Diego."

They rushed to their room and packed several bags, unsure when they would be back. When they were done, Calvin loaded them up in the SUV he had parked at the end of the drive and they headed toward Vegas. As they pulled through the gates, Korbin looked around at the different things that had been put in place around the base for security. Little did he know that he was the one who had signed off on them in the first place.

Calvin didn't miss Korbin's inspection. "Oh, and just a warning… Our intel guy, Timothy? He is a bit...loud."

"I like loud." Stephanie winked, getting into the elevator.

Calvin smirked. "Funny you should say that. The two of you were pretty good pals."

As soon as Stephanie stepped out of the elevator Timothy ran toward them and threw his arms around her. She chuckled and patted him on the back, dropping her bag.

He pulled back and shook his head, wiping a tear from his eye. "Girl, I have missed you so damn much."

Stephanie looked at him a little stiffly. "Timothy, I presume?"

"Ugh, you really *don't* remember. Girl, we were besties! We spent all our free time doing makeup, hair, mani/pedis —whatever we could do to relax and have a damn good time."

Stephanie smiled, but she clearly didn't remember any of it. From his personality and the description of the things they did together, though, it wasn't hard to believe. And he had no real reason to lie to her. He lifted his eyebrows, watching her face and hoping for recognition.

"Here, wait right here!"

Timothy ran off to his room, pulled open the top drawer of his dresser, and grabbed the framed pictures he had hidden, too sad to look at them. He smiled and hugged them to his chest, running back out, doing a grand jeté, and landing in front of her.

She giggled and glanced at Korbin, who had one eyebrow lifted. Timothy shoved a picture in her hand of the two of them doing their makeup together. She smiled, running her thumb over the picture, wishing she could remember. He gave her another with the two of them doing manicures and pedicures in his room.

She turned her head to the side and looked at her face, still shocked that she had actually been there. She recognized herself, but it was like she was looking at another life. Of course, in a way it *had* been another life. A life with a demon inside her, a life of killing demons and working alongside the famed Katie. She held the picture up and showed it to Korbin. He looked closer and shook his head, also not believing that the two of them were who everyone was saying.

"That's a sweet wife-beater," Korbin teased.

"Definitely different from what I wear now." Stephanie laughed, looking down at her white tank and broom skirt. "I like it, though. Seems to have fit me well."

"You have a fabulous sense of style. It was what got us

talking in the first place. I had just gotten here, and you cut my hair and got me going again. After you left I went on mad shopping sprees, trying to dull the ache of your disappearance with retail therapy."

"Did it work?"

"No, of course not. But at least I got a fabulous outfit every other day, and that alone is what makes me get up in the mornings. Now, knowing you are back...well, my whole life has meaning."

Calvin held his hands up to halt Timothy before his enthusiasm ran away with him. "Calm down. They aren't back, they are just here helping me with Sofia."

"Yeah, yeah." Timothy waved his hand. "We'll see about that."

"Wait," Korbin said, looking around. "Is this the military base Stephanie sold? The one that gave us a big chunk of change?"

"Sure is." Calvin chuckled. "We lived in a different one on the other side of Vegas, but demons attacked it and pretty much destroyed the place. We renovated this place, and here we are. Stephanie had a lot to do with the décor, especially the rooms."

"That's not surprising." Korbin winked at Stephanie. "So, I left the leadership position that I had here?"

"No, not exactly. You two were spent after the episode we now call Incursion Day, and Katie decided your love needed a chance to grow. She pulled your demons out and set everything up for you to have a chance to be together. To love without fear."

"Okay, that makes sense. Wait, we fought on Incursion Day?"

Timothy laughed. "Yeah, and kicked some major ass, too."

"Now, not to rush you, but we have plenty of time on the plane to talk about these things. I need you to get down to the weapons area. Do a little refresher on combat, so you are prepared for anything."

"Sounds good," Korbin replied, leaving their bags there and following Calvin to the training room.

The two of them instantly squared up in the middle of the training ring. Calvin stood back and watched them spar, realizing that they actually worked really well together when it came to martial arts and hand-to-hand combat. He really hadn't expected that, but then again, they'd only had each other since they were exorcised.

When they were done, Calvin clapped his hands and nodded. "The two of you still got it. Now, let's get loaded up on weapons." Calvin took a step forward and stopped when Korbin walked straight to the weapons locker.

Calvin laughed and shook his head. What was that? Muscle memory, maybe. Crazy.

Calvin caught up with them and put his hand on Korbin's shoulder. "Hey, how did you know where the locker was? I just watched you walk right over here without any type of prompt like you knew exactly where it was."

Korbin looked around the room and shrugged. "I don't know. I mean, it seems familiar in a way. Maybe I've just been in these types of missile silos before?"

"I don't know about your past, but you designed this place, so it would only make sense that you would have some sort of reaction to it. It just threw me off, that's all."

"Well, hopefully, that means we will be able to jump right back in and protect your girl. We took the job, no problem, and now we have to deliver."

Calvin grinned and slapped Korbin's arm. "Spoken like the Korbin I know and love."

The guys drove through the city in the limo, gawking at all the buildings and people around them. Brock was the only person from his group who had been there before, but even for him, it had been fast and very sheltered with the band. He had to admit the city was a lot more exciting than he remembered it being. The car drove up to the condo building, and several very well-dressed people came out of the doors. The concierge nodded and opened the limo door, letting the guys step out and look up at the tall, mostly glass structure.

"If you would, the staff will follow us with your gear and show you to your rooms."

The guys nodded and handed their bags to the staff. They walked wide-eyed through the expansive lobby and climbed into the elaborate elevator. They started toward the top floor, where their rooms were ready for them.

"Is this a hotel?" one of the guys asked.

"No, sir. This is a residential building, but we keep furnished condos for the use of our VIP residents. Your friend, Ms. Maddison, owns one of the most prestigious condos in this building."

The guys looked at each other but didn't say a word, realizing how little they really knew about her. When they got to the top, the concierge turned left and showed them to their spaces. Each guy got an apartment to himself, each having one bedroom with a kitchen, master bath, and a living room. Each was pretty much the size of a normal New York apartment, but with a lot more charm and style. Each of the guys was let into his condo, and then Brock was taken to his.

"We are here to support and serve all of you, so ask for anything you need. Ms. Maddison has let us know everything is on her."

"Thank you." Brock nodded, and the staff walked back to the elevator.

He shut the door and looked around, chuckling to himself. All of the guys were in their rooms putting their things away and changing out of their uniforms, but Brock hadn't even made it all the way into the apartment before they were knocking on his door. He walked over and opened the door, stepping to the side as his four team-mates sauntered in, talking about their rooms.

"It's like the nicest place I have ever stayed."

"Me too, and I have to say the place is perfect."

The guys all walked into Brock's place, which was just a little bigger than theirs. They were all happy-go-lucky and having a blast until they turned toward the kitchen, spotting the keg on ice in a large bucket.

"Hey, what the hell?" one guy pouted.

"There's a note," Brock told them, picking it up. "It's from Katie's secretary Angie. It says that Katie is out on an operation and will be back soon. We're to avail ourselves of the stuff in our fridges."

Two of the guys looked at each other and darted from

the room, going to check it out. When they returned, they were more than excited.

"We have a ton of shit. The fridge is stocked with food and beer, though you are the only one who got a keg."

Brock shrugged with a smirk. "I guess I'm the one who asked for the date, so I get the keg."

"Yeah, and you also get something else," one of the guys teased him.

"A pair of perfect badass legs wrapped around you." Another laughed. "And you're over here worried about your keg? Maybe your succubus really does have control over you."

The guys all laughed, but Brock just shook his head.

Once Korbin and Stephanie were done getting the weapons they were comfortable with, they loaded into the chopper to meet the company jet at the airport. Katie figured that while they were there it was better to let Korbin and Stephanie have a little fun and relaxation, something you couldn't find on a stuffy flight to California.

"I like this chopper," Korbin said, nodding his head. "I always wanted to learn how to fly one."

Calvin chuckled and glanced at him. Korbin's eyes opened wide, and he pointed at himself and then at the helo. Stephanie patted Korbin on the leg with a smirk, finding it kind of funny how surprised he was at every turn. Calvin gave him a nod, letting Korbin know he had once flown a helicopter.

When they landed at the airport a few minutes later,

Calvin ushered them into the hanger bay and up into the jet.

"We could have flown commercial," Korbin protested.

Calvin waved his hands. "It's just our company jet. We don't use it for everything, but it makes long flights a lot more enjoyable. Just sit back and relax."

Korbin leaned toward Stephanie. "*Just* a company jet. Sheesh, and to think we were upset about the cost of milk at the grocery store the other day."

Stephanie giggled and fastened her seatbelt. "Looks like before we were simple folks with a garden, we were demon-killing business execs with some really cool toys and an old military base as a house."

"I don't know how we survived it." Korbin scoffed.

Calvin laughed, although he was looking out the window and trying not to eavesdrop. It was obvious that Korbin had really become accustomed to his life after the exorcism, but having him talk about the simple life was slightly strange. Korbin had always been obsessed with his job, wanting everything to be perfect, and now he was dreaming of farmhouses and gardens. If he could see himself from the old Korbin's perspective, he would be shocked.

It was really good to have them around again, but Calvin's mind was elsewhere. He had gotten people he could trust to watch over Sofia, but now the real issue came into play...the parents.

9

Katie stretched after she stepped out of the cop car in front of the police station. She had just gotten back from an operation, a small one in one of the hotels. There was a wedding, and unfortunately for the bride, the groom had been out too long the night before and contracted a demon. He had started a bit of a mess at the reception, and when they got there, they realized there was more than one demon in the crowd. Katie ended up pulling the demon from the groom and handing him over to the bride, telling her good luck with *that* one.

The cops were really good at collecting the rest, and all in all the whole thing had been simple. And she got to eat a piece of wedding cake, which Pandora would not shut up about.

Seriously, why is wedding cake so much better than regular cake? Like next week, I want you to go order a wedding cake for us to keep at the house. It was freaking delicious.

I don't think I will be keeping a wedding cake at the house, but we can visit the baker and see what else they have.

Fine, but it better be damn delicious, I'm just warning you now.

Yeah, yeah, got it.

"You coming in for a coffee?" Travers asked.

"No, I'm gonna grab a cab and head back, I have some friends in town."

"All right, have fun, stay out of trouble."

Katie winked. "Me? Trouble?"

Travers laughed and waved goodbye as she hailed a cab and climbed inside. The cab took her back to her condo which wasn't that far away, but she really didn't feel like walking. She went up to her condo and got cleaned up, taking a quick shower and throwing on some actual evening wear. As she waited for the curling iron to heat up, she called Brock's room.

"Hey there, everything going okay up there for you guys?"

"Are you kidding me? This is really awesome, thank you. The guys—they really needed this."

"I'm glad you are having fun. I told you I would show you guys a good time. Sorry I wasn't there when you got there. The police had me on an operation, and it was a mess. Tears, brides, grooms, cake—it was all a clusterfuck, but we got everything under control."

"Good, and I'm jealous of the cake. Wedding cakes are the best."

I missed him. Pandora sighed.

You barely even knew him.

So? He's obviously a genius.

"I am getting changed and ready, and I want you and the guys to get cleaned up and in some nice clothes for the club life. We are going out for a night on the town."

"Oh, boy." Brock laughed. "This is going to be really interesting. These boys have been wrapped up in the war for months, not to mention the fact that you gave us enough alcohol for the apocalypse."

"Normally I would find that funny, but since the apocalypse is a very real possibility right now, I just have to ask you one thing?"

"What's that?" Brock flirted over the phone.

"What alcohol would you want when facing the end of the world?"

They both paused, then said whiskey at the same time. Katie smirked and let out a deep breath.

"Oh, yeah, you are right. This is going to be one interesting night."

The scene was fun, people dancing everywhere. The limo was ready and waiting outside to go to the next club, and drinks flowed like water. Katie knew Brock wanted a date with her, but this was about all of them. She wanted to show them a good time, and allow them to let their hair down and really just be themselves. Katie knew as well as anyone else in the business that it was hard to find time to do things just for the fun of it.

Calvin, Damian, and the rest of the crew had gone out of their way to show her there was more to a Damned life than just hunting demons, and taught her that blowing off steam was essential. She wanted to do that for these guys.

The first club they went to was wild, everyone staring at the plethora of stars who were out. They had no idea how Katie got them in, but they weren't going to question it. They were just going to have fun. All the guys but Brock found chicks at the first club, women they could spend the rest of the night flirting and dancing with as they moved from club to club. Katie kept her glasses on and a drink in her hand, but she was really just watching out for them. Besides, she constantly had Pandora scoping the joint out for hot men, although she wasn't planning on going home with anyone.

Brock hung out with the guys, laughing, and stealing glances at Katie through the evening. There was a definite tension between the two of them, and Katie surprised herself with how cool and nonchalant she played the whole thing. Pandora was pretty impressed as well.

Look at you, being the hot girl tonight.

I thought I was always *the hot girl?*

Yeah, but tonight you got the Pandora Special going on.

Do I even want to know what that is?

The attitude. The 'I'm hot, and I see you knowing it, but don't even think of showing it,' kind of attitude.

There you go again with the rhyming...

Hey, I thought that was pretty great. It's like a sexy rhyme.

Mhmm, Katie muttered, putting her still-full drink on the bar and heading over to the group. A couple of them had their arms around the women. "You boys having fun?"

"Hell, yeah!"

"Where are you guys staying?" one of the women asked.

"Uh, the condos by the park," the guy she was pressed against answered.

She leaned in a little closer. "Swanky! I like it. Why don't we take the party back there?"

The guys looked at each other for a moment, almost as if they were talking to each other telepathically. After a few moments of contemplation, one of them spoke up.

"I think for tonight we are going to take it easy and get some sleep. We don't get much out there in the field. But I would love to get your number, and we can hook up maybe tomorrow night?"

"I'm down," the woman agreed.

"Me too," the other added.

The guys took out their phones and exchanged numbers while the rest of the group drank their drinks and danced to the music pumping from the speakers. Katie didn't care if they had women at the condo; whatever made them happy and relaxed. Brock didn't pay attention to any of the women they met that night, much to their consternation. His gaze was fixed firmly on one woman: Katie.

She hid that she noticed, but it was more than obvious. His eyes roamed her body in a slightly proprietary way. Nothing she would normally encourage, but there was something about the way Brock looked at her that she liked.

When the guys were done exchanging numbers with the girls, they all walked over to the VIP table Katie had bought and filled their empty glasses. The rest of the guys were shocked that they didn't want to bring the girls back to the condos. After that long in the field with a bunch of dudes, they figured they would be chomping at the bit for some tail.

"I have to ask," Brock shouted over the music. "Why not tonight?"

The guys shrugged and one of them said, "We have a few days, and frankly I don't want to answer a lot of questions tonight. You know how people are; they are curious about us. We have demons, but at the same time, we are the good guys. They find that confusing, and I don't want to spend the evening talking about it. Besides, this night is for Lamb. He lost his life fighting the bastards, and I am going to live it up just for him."

The guys lifted their glasses and made a rowdy toast to Lamb's memory. It made Katie think about all the nights at the bar in Vegas, toasting those they lost. She smiled, thinking about the folded-up and crumpled piece of paper in her dresser drawer. The *Prayer to the Damned*, the thing that brought everyone either to tears or to cheers whenever she read it. Just thinking about it reminded her that Korbin and Stephanie were back in the picture, and no matter how nervous she was about talking to them, she was really happy to be able to see them face to face again.

Shrieking from the dance floor drew Katie's attention. Three girls were lifting their glasses, toasting Brock and chanting the name of his band. They were way too drunk to live and half-disheveled, but Katie could tell that Brock enjoyed the attention. She figured the change from rock and roll to demon hunting had to have been quite the adjustment for him, but at the same time, the gun and the uniform fit him well.

He smiled at the girls but begged off, not paying them any more attention. Katie furrowed her brow and walked over, standing beside him and looking at the dance floor.

"You know it's fine if you want to go out there and dance with them. They seem to be fans."

"Yeah, groupies just like all the others. I really am not feeling it tonight. I'd rather hang out with you."

Katie smirked at him and took a sip of her Diet Coke. For a moment she was flattered, but then she realized exactly what was going on. He wasn't uninterested in dancing with the women, he was being bullied by a certain bitchy donut-loving demon from the pits of Hell.

Knock it off, Katie warned.

Knock what off? I don't have a clue what you are talking about.

Don't play coy with me, sister. You know exactly what I am talking about. You are shutting down Brock's game, just like you shut down Calvin's.

Pandora sniffed. *Maybe, but it doesn't affect you. I made a slight change to it, leaving you open for endless adoration and sexy stares across the club floor. He wants you, either way. I'm just taking away the other distractions.*

Yeah, well, not tonight. I have shit to get done tomorrow, and this one is locked. Don't worry, P, you'll get what you want by the end of it all. Just chill the hell out on the guy. Let him have a good time.

The line for the last club of the night was wrapped around the side of the building, even though it was deep into the early morning hours. People in New York didn't have internal clocks, they just partied until their ankles gave out. Katie and the boys were pretty much spent. Between the battles and the bedtimes, they were ready to get a little shut-eye.

Before they even left the club, the stretch limo pulled up in front. The driver got out and opened the door, and waited for the team and Katie to exit the club. There was a low murmur across the crowd as they waited to see who would be coming out to get inside. There was always a chance to get a glimpse of someone famous or super-rich in New York City, and the people waiting outside to get in the club had been there for hours.

The guys walked out first. They were laughing and joking, not paying a bit of attention to the crowd. They put their arms around each other's shoulders, talking about the night and how they had a hell of a time. Several of the girls suddenly squealed, taking out their phones to record.

"It's them—the guys from France," they yelled.

The guys looked over their shoulders and gave them a wave, trying to play it cool. Then, without looking up from the ground, Brock came rolling out the door. Cameras and their flashes were going off right and left, some of the girls yelling Brock's band name and giggling. He was still a star, but it didn't interest him at that point. He was exhausted, and wanted to give the moment in the spotlight to his teammates.

Brock ducked into the limo, giving them a wave before scooting inside. The group turned as Katie walked out, looking in her purse, her hair down over the sides of her face. She looked hot in her tight black dress and booted six-inch heels, and a couple of the girls pouted.

"Lucky hussy," they whispered.

"Uh, no..." one of the other girls yelled as Katie tossed

her hair back. "Try, 'those lucky bastards!' That's Katie of Katie's Killers!"

Everyone in line stopped what they were doing and started taking pictures of Katie. They were screaming and shouting her name, trying desperately to get her attention even if it was for just one second. Katie blushed and smiled sweetly, waving at the crowd. No matter how much attitude she had in the club, it all faded away when she walked out the door. She still wasn't used to being the center of attention, even though she had known it would happen when she had flashed her wings in France.

Her whole life, even before she was Damned, she had done her best to stay out of the spotlight. She didn't want to be the talk of the town, she just wanted to do her job and live her life. She knew, though, that she was saving people she would never even meet again, and that had to have an effect on her popularity. On top of that Pandora had made sure her body was pin-up girl-ready, even before the shoddy publication printed that abomination.

They love you, they really love you, Pandora cooed.

Ugh, I know.

Oh, stop it. Just enjoy the fame while you have it. Who knows, a year from now all these people could be trying to put a knife in your chest because they are all demons.

Let's hope not. That would defeat the purpose of everything I've been doing.

I'm just saying, tomorrow is never promised.

Katie ducked into the limo with red cheeks and scooted over next to Brock, which didn't help the burning on her face and neck. The driver shut the limo door and climbed into the front, putting up the divider between them. He already knew where he was taking them, and after the way the crowd had reacted, he knew they would want some privacy.

"That had to be the best night of my Damned life, and I mean that in both contexts," one of the guys admitted. "Seriously, the women, the booze, the music, and then that? What else could a guy ask for?"

Katie smirked. "A little something-something afterward, maybe? Oh wait, you sent them packing."

"Just for the night," he replied, shaking his head. "Can't the guys just enjoy a relaxing night alone? With you, of course, Katie."

"I'll be one of the guys for the night." She smiled, taking off her glasses.

Brock glanced at her and then back at the guys, chuckling as they started to sing whatever song had been playing with they left the club. He grinned and looked back at Katie, not believing how gorgeous she was. He knew it from working with her, but in the New York City lights with her hair down, her makeup perfect, and those long stems crossed beside him, she had to be the hottest woman he had ever been around—and he had been around a lot of them.

On top of that, he hadn't heard a peep out of his demon since they'd arrived in New York, which for him was a beautiful thing. She was so scared of Katie's demon she refused to come out of hiding. Seeing that he was on a mini-vacation and didn't need to fight anyone, he was perfectly content with having her nowhere in hearing range.

He cleared his throat and sat up, taking the moment

while the guys were distracted by their own conversations to talk to her again. "Thanks again for all of this. You didn't have to do it. The guys are having a blast."

"And how about you?" Katie asked, meeting his eyes.

"Probably the best time I've had in a very long time," he replied, keeping his eyes locked on hers.

She looked at him for a minute and then pushed the hair behind her ears with a shy giggle. It surprised him given how strong and assertive she normally was, but he thought it was sexy. The softer side of the famed Katie of Katie's Killers, a side he was sure that not many people got to see.

Katie and Brock rode the rest of the way back to the condo in silence, listening to and laughing at the guys as they goofed around. They were all drunk; not fall down drunk, but happy. How could they not be? They were off-duty and being shown one hell of a time.

When they pulled up in front of the condos, Katie got out and turned to the guys. "This is where I will leave you. I will pick you guys up tomorrow. I have a little show and tell for you."

With that, she walked away, every eye on her ass.

10

The next morning the guys were moving slowly, still a little muzzy from the night before. They didn't mind. They were having a blast, and they were all excited to see what the day would bring them. Breakfast was delivered to each room with a note to eat, get ready, and meet in the lobby. Brock stood at the window of his condo, sipping his coffee as he stared out over Central Park. For a moment he felt like a normal guy again; not in fatigues, not running from demons, and not trying to get away from crazed fans who loved his music. He was just a guy. He knew that wasn't true, but he was going to let the illusion hang just for a little while.

After breakfast, the guys pulled on jeans and button-up shirts, did their hair, brushed their teeth, and headed downstairs to the lobby. They found Brock there before them, standing with his hands in his pockets, waiting for the others to arrive. He wiggled his eyebrows at them and chuckled. All of them were wearing sunglasses and trying to push through the hangovers to show their excitement of what was to come.

"Do we know what we are doing today?" one of them asked.

Brock shrugged. "I'm just as much in the dark as the rest of you, I promise. Whatever it is, knowing Katie, it will be something wild and adventurous."

Just then the elevator opened and Katie stepped off, her heeled boots clicking on the marble floors. She was dressed from head to toe in her work clothes, her pistols snug on her hips.

She pulled her sunglasses off and grinned at the guys. "Good morning! Everyone still alive?"

"Barely," one of the guys replied with a chuckle.

They all looked at each other's outfits wondering if they needed to be wearing their fatigues. The note had just said get dressed, so they figured they were good to go. Katie smiled at them, seeing the confusion on their faces. She had to be ready for anything. They just needed to relax and enjoy themselves.

"Come on, boys, I've got something for you."

She waved the guys to the curb. They stood there for a second, not sure what they were looking for. Suddenly, rounding the corner, were two huge Humvees showing up to take everyone out. They weren't limo Humvees, but they weren't military Humvees either.

Brock's eyes widened as he took in all the amenities with an appreciative glance. There was no pretense or apology with these beasts. They were *all* for show. The guys laughed and clapped their hands, finding Katie's attempt to mix relaxing with military fun to be absolutely inspiring.

"You know, you keep showing the military a good time like this and you might find a new career."

"Ha!" Katie laughed. "It's easy when people deserve it. I doubt I'd feel as good doing this for some overly-entitled kid graduating from college on his mom's and dad's dime."

They all laughed and climbed inside, ready for the ride. Katie sat in the back of the second Humvee with Brock and one other guy. The other three hopped in the one up front, already hanging out the windows and yelling back to them. They headed from Central Park toward Times Square, which had finally opened back up after the destruction the demons—and Katie, partially—had caused during the attack.

The traffic was bad at that time of day, slowing the Humvees to a crawl. All the windows were down, and Katie was enjoying the air on her face. People on the streets and in cars next to them started to realize who was in the Humvees.

Crowds began to form on the sidewalk, cheering the guys. It was almost like a parade as news spread and more and more people crowded the streets. Katie watched as several people ran up to the Humvee up front to give the guys high fives. One mother carrying her little girl walked up and handed one of the guys a flower. Even the guys melted at this, while Pandora quietly gagged inside Katie.

Katie ignored her, finding the whole thing absolutely enchanting. There was an impromptu minor celebration going on in the middle of New York City, and even the normally grumpy commuters didn't seem to mind getting held up for once. After a while, though, Katie became exasperated. The people were blocking the streets, making a bad traffic situation dire. She took a deep breath and leaned forward, thinking about saying something to the people. Just then, her phone rang, the general's ID coming up on the screen.

"Great." She sighed and pressed the call button. "General, how are you?"

"Moving faster than you are right now, apparently."

She rolled her eyes. "Is this on the news already?"

"Of course, it is. They are the world's heroes. You didn't think you could parade them through the most crowded city in America in Humvees and not attract some sort of attention, did you?"

"I guess I hoped the traffic would be moving faster."

"What are they doing out there anyway?"

"They're on leave, and I am giving them a much-needed vacation."

"I would frown on this, but the live coverage on my television looks like good press. We could use some right now. Between the destruction of one of the oldest historical buildings in France and the incursions still happening, the public needs reminding that the government has their backs."

"That's always a tough one." Katie chuckled.

"You are awful feisty this morning. Am I speaking to Katie and not Pandora?"

"Yes." Katie sighed. "The traffic and mini-parade are starting to get to me. Cool at first, now, not so much. I got things to do and places to be."

The general laughed. "Woman of the world."

Brock elbowed Katie to get her attention and pointed out the window. Standing at the side of the street was a young girl, maybe nine or ten years old, wearing a home-made "Katie's Angels" t-shirt. She was shouting Katie's name and showing her the wings on the back of her shirt. Katie smiled, touched by the gesture.

Pandora was also moved by the sight of the little girl, though she wasn't willing to come out and say it.

Humph. Should be Pandora's Protectorate or some shit like that.

She's nine, I'm pretty sure that she, A, doesn't know your name, and B, has no idea what the word "protectorate" means. Stop being so salty and know that her love for me is love for you too.

Right. I guess I should let you have your moment, I have always been worshipped.

Katie rolled her eyes and asked the general to hold on. She tossed the phone in the seat next to her and rolled her window the rest of the way down. Katie leaned out the window and waved at the young girl with a big smile. The girl screamed in excitement, jumping up and down as Katie pulled her glasses off and tossed them to her. The girl caught them and held them close to her chest, the rest of her year made. Katie flashed her eyes and ducked back in, rolling the window up.

She chuckled and fixed her hair, grabbing the phone. "Sorry about that. Felt the need."

"I saw you on the television. They are doing a play-by-play of the events out there. Personally, I think that was an excellent hearts-and-minds moment. Good work."

Oh Lord, that sounds vaguely like a shitty job coming our

way. I am not the demon you want to parade around shaking sick kid's hands. I never did have that comforting touch.

Katie laughed. *I think you will be okay, I don't think they are dumb enough to send a Damned into a hospital full of sick kids.*

Have you met our military? The higher-ups aren't too bright.

Just then the road began to clear, and the drivers took the opportunity to swing a right and speed off, leaving the crowd behind. The guys in the front pouted, loving the festivities and attention, but Katie and Brock were satisfied to ride along in the quiet.

"All right, General, I'm almost to the thing we talked about. The other cops will be there, too. If anything comes up, you know how to get me."

"Sounds good, Katie, and good job on the morale boost. Not just for them, but for the citizens as well. We all really needed that."

"You know me, a regular cheerleader."

"Ha! Maybe if there are enough nine-year-old little girls, but otherwise I don't see that happening anytime soon."

"You are probably right. Best to not get your hopes up."

The Humvees took them completely out of the city and into the suburbs of the Greek District. They drove quietly through the neighborhoods and out to a small plain cinderblock building inside a fenced parking area. The guys climbed out of the Humvees and looked around, raising their eyebrows at Katie. It wasn't quite the party spot they had been imagining.

One of the guys said what they were all thinking. "So, they throw ragers out here in the suburbs in shady gray buildings?"

Katie smiled and winked. "No, this is actually a surprise for you guys, and some training at the same time. You will find out about the new shit my company is putting out before anyone else."

"Your company?" one of the guys asked.

"Just trust me." She slapped him on the shoulder. "Come on, they are waiting for us inside."

Brock laughed. "Who? The demons?"

"Nooo, the cops." She grinned at the reaction she got.

The guys looked at each other with curious faces. Being in the military, they didn't have any fear of cops, but they weren't sure what she was talking about. The sign on the door said the business was closed for a special event, so they went in and looked around. To their surprise, they were in a gun range. Several cops were milling around the refreshments that had been set up in the back.

"All the fun is in the guns today." Katie smiled, indicating the selection of drinks. "Nobody wants this shit to blow up in the wrong direction, right?" They all snickered at that. Katie winked and continued her reveal of the fun she'd planned. "This is a local gun range, mostly used by cops in their off-duty time to practice and just enjoy shooting. Grab a donut and some soda or juice or coffee and make yourselves comfortable. I have some shit that will blow your mind."

The guys chuckled and headed over to the food, which was no surprise to Katie.

She spotted Angie at the front and walked over to meet her. "Everything ready to go?"

Angie glanced down at her ever-present clipboard and nodded. "Yep. I made sure to give the bags to the detective you told to meet you here, and he set everything up. They are in the back lounging until the presentation begins. Apparently, this is like a family watering hole for gun lovers and cops, so they all know each other."

"That's a good thing. It means they can trust the people they are around." Katie winked. "And by the way, while I have you in front of me, you did a fabulous job planning everything for me. The guys are having a ball, and I can't lie—I'm enjoying the downtime, even though I have to watch them to make sure they don't do anything too dumb. The last thing I need is to lose one of the prized demon fighters in the city."

Angie's eyes sparkled with repressed laughter. "Yeah, that would be bad."

Detectives Travers and Schultz came from the back, nodded to Katie, and took a seat. The rest of the cops followed to watch the presentation, carrying their donuts and coffee with them. Some of them were on duty and some off, but they were all stoked to get an invite to check out the newest demon-slaying ammo that they would hopefully soon be using to help with the incursions. Angie nodded at Katie and took a seat to the side, staying through the presentation to clean everything up afterward.

Katie stood up at the front and took a deep breath, smiling at the group. "Ladies, gentleman, I know you guys are hella busy out there with the influx of minor demons, so thank you for taking time to be here today. I promise you will not be disappointed.

"I am just going to jump right into it. For those of you who don't know, I am Katie Maddison, lead of the mercenary company Katie's Killers. My company supplies the demon-killing arsenal we have all come to love and depend on. Our team is tireless in their dedication to bringing you what you need to fight this war and win. Your feedback has been invaluable to refining the product line. Consequently, I thought it would be fun if you all got to test the newest arrivals to the arsenal."

Katie winked at the guys sitting in the front row; their joy brought joy to her. Those bullets would save their lives during future incursions, and they were clearly stoked to be some of the first to get to use them.

Katie turned and pointed at a dummy in the shooting range. It was modeled after a large demon, with a hide simulated to be just as thick as the real thing. Angie had stuck a couple of donuts over the eyes to lighten the mood.

"Our new bullets have been designed to not only penetrate the flesh of some of the largest demons we have come in contact with, but to continue to work their way through once the ammunition has gone through the first layer. We all know how tough a demon's scales can be, and that has been one of the main concerns. We will produce these bullets in all sizes, so you will not have to switch out your weapons for new ones."

Katie pulled one of her smaller pistols and loaded a magazine of the special bullets. She turned and fired at the target, a small 'x' on the center mass of the dummy. She pushed the button to retrieve the dummy. The bullet hole was smoking and she smiled, looking down at her watch.

"Give it maybe...five more seconds."

She counted down in her head and then pulled the demon hide off of the dummy, holding it up in the air. She looked straight through the hole in the flesh and smiled as the guys clapped. Inside the dummy was a large rubber heart, a hole in it as well and the bullet lodged right in the center.

Katie plucked one of the donuts from the dummy's head and took a bite. "And *that* is how you get it done."

———

Calvin pushed his glasses up the bridge of his nose nervously as Sofia's parents got out of their rented SUV and took care of the valet.

Sofia smiled at Calvin and squeezed his hand, not wanting him to be so nervous. She knew she probably made her parents sound like tyrants, but they weren't. They were just traditional. They had always been supportive of her decisions, which made Sofia want to make decisions they would approve of. She was hoping that today wouldn't be the day that support ended.

They had decided to take her parents to a nice restaurant in the Gaslight District, somewhere they could sit outside on the roof and enjoy the cool San Diego breeze. So far they had been pleasant and welcoming to Calvin, but then they hadn't yet dropped the twin bombshells—that he was much older than their daughter, and that he was one of the Damned.

Calvin was worried they would reject him for being infected, no matter how many lives he had saved or how much time he had spent fighting for the right side.

Calvin opened the door and smiled as Sofia's mother and father entered the restaurant. He followed Sofia in and stood waiting while the hostess prepared their menus. Sofia rubbed her hand across his back.

"Don't be so nervous. They like you so far. I'm sure they will get used to the rest of it," she whispered.

"Why can't the focus just be on my skin for once? Why my eyes? If I am going to be judged for ridiculous reasons, I'd rather have it be something I have a good argument against."

"You do have a good argument. You are a freedom fighter, and you have saved hundreds, probably thousands of lives. Just give them a chance to see that."

They hurried to catch up with Sofia's parents. Korbin and Stephanie followed a distance behind, heading up to the rooftop bar to be able to keep an eye on them. They didn't want to freak her parents out, but they wanted to make sure Calvin and Sofia could focus on what they were doing, not on what everyone around them was doing. So far, there hadn't been a single issue during the trip, not even when Sofia had arrived back by herself for a few hours before Calvin had gotten there. Still, they couldn't be too careful. This was a potentially dangerous situation, and everyone involved had to be protected.

"At least I can have a beer." Korbin smiled, rubbing Stephanie's knee.

Stephanie grinned. "For some reason, something about this just feels normal."

"I was just about to say that." Korbin chuckled. "Let's see how the night goes, and see if we feel the same way then."

"Agreed," she replied, kissing him on the cheek.

She lifted her drink to her lips, but stopped halfway. She narrowed her eyes at a couple of guys dressed in suits standing at one of the cocktail tables in the corner, who were watching Calvin very closely.

"Look to my three o'clock," she whispered to Korbin. "Those guys seem to be very interested in what is going on with Calvin and the others."

"And they are packing," Korbin pointed out, putting down his beer. "Let's move over to the hallway next to them, discreetly grab them and pull them into the bathrooms. We want to eliminate the risk and figure out what the hell they are doing here."

"Good plan," Stephanie agreed, throwing back her drink and getting up.

They walked quickly but quietly across the floor, reaching out as they passed to put a strong hand on each of the guy's arms and drag them off. When they got them to the bathroom door, they threw them inside.

Korbin pulled out his gun and pointed it at them before they could pull theirs. "Put your weapons in the pretty lady's hands, very slowly."

The guys gritted their teeth and pulled out their pistols, handing them to Stephanie with sour looks.

Korbin waved the barrel of the gun toward the wall. "Now back up slowly and put your hands behind your heads, and tell me why the fuck you are stalking Calvin and Sofia."

The guys did what they were told, and the one on the right nodded in compliance.

"We are Mexican federal agents," he told Korbin through a thick Spanish accent. "Check my right breast jacket pocket and you will find my ID."

Stephanie walked over and threw his jacket open and pulled out the ID. She examined it and nodded at Korbin. "So, like he asked, what is the interest in our friends?"

"It's not about them, it's about the parents. They are going to try to take Sofia back to Mexico, and that would cause a problem for both Calvin and Katie."

Korbin and Stephanie tilted their heads and looked at each other, and then back at the agents. Stephanie burst into laughter. "You are worried about Calvin and Katie? This is a riot."

"We are worried about all involved, but they have been important to our country's peace."

"All right, all right." Korbin nodded putting away his gun. "Let's just let you share this with them. I think they can clear all of this up really fast."

They marched the two guys out onto the floor and up to the table, interrupting their dinner. Sofia's parents looked at them nonplussed, then at Sofia and Calvin for an explanation.

"Friends of yours?" Sofia's father asked.

"Actually, they work for me." Calvin sighed. "What's going on here?"

Korbin indicated the agents with a wave. "We found these two stalking you guys from across the room. They are Mexican federal agents, and they are here because they heard that Sofia's parents were planning on taking Sofia back to Mexico with them."

Sofia snapped her head to her parents. "Mom? Dad? Is that true?"

Her parents looked genuinely shocked. "No, not at all true," her mother assured her. She frowned at the agents. "We weren't going to pull our daughter back to Mexico. She has school and a life here."

Sofia's dad swallowed his food calmly and wiped his mouth with the napkin. "I have a few questions. First, why are the two of you scared, even if we were to bring Sofia back to Mexico, and what is going on that the two of you need bodyguards secretly lurking in the back of the restaurant? Let's start with you two."

Everyone looked at the agents, and Stephanie and Korbin released their grip on them. "Calvin and his boss Katie have disposed of a record number of cartel members, including three demon-infected drug lords. We haven't seen this kind of peace in our country for a very long time. It has been a very long road for us, and when they came in, they set our country on a new track. Calvin is very important to us, and we were concerned that you would upset Calvin by taking Sofia from him, which would make it harder for us to continue building communications between his boss and us. We are sure you are all nice people, but our duty lies with Mexico."

Sofia's mother chuckled, looking at Calvin. "I knew you looked familiar. And we would never do anything to stand in the way of our daughter's life, not unless something was hurting her. We are traditional Mexican people, and we live in Mexico. We know what hope his actions against the cartels have brought. Calvin is a hero."

"Wait," Calvin shook his head. "Are you insinuating that if they took Sofia, I would do something to hurt them?"

The agent paled. "We know you care for the girl more than your own safety, señor. We were honestly worried about all parties involved, especially the safety of a pair of Mexican citizens, and the future of our country. You have to forgive us; we are not used to working with the infected. All we know is what we see during the battles. You scare the shit out of us, if I'm honest."

Calvin glanced at Sofia's parents and sighed, taking off his glasses. "Guess the cat's out of the bag."

Sofia's parents weren't sure which issue to deal with first—that their daughter had a demon as a boyfriend or that there were Mexican agents following them around, concerned for their safety and the safety of their country. It was all a shock, and people were starting to stare.

Sofia, on the other hand, was more than a touch amused by the whole thing. Calvin had been worried for nothing in her opinion, and there was no way she would have let her parents take her back to Mexico.

"Okay, I think this needs a bit of an explanation," Sofia admitted.

"I think that might be wise," her father replied.

"You know when I went to Cabo this spring?"

"Yes, for spring break," her mother recalled.

"Well, I didn't exactly come back when I said I did. I have been doing most of my classes online, and rarely getting to come across the border. You see, I met a man when I was in

Cabo, and at first, I thought he was a kind, handsome, well-to-do businessman. He was just a few years older than me, and…well, I got caught up in the glitz and glamour of it all. He spoiled me rotten, convincing me to stay a little longer, and a little longer, putting me under this spell I didn't even realize I was under." She looked down and brushed her hair behind her ear. "Then the truth started to slowly seep out. I found out he was married, and that the house he had welcomed me into wasn't his main residence. Of course, immediately I wanted to leave, but his hooks were in, and he revealed the truth. He was Manuel Sosa, the heir to the Sosa drug cartel. He lived with his wife and children at the family compound, and I was his mistress, a possession he was not willing to give up. After that, I found myself guarded at all times, watched like a hawk. He would send me nice things, send me on trips, send the other mistresses with me to try to keep me happy, but in the back of my mind, I knew I had to find a way out. I tried to contact you, but he threatened to kill my whole family and me. After that, the abuse came often, always in places that people wouldn't notice, but it put the fear of God into me. I felt like I couldn't get away."

Her mother reached out and took her hand. "Oh, sweetheart."

Sofia breathed out heavily. "Then, one night when I was escorted out with the other women, another cartel attempted to kidnap me. That was when Calvin showed up. He rescued me, and got me on a jet to the States. Then he faced Manuel and the men from the other cartel at the border. He was heroic, taking them all down; not without injury to himself, but successfully. After that, we came to my home here, and a few days later more men came after me to get revenge for the new leader's fallen cousin. Calvin quickly shipped me to his base in Nevada. He is a mercenary with Katie's Killers. They took care of me there while Calvin and Katie went to the family compound and exorcised the Mateo's demon. That was where I was when you called—Nevada. We wanted to make sure it was all over, and that no one else was coming for me."

"And that is where these two come into play," Calvin interjected. "They are very trustworthy uninfected friends of mine who have agreed to watch out for Sofia. I have to get back to work soon, and she needs to go to school. Until we can figure out the rest of it, they are willing to stand guard over her."

"Do you think she would be safer with us in Mexico City?" her father asked.

Calvin shook his head. "I wish I could say yes, but I think that would just put all of you in danger."

Sofia's mother grasped her father's hand, thinking about everything that was just said. They looked at Calvin, who was smiling sweetly at Sofia and holding her hand gently. It was obvious that he cared for her deeply.

"I don't know if I speak for my husband, but I am going to speak anyway," her mother began. "You are an adult, Sofia. A beautiful, mature, and obviously well-protected adult. Normally, we would not only caution you about dating an infected, but dating someone so much older than you. However, it looks as if this situation is unique. Calvin has shown that he cares for you. He has shown his bravery and his dedication to your safety. You found yourself in a very dangerous situation, one all parents fear, and without Calvin, I can't even begin to think where you would be now. It was he who saved your life—more than once, it sounds like—and it was he who continued to do so for not just you but for all of us as well. In my opinion, that makes him more honorable than most men I know—besides your father, of course."

Sofia's father smiled for the first time that night and squeezed her hand. "I would have to say that my wife put it beautifully. Sofia, I am sad that this happened to you, and though I could be disappointed, there is no reason to be. You found yourself in a situation, blinded by the beauty of an idea of love, and did your best to survive when it fell apart. As far as I am concerned, I owe Calvin here a huge debt for making sure you were safe. I think we can agree, your mother and I, that we wish both of you the best."

Sofia smiled, and Calvin nodded at Stephanie and Korbin. They nodded back and took the two guys gently by the arm, escorting them down the stairs and out of the building.

Stephanie handed them their guns. "We are sorry for the confusion, but maybe next time you should find out the details." Korbin raised an eyebrow and nodded, watching them walk away.

K atie had demonstrated several of the new bullets and was holding up a new design for the grenade smoke bombs. Detectives Travers and Schultz had left over an hour before, having been called away in the middle but not involving Katie. She was explaining the timer located on the side. They were a new design, meant to prevent the infected fighters from getting caught in the crossfire.

"If you pull the pin and let it go, it will give you fifteen seconds to get away. However, you can program it on the spot, or pre-program these for a longer time period. This will help you get out of tight situations without being taken down by the smoke. I believe that these would also work well when you are setting a trap. If you know where they will be gathering and what time, you can set these in nondescript places and put the small carrying bag around them. That will shield those on the outside from the light of the timer. Then set them for a time when you won't be in the building but demons will be. Drop them where they stand, and then you can go in with gas masks and clear the field."

Katie's phone rang and Angie picked it up, walking away for a moment. She nodded and talked quickly, then walked back to Katie. She whispered into her ear, "It's Detective Travers. He says it's an emergency."

Katie nodded and looked at the crowd. "Okay, boys, feel free to try out the new ammunition. Just not the grenades. We don't need that kind of mess today."

Katie took the phone from Angie and walked to the back of the room. "Travers, what's going on?"

"I'm sorry to interrupt your fun, but we were waiting for some intel before we brought this up, and we finally got it, I think. Something big is coming, but we couldn't pinpoint when or where. We've been tracking this for days now, noticing the shift in how the demons have been attacking. Our ability to track these things on our level is difficult, but we are running out of time. We think something could happen as soon as the next few hours. Whatever it is, it is big. Bigger than anything we have seen before."

"I had a feeling there was something in the works." Katie sighed. "Have you contacted the government?"

"Sure, but they don't find anything credible until they see it with their own eyes. They laughed us off for talking about a gut feeling."

Katie rolled her eyes. "Yeah, they don't use their intuition very often."

"That they don't, but this is too big to wait. By the time they see it, confirm it, and start sending troops, it might be too late. We don't want to just sit back and let that happen, but we need help with this one."

"All right. Actually, I know the perfect person to help. I'm going to put you guys on hold for a minute. Don't hang up."

Katie put them on hold and called Timothy's line in IT. "Hey there, boss lady. Are you calling with some good news?"

"Well, good if you want something to do, bad if you don't."

"Uh oh."

"There is some rumbling going on, Timothy. The detectives out here have tracked it. Normally when someone says they know but don't have evidence I would shrug it off, but to be honest, neither of these guys is the kind to jump to conclusions. The problem is, they are city cops. They can't really search for intel, so we are teaming up with them. I am going to switch over and introduce you, and we will work together to find the surge that will tell us where the portal is going to open. I know it's out there, and may even be open already, but we need to be able to locate it either way."

"Got it."

Katie added Timothy into the call with Travers, Schultz now on speakerphone with them. "All right, Detectives Travers and Schultz, this is my intel and technology whiz Timothy. He is going to use our systems, which at times are more useful than the military's, to help track this incursion. I need you to give him coordinates of the hotspots you've been tracking. He will be able to use those to narrow down the energies that shouldn't be around New

York and pinpoint any high levels of heat that would be coming from a large portal."

"All right, we can do that," Schultz replied. "I have the map on my desk, Timothy you just tell me when you are ready."

Timothy typed quickly on his computer, Travers and Katie standing by. Schultz read out the coordinates, starting with the most crowded areas and moving down the list. Timothy typed quickly, watching the infrared on the other screen and looking for anything out of the ordinary. The areas had action, but it was small; individual demons, or small groups. Nothing that would put them on alert for a large-scale incursion.

"Everything so far seems legit."

"Okay, let's move over to Brooklyn. There are a lot of residential areas over there stacked on top of each other. A very populated area, but not a lot of tourism. You might find more individual activity than in others. This area has been kind of a hotspot for random infected to congregate."

"It tends to happen that way. Places out of the main line of sight," Travers added, "would make the perfect place to sneak in a portal."

He gave the coordinates of a residential area on the edge of Brooklyn and waited to give the next. Timothy input them and looked at the screen, scanning the area and stopping. He zoomed in on one specific area, shocked to see the exact information and location they were looking for.

"Wait, this is way too much heat for just a couple of rogues. It's on the edge of the coordinates you gave me; an apartment complex, it looks like. I can't tell exactly from the screen. It's just infrared."

"I know that area very well." Schultz sighed. "We have a lot of poorer residents over there. It's a high-crime area, but surprisingly, up until this moment no demons have been taken from there."

Katie rolled her eyes. "Pain-in-the-ass demons just have to go and fuck up my day."

"Hold on, let me pull up the real-time satellite feed. I can give you the direct information on the location."

They could hear Timothy typing away, pausing, and then typing some more. Katie grabbed her jacket and threw it on, knowing that she would be heading out soon.

After a couple of minutes, Timothy came back on the phone. "Okay, I got it. It's a very large gate over an old cemetery from centuries ago. There was a twenty-two-story building constructed over it, and from the looks of the real-time feed and the infrared, I would suspect the gate is opening in the basement."

Travers sighed. "This is going to be a bitch to clean out and clean up."

"Hold that perimeter for me, Schultz," Katie replied. "Go ahead and send people out, as many as you can. Cordon off the space, but don't get too close. If the gate's as big as Timothy is describing, I just want you to keep it contained until I get there."

"What are you going to do?" Schultz asked.

"My job," she replied. "I've got a team. I am pretty sure they will be more than happy to make a house call today."

"Sounds good, Katie," Travers replied. "I am going to hold back a medium-sized unit, just in case we are looking at a situation like France. We don't want to fall for it twice and have another portal open that we aren't prepared for."

"I agree, but I would go ahead and put a call in with your captain. You may want to have the military on standby. These things can quickly get out of hand, and there are a lot of innocents in a very small space around there. The fewer casualties, the better, especially with the way people tend to panic. We don't want to set off a panic and have everyone taking to the streets. That will only compound the problem."

"Got it," Travers replied. "Thank you, Timothy."

"No problem, all in a day's work."

The four of them hung up and Katie stood there for a second looking at her phone. She heard a shuffle of feet behind her and slowly turned around, finding the guys standing at attention with their go-bags over their shoulders. They had been listening to the conversation, and they were ready to go. She held back a smirk, knowing she could count on them.

"All right, boys, it looks like we have a big one. The gates are opening, and this time it's no joke. This is not a Times Square incursion. This is like France, only we have no idea what might come after it. I know you are on vacation, and I didn't want to do this but..."

Brock smiled. "Why apologize? You didn't exactly send them an invite. Fuckers insist on gatecrashing our liberty, we're gonna kick their asses back to hell. That is what we're here to do."

Oh my God, I didn't think they made them like this anymore, Pandora purred.

Katie grinned. "Good, then suit up, boys. We're going in."

The guys high-fived and cheered, then ran to the table of weapons and picked out what they needed. Several of the cops who were there went out to their cars, bringing in flak vests for the team to wear. They were all nice shirts, not really optimal for fighting demons. The guys geared up, getting more and more motivated by the prepping and mental stimulation of the buzz in the room. Several of the cops were going to head out with them. Katie stood, making sure she was fully locked and loaded.

Oh, some action at last. I was starting to get fucking bored. Although it's not exactly the kind of action you promised, an ass-kicking is always a pleasurable thing to give.

Katie smiled, pushing the magazine into her pistol. *Right? It's been a couple of days with no asses to kick. I was thinking about taking a walk in the bad part of town later just to get my fix.*

I was thinking of making you so damn horny you had no choice but to jump Brock, but hell, this is just as good.

You think this is Moloch?

If it's not him, it has to be one of the other high-level demons. That kind of gate doesn't just open for some idiot cult members. I'm not really surprised. It may have been busy lately, but it was all petty little shit. The boys downstairs have been quietly plotting their next attack or attacks.

I just hope we are ready for what we are walking into. Brock doesn't even have his whole team. One of the guys went to visit family, and one was just laid to rest.

They will be fine. Remember, you don't have your old team either, but you are still a badass.

Katie walked over to Angie. "If you can get whatever is left back to the house, leave the food for them, minus two boxes of donuts."

"Already got that covered."

"Good, and put in a call to Calvin. Just let him know to be on standby. I'll only call on him if it gets out of hand. I want him to know what might be going down, though."

"Check. Be careful out there, and don't let those boys walk in with their egos."

"You got it." Katie smiled. "It's all about the mission."

The sky above the city was starting to darken, and the lights outside the windows of the cop cars were twinkling. There was a stillness in the air that sent shivers up everyone's spines. Something was different about this fight, something that none of them could quite put their fingers on, but it was there. The cops' sirens echoed off the buildings, and Katie rolled her window down, feeling the stale air waft over them. The closer they got to the building, the hotter and stuffier the air felt.

Katie and the team rode in the police vehicles. They'd jumped in with the cops to get there as fast as they could. They were hauling ass down the streets, weaving in and out of traffic and even coming up onto the sidewalk when it was safe in their rush to get through. Cops and SWAT from all over the city were converging on that one complex in Brooklyn. The people in the buildings around shut their doors and hid, feeling the air of wrongness that pervaded the area.

The cars pulled up halfway up the block where they had set the perimeter. They stepped slowly out of the car and could feel the darkness pulsating from the area. Katie put her hand to her chest and rubbed, trying to soothe that burn she'd begun to feel before they even left the shooting range.

They could hear screams echoing from the building, from the bottom up to the top. All around the building the cops were setting up roadblocks, lines of officers ducking down below them, resting their weapons on the cement blocks. Every few minutes a burst of gunfire could be heard when a demon came out of one of the exits of the building attempting to make a run for it.

The cops were all equipped with the special bullets, and had finally learned to aim for the head. There was already a pile of dust building up on the sidewalk. The captain had arrived shortly before Katie and the guys and he walked over and stuck out his hand, shaking Katie's.

"It looks like the demons are coming from inside the basement. That is also the closest point to the old cemetery this building was built over. They are exiting the gate and making their way up one floor at a time. The people inside are attempting to barricade themselves in, but we are unable to tell at this point how many casualties we are facing. The city sent over the specs for the building, but it is a very simple layout. One set of stairs, no elevator, and a straight hall from front to back, lined on each side with apartments."

"Are they all occupied?"

"There are six vacant units on the first three floors. The

rest are occupied, but we have no idea how many were home when this began."

"Thanks, Captain." Katie looked up at the top of the building. "I'm going to get up there. Get above the bastards and drive them down. Your guys are doing a great job keeping up with the ones coming out, but you need more men on those posts. If there is a surge, you could be hit by hundreds of demons."

The captain swallowed hard and nodded. "Got it."

Katie needed a way in from the top, and she didn't have time to wait for a chopper. She glanced at the building next door and smiled. "I got this!"

She turned to the guys, who were standing by waiting for instruction. "I want you guys to get ready to go in. You will know when it is time to rush the place. Be safe."

With that, she took off down the street and up onto the sidewalk, sprinting into the building next door. The guys all looked at each other and pulled out their weapons making sure they were ready to go. The SWAT team loaned them some helmets and jackets to wear over the bulletproof vests, and they stood listening to the silence, wondering what their cue would be. Suddenly, one of the fifth story windows shattered, and glass exploded outward and fell to the street.

Katie dived out the window, and her wings unfurled before she dropped too far. A few beats and she was level with the fifth-floor window she'd chosen as her ingress. The steady beat of her wings as she held herself steady with Tom and Harry raised caused a downdraft. She fired, and one final flap propelled her through the now open window.

Brock raised his eyebrows. "I guess that's our cue!"

Before they could take a step toward the building, they were knocked back by a massive concussive wave. Brock and the guys dived for cover as glass exploded from the buildings and cars all around them. They regained their footing and started toward the building, wishing they had seen whatever just happened with their own eyes.

The cops standing by watched with wide eyes as the guys ran toward the building and disappeared inside.

Gunshots echoed as total chaos erupted inside the building and the night was filled with the song of demon screams.

12

Katie rushed across the sidewalk and into the building next door. She hit the stairs and climbed until she hit the fifth floor. She ran down the hall and pushed into one of the apartments, finding it lived in, but unoccupied. She raced over to the window and looked out, trying to make out her plan.

Okay, here's the deal. It looks like that apartment straight across is vacant. I need to get from here into there.

You can't be thinking what I really hope you aren't thinking.

I don't even know what that means. I am going to shoot out this window, make a run, leap across, and use my wings if it's necessary to get across the gap. While that is happening, we will shoot out the adjacent window and dive through, landing in a nice roll on the floor.

That all sounds absolutely poetic, but in reality, you are going to try this wing thing again. I don't like it.

You don't like it because it's an angel thing and you can't control it.

I don't like it because humans and demons aren't meant to

fly. We climb, we run, and we fall, but we do not act like pigeons on a New York apartment windowsill.

Okay, but what do you have to really give me? You refuse to tell me about the armor and sword thing Gabriel wanted you to share with me, so I would like to know what you have to add. If you have a better idea, by all means, give it to me. I am all ears.

First of all, Gabriel doesn't know you. You are not ready for the sword and armor "thing." Secondly, we have been marching right into the thick of it this whole time and now that you get angelic tingles in your thighs and some feathers on your back you want to change what has always worked. Besides, I didn't even know about the whole armor thing until he said something. I had to figure out what it was, and unlike some creatures, I don't give you details in bits and pieces and hope that you can piece enough together not to die.

I like to think that after all this time fighting demons, you would have learned that it is better to take the safer route than the gung ho, jump-into-hell route. It's only a matter of time before we end up with a bullet in the gut or our head bitten off.

Oh, so it's okay for you to send the heroes in that way?

They don't have wings, and they are trained to do whatever is necessary. Why do one thing when I can help from another angle? You are really an impossible bitch today.

Pandora gasped. *How dare you!*

Oh, shut up. You are a bitch and usually very proud of it.

Katie looked out the window and saw that she wasn't quite at the angle she needed to hit the opposite window straight on. She headed down the hall to the first bedroom on the left and kicked open the door. She ran over to the window and checked the angle from there. She nodded, finding it perfect for her plan, waiting a moment for Pandora to shut the hell up.

Why don't you just let me take over? I can jump that and climb down.

Because we are too close to the ground, so everyone will know it's not me. And we are walking into a fight with a team that has no idea I can morph into you. We don't need to distract them. They aren't as strong as we are, and they've already lost one teammate this month. Now, if you are done, I would really like to get in there before the battle is over and Earth is swallowed by a giant portal to hell.

That can't happen. Pandora scoffed. *You and your imagination. Humans are so silly with that.*

You are a demon from another realm, I think I have the okay to start thinking that the crazy just might be possible.

Yeah, maybe, but let me tell you right now, it's not glittery-vampire possible. You got to keep those feet somewhat grounded, or you'll be chasing down faeries and talking to invisible trolls.

Katie just ignored her, seeing that the guys were down on the street waiting for her. They were getting their gear ready, and more demons were pouring out of the front door. She kicked the stuff off the floor around her and walked back to the center of the room, then ran toward the window. She drew Tom and Harry, firing both as she coiled and leapt through the opening the bullets created a split second before she hit the glass.

As soon as she cleared the window her wings appeared. She flapped them once, twice, the powerful beats sending a gust of warm air down to the ground. She turned a tight somersault in the air and raised Tom and Harry again and fired, hitting the closest window as she turned her body to go through.

Ohhhh nooo! Pandora grimaced. *Please for the love of Lucifer don't miss. It will fucking hurt, be embarrassing as shit, and then we will go splat on the ground as a not too funny encore. I don't want to have to put your entire body back together in a dirty alley in Brooklyn.*

Katie aimed and closed her eyes, ducking her head as her wings collapsed and she flew through the now open window. She rolled as soon as she was inside, tucking her body as she hit the floor. She whirled around on the hardwood, her body spinning as she crashed into the wall on the opposite side of the room.

Well, that *was fucking graceful.*

Hey, I landed, didn't I?

Pandora sniffed. *Kind of. I still think we should have done it without the wings.*

Katie groaned and pulled herself to her feet, listening to the screams tearing through the hallways. The apartment she was in was empty, which was good because she really didn't want to put anyone else in danger. She looked back out of the broken window at the guys, who were just figuring that was their cue.

She turned back around on instinct, just as her body was wracked by a pulse that began in her chest and exploded outward around her.

All the glass around her disintegrated

What in the hell was that? What? Are you a fucking Avenger now or something?

Wasn't that you?

Uh, no. I don't do weird alien Superman shit like that.

146

Huh, it must have been my angelic powers then. That's pretty fucking cool.

Oh yeah, sure until you go out there and find all the humans have turned to dust or something fucking weird like that. I'm telling you, these angels aren't as angelic as you really think they are. They aren't above dishing out some collateral damage to get their point across.

I can feel the energy around us, Pandora. They are still alive, and so are the fucking demons. From the sound of it though, they don't like it too much.

Katie walked out of the bedroom and flung the front door open. She cringed at the sound of demons screeching in agony all around her. Wherever they were, anything demonic in the range of her energy discharge didn't like it too much. It was like she had the same power that her special metal ammunition had, only it was inside of her body.

She stepped out into the hallway and looked down at the staircase at the end of the hall. She started to run but slowed as the sound of screaming got louder. There was an open apartment door to the right and she peered around, finding two demons writhing on the floor, holding their claws over their ears and clenching their eyes tightly shut.

She stepped inside, stopping with a hand to her chest when she saw the entire family dead on the ground. She knelt by the body of the daughter and touched her fingers to the little girl's eyes to close them.

Katie gritted her teeth, and her eyes glowed red. She stood up and stomped over to the demons. She used her momentum to pack a little extra into the foot she planted in the demon's balls. Katie continued to kick him, each strike calculated to cause the most damage.

"You sick sonsofbitches, you come to my motherfucking world and kill *my* motherfucking people? This is what happens to pieces of child-killing shit. How does that *feel*, you dick-sucking asswipe?" She punctuated each word with another kick or stamp, and the demon was mostly a smear on the floor by this point.

I hate to break this up, it's rather enjoyable to watch, but I have to tell you, there are about a gazillion other demons and humans that actually are still alive.

Katie kicked the demon one more time, her chest heaving from the effort. She wiped the sweat off her forehead and pulled a large knife from her waistband. She grabbed the first demon and turned him toward the second, pulling his head back to expose his neck. She sliced the demon's neck and threw him to the floor, then grabbed the other by the shoulder. Holding it up in front of her, she sunk the knife into its gut and sliced up through its chest and into its throat, spilling its sludgy entrails all over the floor.

That stain is never going to come out.

Katie shook her head and tossed the demon to the floor, turning and taking one last look at the little girl while the beasts turned to ash. She walked back out of the apartment and took a deep breath to get her emotions back under control. She was livid, angrier about the death of that little girl than she had been about anything in a long time. It was running through her veins, the revenge, the anger, the bitterness. She could feel the angelic side of things pushing back against it, but she wasn't going to let it go.

She sensed a demon across the hall. She pulled out her pistol and stomped over kicking the door straight off the hinges. There was a mother and her child crying and shaking in the corner and a demon was stalking them, his big claws out and ready to strike. She raised Tom and pulled the trigger, and the demon's head exploded all over the wall. The mother shielded her daughter from the sight and waited for the demon to turn to ash before picking her up and running toward Katie.

"Thank you so much," she cried.

Katie nodded. "Go down to the third door on your left, it is an empty apartment. There is a broken window with a fire escape. Get out of the building, but make sure they see you when you are coming down. There are cops ready to take care of you."

The woman nodded, and the little girl turned, looking up at Katie. There was a flash of red in the little girl's eyes, but she smiled, reaching out to touch Katie's face. Katie was stunned as they raced down for the empty apartment, never before having seen a child so young infected.

Looks like they are starting them young now.

I don't even have words for that.

Probably better. There is a lot of ass to kick, and we are running out of time.

Katie jetted down to the staircase and looked up and down making sure there was nothing bigger than her or equal to her anywhere around. The demons were fleeing which was strange to her. She shook her head ready for anything, heading down the stairs to find the others and shut this portal to hell before it was too late.

Brock and the gang plowed through the bottom floor, taking down six demons just as they entered into the large open entryway. A couple of the guys grabbed several metal pipes from a pile of renovation tools in the corner and slid them through the doors to impede the demons' exit. They looked at the doorway leading to the basement, the door knocked off the hinges and waves of heat shimmered in the air. The paint on the walls all around them was dripping with sweat, and the floors were hot even through their shoes.

A demon shot out of the top of the door, then clung to the ceiling and scurried across. All five men pointed their weapons and opened fire, taking the demon down. One by one they shot demons trying to escape the basement. There didn't seem to be a lot of them coming at one time, which made it easy to keep them from entering the high-rise.

"This isn't so bad. Are we sure the gate is as big as we think it is?" one of the guys asked.

Suddenly the ground began to shake, and dust cascaded from the walls. All five men turned and stared at the doorway leading downstairs to the basement. They could hear the roars of hundreds of demons echoing as they swarmed up the stairs and walls toward the door. The same guy looked at the others and lifted an eyebrow. "That can't be a good sign."

Suddenly a flood of demons came rushing out of the door and burst out into the space. Several of them ran right into the glass like pigeons while others roared and screeched as they pulled on the front doors. The guys just shook their heads and started shooting, backing up to each other to cover every angle. It was like shooting apples in a barrel at that point there were so many of them. The floor was coated with a thick layer of demon ash, but there were so many of them Brock and his team were getting swamped.

Brock shouted to be heard above the squall, "We have to move or we are going to be overwhelmed. I don't know where Katie is, but they are coming faster than we can take them down."

"There's no place to go! Katie is pushing down, we are just killing!"

The sound of gunfire and crashing glass was all around them, and they stared wildly as the demons spun around the room, jumping over others as they turned to ash. It was the craziest thing Brock had ever seen. He pulled his finger off the trigger for a moment and looked around, noticing that it wasn't a normal attack.

"Guys, guys, stop shooting for just a second."

One by one the guys stopped shooting and looked around them. Brock sighed in confusion and turned toward the men.

"They aren't coming for us, just shoot them as they go by. Don't let them out the front doors or into the upper stairwell!"

The guys started working to slow down the hordes, knocking them down as they attempted to escape one way or another. However, as the guys aimed at a surge coming through the doorway to the basement, three of them to the right changed course, heading straight for them. All five of the guys turned, forming a line and blasting into the charging demons. They started to surge, joining the attackers coming at the guys like a wave.

Brock unslung his automatic rifle from his back and planted his feet into the ground. He focused and pulled the trigger spraying bullets back and forth across the surge until every last demon fell to the ground in a huge pile of ash. The guys stopped shooting, the other demons still running around them and stared at Brock. He wiped his forehead and took the gun strap from around his neck, tossing it to the ground.

"What? Sometimes you need more than skill and luck. Sometimes you just need to pump the motherfuckers full of bullets."

Just then another demon jumped from the adjacent wall with his claws out at Brock. Brock rolled his eyes, raised his sidearm, and shot the demon.

Don't they ever learn? They make me ashamed to be a demon.

The demon groaned and then fell to the ground, turning to ash as he hit the floor. The guys tilted their heads at Brock and then cheered, finding that he was becoming more badass with every passing moment.

A couple of floors above them they could hear Katie's huge guns blasting away demons. They continued to fight, thinning out the horde as they continued to pour through the door to the basement. They knew they were going to have to go downstairs and somehow close the portal, but there was no way in hell they were doing it without Katie. They were badasses, but they weren't sure what would be crawling out of that portal at any minute.

"This isn't quite what I thought when you said a good time in New York," one of the guys shouted. "But fuck if I am not having a damn good time. I will definitely have my fill of demon heads by the end of all of this."

Brock chuckled and killed a couple more demons before reloading his pistol. "At least we can say we helped New York City while we were here."

"All I know is this better get you fucking laid."

13

Katie thought that finding the others was a hell of an idea, if she could get out of the fucking stairwell first. As soon as she started moving down the stairs to the fourth floor, a demon dropped down in front of her, snarling and swiping his claws at her. She rolled her eyes and kicked him hard in the chest, sending him stumbling down a few steps to the landing. He continued to growl and snarl, putting both sets of claws up in the air and waiting for a fight. Katie had neither time nor patience, she wanted to get this the hell over. All the rest of the demons that were around were running like they had a bus to catch, but not this fool.

Katie reached back and pulled out two halves of her staff. She pressed the buttons, and the blades flipped. She smiled, tapping the metal against the railing of the stairs. The demon continued to snarl, finally swiping his claw outward. Katie swung a staff, slicing the demon's arm off above the elbow. The limb fell to the ground, and thick black blood squirted everywhere. Katie leaned back to avoid the spray, watching for a moment as the demon snarled and screamed and then regained its composure, lunging toward her. She moved to the right as the demon flew past, landing on the steps and then turning quickly around.

She swung her staff again, this time she struck the demon in the neck. The blade stuck in his throat.

Katie sighed and applied her foot to the demon's chest to dislodge it. The staff finally dislodged, and she stumbled backward onto the platform below. The demon glared at her with wide red eyes before bursting into dust.

"This just couldn't be simple, could it?"

When she opened the door to Level Four, she stood back as the demons churned past, paying her absolutely no mind at all. She tilted her head when she caught sight of a straggler that looked more like an orangutan. The oddly-shaped demon fell a little farther behind, and Katie saw the leg it was busy eating.

Katie stepped out from the stairwell and cleared her throat, which didn't get the demon's attention.

"*AHEM!*" she yelled.

The demon slowly turned, its eyes blaring red. Katie chuckled at its huge belly and short legs.

"Where you going?"

The demon snarled and turned to continue on after the others, but Katie was not going to be ignored. She drew one of her small throwing knives and flung it to stick in the demon's back. The demon stopped and reached back with an overly long arm to pull the knife out, then turned with a speed that belied its odd frame and threw it back at her.

Katie dropped her staff and caught the knife between her palms right before it struck her in the eye. "Look at you, a crazy little fucker. Have you met Tom?"

The demon tilted his head at her and blinked vacantly. Katie pulled Tom from its holster and pulled the trigger, blowing the strange little demon's head right off its shoulders. The round body wobbled back and forth before collapsing into a pile of dust.

Katie turned around and headed down toward the bottom floor. She was almost hit by several demons that busted through the second-floor door, making a run for it. She walked onto the floor and looked up and down the hallway. The lights flickered, and Katie caught sight of one apartment door that was wide open.

A little girl, frozen with fear, crouched on the floor in the doorway, her hands in her mouth as she tried to stifle her hitching sobs. Just as Katie relaxed her shoulders, a paw swung down from the ceiling, knocking the gun from her hand. The demon dropped onto Katie, and the two tumbled across the ground as Katie worked to bring its arms under control.

The terrified little girl's feet scrabbled against the floor as she tried to push herself backward.

Katie kept her eyes on the fight but called over some reassurance for the child. "Just one moment sweet-ie...ouch." The demon clipped her cheek with its claw, opening a hot line across the skin of her cheek.

Just as fast as it was torn, Pandora closed it. Katie smashed her forehead into the demon's nose and then thrust upward with her hips to fling it off. It landed in an ungainly heap against the wall and Katie flipped to her feet and kicked it in the face for good measure.

"What is with the heavy-assed demons tonight? What are they feeding them down there?"

Probably a high protein diet of fried chinchillas and human thighs.

I'm sorry I asked.

The demon stood up and leapt at Katie and she darted for her weapon, tucking into a roll to avoid the demon's claws. She scooped Tom up from the floor and rolled over on her back as the demon soared overhead, aimed for its head on her next breath, and pulled the trigger. The demon fell on Katie's legs before turning to ash. She grimaced, shaking the grit from her legs and pushing herself to her feet.

She grabbed a teddy and a blanket from the couch and took the little girl to the closet in her room. "I have to go and save some more people, you stay in here, okay" The child nodded blankly. "Someone will be here soon to save you. Do you understand?"

The little girl nodded again and took the blanket and bear from Katie.

Katie didn't know where her parents were, but she didn't really have time to think about it if she were to save more lives. She was the blunt instrument sent in to clear the danger, the people whose job it was to provide care would be able to get in just as soon as she had completed her part.

She left the apartment and headed back to the staircase. The stairs were empty again, and she hurried toward the first-floor door. She could hear the gunfire inside and knew that the team had to be inside. She needed to get to the portal. Just then another demon ran up the stairs from the door below and stopped right in front of Katie. It snarled and gurgled, which was getting a little boring.

Katie rubbed her face. "I'm so done with this. Come on, already, asshole. I don't have all day."

The demon jumped at her, and she grabbed its arm as she twisted out of its reach. She kicked open the first-floor doors and dragged the demon in behind her by the arm.

The guys looked up as she dragged the demon to the open space by its arm and slammed it on the floor on either side of her a few times before she hurled it through the window.

Brock chuckled and nodded as the ash rained down outside the window. "Nice of you to finally join us."

Katie's fist tightened momentarily on the demon arm before it too turned to dust. She looked down at the resulting mess on her boots and sniffed. "Yeah, well. I had a little cleaning up of my own to do."

"They just keep coming, but most of them don't want anything to do with us. They are running from something."

"Or *to* something," Katie replied. "I think they are supposed to flood the city, but they can't get out of the building at the moment."

"What do we do?"

"Well, we could stand here for the rest of our lives shooting at them, taking them down one at a time, but they will just keep coming. I promise you, the demons in hell have a lot more time to waste than we do. We could be stuck here for the rest of our days. We have to keep moving. Kill anything that comes after us, but we press forward. From the heat rolling out of that doorway, I am assuming the portal is in that direction."

Brock nodded. "That seems to be the case. At least that's where they are all coming from."

"All right. I want two of you in front of me and three at my back. Kill anything that moves, minus the people of this building that are hiding. We need to get down there, and then I can figure out how to close this gate. The bastards don't want *me* jumping in after them."

Brock nodded and turned to the men. "Jones, Eros, you are up front, clear the path down to the basement. Richards, Thompson, and I will bring up the rear. Kill anything that comes after us. We need to get down to the basement. Keep Katie in the middle. She has a plan."

Katie grinned. "What, you think I need you boys to keep me safe? That's cute, but I'm really the one trying to keep you safe."

Slowly they moved down the steps, killing every demon that came their way. When they reached the bottom, they all put up their arms to block the massive waves of heat coming from the portal.

Katie walked over and kicked down the stack of bricks and stones holding up an old-looking artifact that seemed to be helping the gate stay open. She shook her head, looking at the gate. It was huge—twice as big as any she had seen before—and she could see land on the other side.

Curiosity got the better of her. She stepped through the portal onto the obsidian landscape beyond and gazed open-mouthed at the burning expanse. Lava flowed in thick rivulets just a few feet away from where she stood, and the sulfur stench of brimstone was enough to make Katie catch her breath. She spied mountains in the distance. No, not mountains. Mountains didn't move.

Titans.

The giants paused in their progress and turned as one to inspect her with red eyes the size of small suns. Katie felt small and insignificant in the light of their glare.

Pandora, why are they all looking at me?

They sense the angel in you. I'd step out and let the portal close before they decide you're worthy of more attention.

Katie nodded, chilled to the bone by the extremity of the hellscape.

Katie!

Huh? Oh, yeah. Close the gate. This is not a vacation.

Some vacation that would be. You would have a sunburn within ten minutes if your body didn't dry up and turn to dust first.

Katie nodded and stepped out of the portal into the basement. Brock pulled her back as the gate snapped shut.

Katie frowned. "That was a bit easier than I thought it would be."

They sensed you are part angel. They didn't want to take the chance of you climbing back through with friends of the angel variety.

Umm...I don't have angel friends.

Yeah, well, it's a stigma. Sorry, everyone in hell assumes every angel loves every other angel. It's all a disgusting love-fest up there, and I really don't know where that came from. Probably because they are the warriors of God.

Does that mean I should be going out to find some angel friends?

Good grief, no. We already have one too many nosey angels hopping around this place.

Are you talking about Gabriel or me?

Both, but mostly Gabriel.

I'm sure he's not really that bad. You are just predisposed to hate him.

Oh, yeah, totally overreacting. His kind only tossed our kind down to hell. No biggie.

Safety first? Katie wasn't sure what else to say. She knew how hurt Pandora was by the whole thing. However, she couldn't exactly make a choice between her angel side and her loyalty to Pandora, since both were immutable parts of who she was. She hated things like that, things that tore friendships apart. That was why even before she became a demon she stayed away from most political debates, and almost all confrontations.

The sound of firing echoed from above them, and Katie realized all those demons trapped in the lobby had been able to get out the small windows. Still, it sounded like the cops were in badass mode. Precinct 19 was still getting shit for letting the one infected get away, and they didn't want to deal with that level of humiliation if they let one slide by.

Brock grinned. "Sounds like they have it under control up there."

"Good. I'm wiped and disgusting," Katie replied. She looked down at the demon blood splattered on her chest and arms and grimaced.

"Well, it sounds like you taught them well."

Katie sat down on an old chair and put her feet up on a pile of rubble. "I'm just gonna wait and let them handle this. You know, for morale purposes."

The guys chuckled and took a seat, some wiping the grime off their faces, others just taking a minute to be still. A hell of a lot of demons had come out of the portal, and they had gone through almost all of the ammo they'd brought. It had been a huge incursion, but not as deadly as the others.

After about fifteen minutes the gunfire stopped. Katie stood up and held her hand up to the guys. One more round blasted, and Katie smiled, nodding. She twisted her finger through the air and pointed at the door.

"Okay, boys, it's time to get the hell out of this hot, dingy basement."

As the guys climbed the stairs toward the first floor, they talked about the new weapons they had gotten to use.

"This ammo was badass. The demons were dust with one shot. There was no need to cut off any heads or shoot them multiple times. Even the ones where the bullet lodged in their flesh, fifteen seconds later it wriggled into their brains and *poof*."

"I know, right? And the looks on their faces, like there had been an electric shock to the brain."

"Hmmm," Katie mumbled, bringing up the rear. "Electric shock. Now *that's* an interesting idea."

They climbed up to the top floor, and the guys in the front killed the last two remaining demons that weren't smart enough to figure out how to get out the broken window. Everyone else stepped over their ashes and the guys grabbed the poles in the front doors, sliding them out and tossing them to the sides. They came out tired, nasty, and ready for bed, but that didn't stop them from waving to the cops, who were all cheering for them as they walked out.

"We're like the fucking Ghostbusters."

"What does that make me?" Katie asked.

Brock laughed and looked back at her. "Slimer?"

He'd better watch that shit. I control that dick.

Calm yourself, Pandora. It's all in good fun.

Hmmm...

Travers walked around, shaking hands with each one of the cops. He made his way over to Katie and handed her his handkerchief. She smiled and wiped the blood off her face before handing it back to him.

He held it up with the tips of two fingers and dropped it to the ground. "I have a million of them. Good job in there. You guys really kicked some ass."

Katie grinned. "You guys weren't too shabby either. I heard the gunfire."

"Yeah, they really knocked it out of the park. Not a single one got away. Now we have to go clean up and get the survivors out of hiding."

"Oh, that reminds me. Floor two, Apartment 2c, there is a little girl all alone in the closet with a blanket and teddy bear. I have no idea where the adults are. I told her you guys would come and get her when it was safe."

Travers waved a nearby cop who was eavesdropping to go get the girl. "Sure, sure, we got this part. You guys get out of here. We've taken up enough of your vacation time already."

The guys were already halfway down the block when

Katie caught up with Brock. They reached the main road and looked around. Across the street was a donut shop, with a pizza place next door. The guys turned around and looked at Katie.

"Hell, yeah. You can't offer me donuts and expect me to pass that by."

Yass, you are learning. I thought you never would.

I'm also fucking starving.

Hey, I think you deserve a snack. Pandora chuckled. *Except for the whole wing thing. That is like five points off.*

Let it go. They aren't going anywhere.

We'll see about that.

Katie chuckled and followed the guys across the street, ready for some delicious food. They all deserved a break, and Katie was going to treat them. She grabbed her donuts and met them next door, sitting down by the window and chowing down.

It felt like old times, she could get used to the idea of having a team again.

14

"Remind me again, how many spots did we hit at once?" Baal asked, walking beside Moloch.

"Thirteen my friend, thirteen glorious places and Lilith could only be at one. Three of those bad boys were complete and total destruction. There wasn't a human left for miles around."

"Nice, but New York was a bust."

"Meh, doesn't matter. New York was a distraction really, something to keep her and her crew focused on what they thought was going to be a massive incursion. Half the demons didn't even pay them any attention. They were too worried about getting out of the building. I told them anyone who died in the building would serve an extra century in the pits. They were clawing through the walls to die on the pavement out front."

"Genius, pure genius."

"We will attack the US again, but we need to really show that this battle has no borders. That we are coming on strong and are not backing down. I will not have some lowlife demon bitch who thinks that because she was queen, it gives her the right to get in the way of my plans. That bitch can suck it."

Baal laughed. "Let it all out there."

"You know what?" Moloch replied, all amped up. "Let that bitch come, she can clean up a few heads as the humans scream her name. It's time we fuck with *everyone*, no holding back. We are in hell, for fuck's sake. Just because the slut changed sides for those damn donuts doesn't mean we don't still rule with a hot iron fist. We are holding back and getting crushed for it at every turn. Well, no more, this shit is going to be on point from now on."

"I like it. Has there been any word from Lucifer?"

"Nah, he'll stay out of it until he knows we can't lose. There is too much at stake for him. If the angels find out he is involved, they will smite him where he stands. He has to be the one playing politics with this shit. He has to have deniability. I'd rather work just like this anyway. It's quiet, and we get all the glory for it."

Baal chuckled. "We also get the shit, too."

"I can take the shit, it doesn't bother me in the least. There is never victory without a few losses along the way. We just had to find our rhythm, figure out how to get around these asshole humans and their technological advances. Now there is no holding back, we are out for blood and entrails. When this all comes to a close, I am going to decorate my office like it's fucking Christmas with human guts hanging like garlands."

"Fancy." Baal chuckled. "Don't forget the balls for ornaments."

The two demons laughed loudly, reveling in their

success, thinking about what came next. They were heading out to explore their victories, but they had to ensure that Lilith and her meatsack were too tired to even notice. From what Moloch sensed, they didn't even know the whole story yet.

They were oblivious, and that was exactly how he wanted it.

When they got back to the condos there was no real conversation, everyone went upstairs, shut their doors and passed the hell out. They were spent, mentally and physically from the start of the trip through the incursion. On the kitchen counter in every room was a six-pack of donuts and the coffeemakers were filled and ready to go, so all they had to do the next day was press the button and they would have a fresh breakfast.

Katie walked into her apartment and tossed her bag onto the floor, letting out a deep sigh. As usual, the house was immaculate. Angie made sure that nothing was awry, and kept the house very clean. Katie dragged herself to the kitchen to grab a bottle of water and looked up on the shelf, finding three dozen fresh donuts waiting for her for the morning.

Look, P, someone is watching your back.

I know, right? It's about time. That girl was the best choice you've ever made. We are going to get along just fine.

I like how for me it takes a perfect body, stuffing myself to the gills, sex, and about a thousand other things to make you happy, but for anyone else, it's three dozen donuts and a smile.

What can I say? I hold my vessel at a higher standard than everyone else. They don't have to carry my ass into battle, you do. Being in here, I know better than you do what you need.

For some reason, I don't think donuts are on that list.

No, I need those. But then again, who's to say where I stop and you begin?

That's kind of a freaky thought.

You're welcome. Now, when are we giving the old Brock-meister the big V?

Please don't call him that. I had a note sent up to him earlier. You will get your happy ending tomorrow. Relax.

I'll relax when the big O tells me to.

Gross. I have to share everything else in my life with you, and now this too.

I know! It's great, isn't it?

Katie rolled her eyes and chuckled. She finished up a bottle of water and headed straight to bed.

Upstairs, Brock took the time to shower, then stood in the kitchen drying off and drinking some OJ. He looked down at the coffeemaker and picked up a folded note. It was from Katie's assistant, letting him know he would be meeting with Katie the next day at two. The condo number was listed after a personal note from Katie reading, Come on down for a drink.

Oh yeah, sure, a drink, his demon scoffed. *Followed by demon sex, and she may or may not bite your head off your shoulders afterward like a praying mantis.*

Brock laughed. *I really don't think it will be that horrific. She doesn't seem like the kind of woman to go all primal on me after the fact.*

You don't know her demon. When I was in hell, I heard

rumors that she would line up demons just to look at who had the biggest junk and everyone else got their heads ripped off.

That's interesting. Brock yawned. *Well, I'd better get a good night's sleep if it will be my last.*

Go ahead, joke about it. It's all fun and games until someone loses a fucking testicle!

Jesus, he replied rubbing himself. *Enough with the evil comments, my body doesn't want to picture that whole event.*

Just giving you a friendly warning, that's all.

Goodnight. See you on death day.

The next day Brock woke up with a pep in his step. It wasn't a given that he was going to get laid, with Katie he never really knew what to expect. But it was definite that he was going to get some alone time with her. He hadn't been alone with a woman since before Incursion Day, and for the first time since...well, his first time, he was slightly nervous. At the same time, he couldn't tell if those nerves were coming from his own demon or were all his own about what was to come.

He spent the day relaxing. He ate his donuts, drank his coffee and just enjoyed the luxury of being alone for a while. The other guys went out sightseeing, so there was no one there to bother him. They'd all had their fair share of excitement for the week, and having a day without any was a welcome respite.

His alarm went off at one to remind him to grab another shower, tighten up anything unsightly, and get ready to go up. He kept the information from his brothers, not wanting to get the rousing applause he knew they would have given him. He could already imagine it, leaving the apartment while the four other guys stood outside their doors clapping for him as he got into the elevator. That was not the type of start he wanted. He still couldn't wrap his head around why he was so nervous.

Probably because she's terrifying. I mean, you're going up there all hopeful... You remember what I told you about Lilith. Your dick is at risk, my friend. I'd be nervous too.

Katie is still a woman underneath the demon and mercenary shit. A woman with needs.

Well, as long as her needs don't end with you bleeding out, I'll keep out of it.

That's so generous of you. Nothing to do with what her demon will do to you if you dare object?

His demon was silent.

That's what I thought.

Brock stood in front of the mirror and ran a hand over his buzzcut. His teal button-up shirt was wrinkle free, and he smelled good from the cologne he had spritzed on. He tilted his head to the side and flexed his chest muscles, realizing that all the action was starting to pump his muscles. The clock beeped again, catching his attention. He grabbed his keys and left the condo. He took the elevator down to her floor and made his way to her door.

Brock knocked on the door and waited patiently for her to answer the door.

A moment later he heard soft footsteps. Katie opened the door wearing a flowing, knee-length coat that was totally at odds with her bare feet. "Hi, come in."

Brock smiled nervously as he entered her apartment. "Nice coat. Should hide all the weapons nicely."

Katie's mouth lifted at the corner as she pushed the door shut with her foot and dropped the coat. "This? It just hides a lot of skin."

Brock's breathless reply could be heard in the hallway. "Oh wow... Really creamy. Ohhh, mmmm..."

15

The guys had been left to their own devices for the rest of the night. Brock and Katie hadn't surfaced for air the whole night. The alarm clock blared, and Katie rolled over to turn it off. Brock groaned when she slapped his bare ass and laughed.

"Wakey wakey! You'd better get back before they send a search party for you."

Brock turned over onto his stomach and wrapped his arms over his head with a groan. "I suppose you're right, we don't want any drama like that going on."

Katie slapped his ass again and got out of bed. "Go pack, I'll meet you all in the lobby."

Katie sauntered off to the shower and Brock climbed out of bed and threw his clothes on. He couldn't stop smiling the whole way back to the condo upstairs. He packed his duffel and quickly showered and changed his clothes before he headed downstairs. The other guys were all waiting, takeout coffee in their hands. One of the guys handed Brock a cup, and he nodded in thanks.

Katie escorted them back to the airport to take her private jet back to base. The other guys thanked Katie and gave her a hug before climbing on. Brock stood smiling sweetly at her at the base of the steps. Katie smiled back, walking over and kissing him on the cheek.

"Will I see you again soon?" he asked.

"I'm sure you will," Katie told him gently. "Just remember who we are. There are no permanent relationships for people like us. We don't know if we will be dead by tomorrow. What we had last night? That's the best I can offer."

Brock smiled and leaned in to kiss her lips. "And it was fantastic. I get it. Don't worry, I'll be okay. I have lots of memories to hold me over—especially that bobcat twisty-leg thing you did."

Katie laughed and slapped him on the leg. "Get up there. They are all waiting."

"Yeah, yeah. Stay alive, demon angel," he replied, waving over his shoulder. "That way next time I see you we can have a repeat of last night, but maybe more than just four times."

Katie shook her head and laughed, not knowing if she could handle more.

Pandora scoffed. *Please, you think I can sustain you through a twenty-four hour all-out battle but not through more than four times in one night? You are underestimating my abilities, sister. I only let him off at four because he was clearly exhausted by the battle.*

He climbed the steps and walked into the cabin, and all the guys gave him a huge round of applause. He laughed and bowed to them, taking a fresh cup of coffee from the flight attendant and sitting down in his seat. Everyone was in a great mood, so much more relaxed when they had first gotten there, even after a major incursion. He accepted the last high five and buckled in for the long flight back. He took a sip of his coffee and looked out the window, smiling at Katie, who stood there in her shorts and tank top with her hair still damp from the shower, waving them all off. She didn't even notice that Brock was looking in her direction.

He realized at that moment that not only had he have a wild night with a Damned, he'd made love to an honest-to-god angel. How many guys could say *that*? Just as the plane started to taxi down the runway Katie looked up at the window and smiled, a flash of red in her eyes. He chuckled, remembering she might be part angel, but she was a badass chick, which was what had attracted him to her in the first place.

Nothing may be permanent, nothing may last more than one really hot night, but he was going back with a smile on his face and a group of guys who couldn't have been happier. That was what the whole trip had been about, and it had been a complete and total success. Now all he had to do was start figuring out how to get gigs in New York and he would be set.

"You have a good time in New York?" his buddy asked.

"Hell, yeah, I did. You?"

"Damn straight, brother. Just with..."

"Yeah," Brock replied, thinking of his fallen comrade. "Me too, but we gave the city hell for him, and he is wherever we all go when we die, giving us the fucking finger and laughing his ass off surrounded by a hundred hot French chicks."

They both laughed, staring out the windows as the plane took off, leaving New York and KatieDora behind to kick ass and take names.

Angie leaned back in the office chair and put the end of her pen in her mouth as she listened to Timothy tell her a story about where he had gone shopping a few days before and how he scared the hell out of some rude saleswoman with his red eyes. They both laughed hysterically into the phone, relaxing for a moment before diving into the real conversation.

"So, I want to first off say you did a fantastic job the other day nailing down that location of the incursion. It was like two seconds and *bam*, you knew where they were going, the history of the building and even the approximate size of the gate. Now, I'm just learning this stuff, but I was impressed, I won't lie."

"Girl, let me tell you. I was hacking and packing my way through life long before this demon shit. This new life just gave me something better to do with my time than just sit in internet cafes pulling pranks on assholes and building websites in my free time for cash."

"Doesn't mean you aren't talented at it."

"Well, thank you. It's nice to be appreciated every once in a while."

"I hear you." She chuckled. "Katie is really good at doing that for me, but I know she gets caught up in the battle, so I wanted to say something. On that note, I had an idea."

"I like ideas! Girl, give it to me."

"I was thinking that maybe we could figure out how to take that and use it for governments all around the world. I mean, seriously if they'd had someone like you in France that day then things might have turned out a hell of a lot differently. I'm not saying you do it for the whole world, but some sort of system that gives off level detections. When the heat starts to rise above a single number we know, and maybe can even be there before the gates fully open."

"That's interesting," Timothy said thoughtfully. "It would be like a software tapped into a system with my brain. I have always wanted to be a virtual superstar."

"I figured as much." Angie laughed. "But we are hanging over a precipice with the demons. What we have now won't be enough, and new armor and weapon technology only goes so far. Early warning might be a game changer for us."

"The first thing I would have to do is run it like it's live. So basically, set it up on a small scale and go through every motion, making a note of everything the system would have to be able to do. Then from there, I could put it together into a format that could be translated into a system or software."

Angie's eyes glazed over. "Right. I think I got you."

"The only thing is that the general might have issues with it at some level. I know we are contract workers, but we are a huge team, and I don't want to piss off the man who signs the paycheck. The government is more than capable of creating something like this, or even having enough hands on deck to do it without a program, but that is a lot of work for other countries."

"Yeah, but if it helps the demon problem?"

"I don't put anything past the government, sweetie. If this demon problem ever becomes lucrative moneywise for them you will see them doubling down their efforts, trust me. What's good for the bank account is good for the government. But I will spec out what is needed as far as hardware and figure that part out. You are in charge of getting the General's go ahead. He likes me and all, but he will need a little sweet-talkin' from a pretty little thing like yourself. I have no effect on the man in that department. If I did, we would have all kinds of fancy toys to play with. I'm just good that way, if you know what I'm saying."

Angie laughed. "Okay, I can do that. I haven't ever talked to him before but he and Katie are on each other's speed dial, so I'm sure he would take a call from me."

"Good, you do that and I'll do this, and then, we will take over the world." Timothy let out a deep evil laugh. "Just kidding. More like save the world from an evil takeover. Lord, I never thought I would say that in my lifetime."

"Me either." Angie sighed. "Until Katie pulled me out of relationship hell, I didn't even really know the demon problem was that much of an issue. I thought they were overdramatizing on the news."

"If anything, they are playing it down. Humans are too fragile for that shit."

16

"My beautiful assistant, what can I do for you?" Katie asked, chewing loudly into the receiver.

"Hey, you busy?"

"Busy filling my body with something other than donuts while I can. Other than that, no. I was going to check in at the station after this. What's up? Do we have a call?"

"No, actually this is more along the lines of a business venture since you haven't had the time to put into that part of things lately."

"Mm, good, let's hear it."

"So, after the last incursion, I started to think about Timothy."

"Oh, girl, let me just break it to you now. You don't have the right anatomy, if you know what I mean."

"No, no, that wasn't what I meant. I meant, because he has some badass skills, and if he hadn't detected the whereabouts of that gate, things would have been a hell of a lot harder for you and the team. That got the wheels turning, and I thought, what if we could take that—Timothy's skills —and put them to use? We could create a system of detectors every government in the world could use. They could monitor heat and energy levels, and before a gate even fully formed, they would know about it. We could get men to the scene before a single demon came through. That might help lower casualty rates and keep the cities physically intact."

"Look at you, coming up with the master plan. What does Timothy say?"

"He thinks he can do it, but he wants your and the general's okay first."

"I would agree, but I want him to start with just New York as a test. And it needs to be at a reduced rate, so keep the hardware costs down."

"Perfect," Angie enthused. "I'll call Timothy right away."

"Great, and you can call the general too. I don't want that headache today."

"What is it with this man? No one wants to call him." Angie sighed. "I will call him right after I get off with Timothy."

They hung up and Angie immediately dialed Timothy's number. "You are fast. Did you talk to Brushwood?"

"Oh, uh, no not yet," Angie replied. "I talked to Katie first. She said it sounds great, but she wants you to start with New York only, and she made a point to say that she needs you to not go nuts with new hardware. Keep the cost below reasonable."

"How about zero dollars? That's reasonable right?"

"Uh, yeah," Angie chuckled.

"Good because I looked at everything and I won't need

any new hardware if I am just doing New York twenty-four hours a day. It is not a very big place, and once I get the automation up, it'll basically run itself with me scanning and pinpointing the specifics."

"Perfect," Angie replied. "Go ahead and start your setup, I'll give the general a ring and get the final okay."

Angie went through the list of numbers Katie had put in her phone in case she was unable to make the call herself. The general was one of those. She took a deep breath and dialed, holding her head high as she waited for him to answer.

"This is General Brushwood."

"General, this is Angie, Katie's assistant."

"Angie, this is a surprise. Is everything okay? Is Katie okay?"

"Oh, yeah, everything is fine on that front, sure. I wanted to introduce myself so you would know who I am."

"Well." The general chuckled. "We already know all about you. We know who you are, where you've been, and even those few...indiscretions, shall we call them? The ones from your younger years."

"Oh, you... I see. Hmmm."

The general chuckled dryly. "Did I catch you off-guard?"

"A little, yeah. I mean I didn't think that a nobody like me would be so interesting to the federal government, especially enough to be researched to the depth you apparently did."

"You have to understand, it's nothing personal. Katie is one of the greatest assets we have. In fact, she is one of the greatest assets that the entire world has. Anyone on Katie's team is considered a person of extreme interest. It's kind of our way of protecting Katie, and at the same time, covering our own butts."

"Right, and does Katie know you do this?"

"I'm sure she wouldn't be shocked. In reality, whoever works with Katie ends up working and communicating with us as well. It's very hard to separate those two things in the line of work we all do. It's better for us to dot all the I's and cross all the T's before we need to communicate with a person. Otherwise, we would lose valuable time or even compromise everyone's efforts by confiding secret information to someone who may not be authorized to have that information."

"Right," Angie replied, trying to work through the eerie feeling she had in the pit of her stomach. Knowing that the federal government knew most of the intimate details of her life without consulting with her first made her really uncomfortable. She had to get over that, though. She was in that world now, and things weren't as simple as she wanted them to be. She pushed the feeling aside to move to more pressing issues.

"Anyway, I was calling today to talk to you about something. We…no, I guess I should say *I*, wanted to talk to you about Timothy's skills, and packaging and marketing those for retail purposes. He is a hell of a tracker, and we believe his program could be useful not only to us, but to the world as a whole, especially with the most recent attacks. The ability to hone in fast on an incursion could be vital to other places, and at the same time save millions of lives."

"Hmmm," the general replied, thinking about what she was saying.

He had a team right down the hall from him that could do that at the drop of a hat, and they covered most of the US. At the same time, they didn't have a budget to focus their efforts tight enough to catch it every single time, like Timothy had done with the apartment complex in Brooklyn.

"I have a team in place in New York City, but I'm thinking that it might do us good to have that additional service, especially if it is approved by the department. On top of that, you are correct, while my job is to focus on this country unless otherwise directed, the other places around the world desperately need a way to be able to watch the demons, the gates, and be prepared ahead of time for any incursions that might pop up."

"Exactly. It's like backup, but better." Angie grinned.

The general laughed. "Now I just have to figure out how Timothy would prove that he was enough for the task, and I love messing with him."

"I got that impression from how he talks about you," Angie replied.

"None of them would call me, would they?"

"No, sir."

"So you were stuck with the task."

"Yes, sir, but I am enjoying the time."

"Well, Angie, like Katie, you are a good saleswoman. I will give my stamp of approval on the trial of this, but just in New York. If they need to move outside the state, I will need someone to call me to get confirmation."

"Of course, sir. That will absolutely happen."

"Good. Now, why don't you let me call Timothy and give him the good news?"

"Of course. But sir, don't get him too riled up. I need him to focus."

"Ha! If this old man can push him around, he needs to toughen up a bit."

"I won't lie. You are a little more intimidating than I expected you to be. Just saying."

"And you are a lot sharper and a lot more intelligent than I expected you to be. I guess that means I need to start judging people *after* I meet them, not before, no matter how much intel I read."

Angie smiled and chuckled. "That would probably be good. People can surprise you."

"Ain't *that* the truth." The general scoffed.

Angie and the general got off the phone, and Angie put it down on the table, clapping her hands together and smiling. She had actually been able to get something planned out and approved within a twenty-four-hour window. Maybe she wasn't giving herself enough credit. Maybe she really *was* good at doing whatever needed to be done. Little did she know, Katie had seen those traits in her before she saved her, which was how she'd known that Angie would fit in perfectly.

The general sat back in his office chair and smiled, picking up the phone and dialing Timothy's number. He loved messing with the kid. It was too easy, and so much damn fun. It was one of the few entertaining things he got to do with his time.

"This is Timothy."

"Timothy, it's General Brushwood." He could almost hear the grimace on the other end.

"Morning, sir. How are you?"

"Good. I just got off the phone with Angie. Bright young lady."

"Yes, she is, sir."

"She told me about the idea to use your skills. I like it. You are good at what you do, and I think if it works it will be an asset to many. I am, however, only giving you a temporary approval on this. You will work strictly within New York state, and prime the information for use by your team and us. To move on from that point, not only does it have to be tight, no flaws, you will have to create some sort of test to confirm that whatever company is used is good enough to provide this service. I don't want some crap company with loose security and minimal skills messing this up. It has to be fool-proof."

"Of course, sir."

"Unless, of course, you want to work on selling this service to three million municipalities around the world, in one hundred and twenty-two languages at a minimum?"

"Holy shit, no." Timothy had just realized the enormity of the project. "Uh, that's a lot, but this service is impor-tant. I will say, I can't tell you that Katie wouldn't be willing to do that. She is motivated in that way and looking to expand her businesses. However, if it's something too large that she doesn't want to take on, then I would be willing to do it for sure. If she doesn't want the responsi-bility, that is. This can't end up in the wrong hands."

"That's good to hear, Timothy. You have your work cut out for you, so good luck. If you need anything from me, don't hesitate to pick up the phone or have Angie do it for you."

"Yes, sir," Timothy replied with a chuckle, knowing they had been had.

The general hung up the phone and stretched his shoulders back, drumming his fingers on the table. His mouth curled into a smile, and he started laughing to himself. This time, he had finally gotten one over on Timothy. He had a hard time believing they would come to him with an idea like that and actually expect him not to screw with them, at least a little. The general knew Katie probably expected it, which was why he hadn't heard a peep out of her all day. She had her people taking care of the details, putting them through the initiation of dealing with him. All in all, though, the whole thing sounded absolutely perfect. He just hoped it worked.

We just ate a sub like three hours ago.

So? I'm hungry, and I want Chinese, Pandora insisted. *Since when was I ever the one to stop and be worried about when the last time I ate was?*

Never. That would be never. You would eat all day every day if I let you.

Gotta get the calories, my dear. Demon life is strenuous.

I'm sure it must be exhausting lounging around in there doing absolutely nothing ninety percent of the time.

Hey, I fight, remember, even if I'm fighting through you and these days that is at least 50% of your life.

Katie sighed. *I suppose you're right.*

Katie pulled out her phone and found a decent Chinese restaurant about three blocks from where they were. She walked along the streets with her head down, trying not to attract any attention. She had gone out in a pair of flare jeans, flip-flops, and a sweatshirt; frumpier than she usually dressed, trying to hide her identity from everyone. Sure, she appreciated the praise, but she didn't want to live in a constant halo of it.

When they arrived at the restaurant, they went inside and took a seat in the back booth. The waitress came over and took her drink order, and Katie skimmed through the menu. Pandora was there, but not focused on the food. She was too busy giving Katie a play by play of her night with Brock like she hadn't been there.

See, I told you it wasn't about your vagina of death.

He hasn't been back out in the field, so the results aren't conclusive.

You can't blame that on your homicidal slit of horror. That's just the breaks for living a life like you guys do. He left with a smile on his face, and that is what really matters.

Yeah, until a demon takes his head off his shoulders.

Pandora sighed. *What you really need to start thinking about is position. You guys tried a few during the night and I was proud of you, but you need to really get creative. If your v does kill the guy, you can at least give him a wild night before he bites the big one. Missionary is fine for housewives and church women, but you're flexible. Use that fact.*

I think he was more worried about the feeling than whether my leg was behind my head.

Oh sure, sure, until you put your head behind your leg and see his reaction. Trust me, this isn't just for him. I'm a selfish demon bitch. I want you to have multiple O's. This advice is to get the most out of your time. You should be fucking exhausted by the end of it.

The waitress walked up and put Katie's drink down with a smile. Katie started out with an appetizer or two and ended up working her way through seven different plates during the time they spent at the restaurant. Not only that, she finished every single one of them. The server and kitchen staff kept poking their heads out to watch Katie from a distance.

"How does she eat all of that food? I wouldn't think it was humanly possible?" the chef whispered to the server.

The server shrugged. "Maybe she isn't human...or she has a tapeworm...or an iron stomach."

Katie and Pandora talked the entire time they were eating, which was mostly the reason why Katie didn't even realize that she had gone through so much food. She had gotten to the point where she just ate until Pandora was full, which gave her the nod in her stomach to stop. There was no point in fighting over it or trying to avoid it. She either listened to her bitching or went with a really aching belly because Pandora would inflict major hunger pains until she gave in, or just eat the food and deal with the repercussions later. She liked Chinese food a lot, too, so it wasn't really that bad. All the rice though made her wonder if she was going to blow up like a pigeon.

You know what really gets me? Katie whined.

No, but I'm sure you will tell me.

On the way over here, I was slammed into by seven—SEVEN —different people. And every single one of them was extremely fucking rude. The only thing they said was either "oomph," or "get out of the way."

It's New York.

Every single one of them had a fucking New Jersey accent. How is it that an entire state can be so damn rude? They have no respect for anyone else, and they act like I should be the one to apologize when they *rammed into* me. *And at first, I thought, oh, it's just the ones in the city, but no. I went to Jersey, and they were the same damn way. It's like they were born and raised to be fucking assholes. I don't get it.*

Maybe it's you. Maybe you are just a bright shiny target for dickheads. I tell you, I had that exact problem when I was topside before. It was like every man I met was a complete and total asshole. Of course, at the same time, I liked that. The nice guys made me want to barf with their romance, hand-holding, and lovemaking. Just give it to me and leave me be, damn it.

Are you even in this conversation, or have you checked out into Pandoraland?

Sorry to tell you, but you are always in Pandoraland. If we check out, it's to hover on Earth for a few and then head back to the happy place.

That sounds absolutely miserable, and if it's true, it is why I am so pissed off all the time.

That's just because you are a raging bitch.

Look who's talking. Seriously, though, Jersey is the fucking worst and for no reason. It's not like there is a demon that can do that, infect an entire state with the asshole virus.

Pandora cleared her throat nervously. *Well, I mean, there actually are demons large enough to affect big areas of land. They are very few and far between, and they tend to stick to rural communities.*

You are just telling me this now?

I mean, it's really not that big of a deal. There are all kinds of demons out there, and to be honest, I don't think many people would complain. Humans like to be miserable.

No, we don't.

Sure you do. You go on crazy diets where you can't eat bread, you wax shit off your body, you date people who make you miserable and you refuse to change your ways if it doesn't work. It's seriously like a planet full of masochists.

I think you are seeing us all wrong.

In reality, there is probably a much more practical answer to Jersey than an emotion demon. Like maybe the people in Jersey are just all assholes. I know, it sounds unlikely to have so many in one place, but who moves in or out of Jersey really? Not many people. They breed their doom and gloom and stay in their smelly dirty state. I would be an angry bitch all the time too if I had to tell people I was a resident of New Jersey. It's like saying I like the off-brand makeup because it's just shitty and I'm shitty too, so we are the perfect match.

Katie put down her fork and took a deep breath, looking up at the waitress who was bringing the bill. She smiled kindly at Katie, but Katie knew they had all been watching her. It really didn't even bother her anymore. She was used to stares, especially when it came to eating in public. Her eyes opened wide looking at the number of zeroes her bill was showing. That part hurt her feelings every single time. She had never in her whole life spent as much money on food as she did with her demon. She could have bought ten houses by that point just out of the amount she spent on donuts and Italian food.

But then again, what would she do with ten houses? At

least with the food, she got a little peace and quiet every once in a while.

She dropped a wad of cash in the bill holder and closed it up, leaving it sitting on the table as she got up, stretched and headed back out of the restaurant. Before she exited the doors, she pulled the hood of her sweatshirt up and made sure she had everything. Katie slid her sunglasses on her eyes and squinted as she walked out into the sunshine. Luckily it was starting to become fall, and the air was crisp enough for her not to burn alive inside of her sweatshirt. She put her hands in her pockets and walked with her head down back toward the direction of the park. She wasn't feeling people today, and she wasn't feeling any work either.

It's all the Chinese food, Pandora replied. *You'll feel better once I get it metabolized.*

I really hate eating that much food, especially when I'm about to roll up to the police station. You never know when they will throw me a flak jacket and send me out to an incursion. It would be really bad manners to puke all over people during a battle.

I don't know, might get their asses moving faster.

I would probably stab someone if they puked on me while I was killing demons. It's like super freaking rude. You know?

Pandora laughed. *I have never puked before, unless you include word vomit. If you include that, well, it's a constant stream of it.*

Isn't that *the fucking truth.*

Angie walked around the condo, dusting things off and making sure that everything was straight. She headed into the kitchen and poured herself a cup of coffee, staring into nothing as she added the cream and sugar and stirred it. About five minutes later she pulled herself out of it, shaking her head. She had been in a trance for days, unsure what to make of it.

She took her coffee and walked over to the computer, pulling up both their schedules. She ran through hers to make sure it synced perfectly with Katie's. She needed to know where Katie was at all times and what she was doing. She didn't want to be caught off-guard, especially not with a boss who had a lifestyle like hers did.

Angie sat back in her chair and tapped the pen against her lips, looking at the few empty days of the schedule. She looked around the room for a moment and then leaned forward, typing an appointment with the police into her schedule. She bit the side of her lip, knowing it was made up, and then clicked the Share button, putting in Katie's information. She hovered the mouse over the Send button for several moments. Finally, she let it go, clicking and then shutting her computer. She looked around, holding her cup of coffee to her lips, hoping she had done the right thing.

17

Katie had found a local boxing gym. She liked having a place to work out where no one bothered her. It was much easier than working out in the condo's fitness room or going to some gym where she couldn't work out without the eyes of almost every guy in the place focusing on her tits instead of their own damn business. That wasn't even taking into account the extra attention she'd been receiving since her public revelation. The last thing she needed was to be peppered with a million questions when all she wanted to do was burn off some energy and lose herself in her thoughts while she worked on her kicks.

She hadn't really thought that part through when she'd bought the condo, but it was okay. It got her out of the house and motivated to work out. Otherwise, she would stare at the weights from the couch every night, and the only thing she'd lift would be donuts. While Pandora could build muscle, she couldn't maintain it or optimize it to make Katie stronger and faster. That was all up to Katie.

Katie pulled out her iPod and put the buds in her ears.

She turned on some trance music and found her groove, ignoring everything else going on in the gym. She didn't like to lose concentration, and the owner of the gym knew that. He made very sure everyone else knew that too. The guy was cool. He understood her need to train and had offered to spar with her anytime she wanted. Those days she felt like she needed it almost all the time. Not having a team to practice with was hard to swallow.

The doors up front opened but Katie didn't pay them any mind. Everyone who worked out there was cool, and she was in her own little world. The new guy walked in with his bag on his shoulder and set it down on one of the benches. He reached in and pulled his towel out, nodding to the guy next to him. As he looked across the gym to get acquainted with the place, his eyes fell on Katie. At first, her ass and hips caught his eye, but as she swung her long braid out of her sweaty face his mouth dropped open.

"Holy shit! That's the mercenary Katie, from Katie's Killers," he said to the guy next to him, slightly freaking out. "I've only ever seen photos of her. Never thought I'd actually meet her face to face. She's even hotter in person."

Another guy across from him looked at the other regular, and they both stepped forward, shushing him.

"She's here because we treat her like a kid sister. We don't make any big deal of her being here, and we don't for *any* fucking reason tell anyone she works out here. She can come here and do what she needs to do without the hassle of the people who want to ask her a shit-ton of questions and fanboy out on her. She specifically told Harry, the owner, that she would continue to come here, and pay damn good money too, if we all respected her rules and made sure to leave her be. Do you get that?"

"If not, you will need to make other arrangements." The guy held his hands up to show he wasn't starting anything, but he also moved to block the newcomer's view of Katie. "No disrespect, you know, but she is now gym family to us and fuck knows we spend more time here than with our own damn families."

"Right, no I get it. Lips tight, and leave her alone." He nodded his understanding. "Wait, so this is her...what?"

"Dude, seriously?" the guys repeated, putting one hand on his shoulder and a foot up on the bench to talk closer. "We are her place to hide. Her safety before she goes out there and kicks major fucking demon ass. The deal is, if she wants to talk she will let us know. If she wants to spar, we spar with her. We all know she could and has kicked our asses all over this fucking gym."

"Yeah." The other guy scoffed. "Her and Calvin. That dude packs a fucking *punch*, I won't lie. I'm a big guy—bigger than anyone else in here—but that guy puts out ten times the strength I can. Maybe it's the demon inside him, or maybe just the fact that these mercs are used to training harder than fucking Olympians. Now I understand what the demons feel when they are going wild on their asses."

"Who is Calvin?"

"Calvin. You will see him, trust us. He works right alongside Katie. They are a team, and he has been a merc longer than most. They are the remaining members of Katie's Killers, still holding it down for the city. Calvin was on the news in France, kicking demon ass with Katie. He is quiet. Less followed, but just as badass."

"I don't know if I'd say just as." The other guy chuckled. "Katie is like a fucking hurricane and tornado all twisted up into one giant storm."

"Man, so do they spar with just anyone?"

"Nah, Harry picks who can spar with her. He wants to make sure that not only do they get a workout that's worth their time, but that whoever is the lucky one to be on the receiving end of the hit can take it. The first time they got up there Katie sparred with Big Boy John, and within three minutes she had laid him out cold. He was out for two days."

"Big Boy John? As in, the heavyweight amateur who almost took the world title last year?"

"Yeah." The guys chuckled. "When he missed the pageantry match in Las Vegas two weeks ago? That was because Katie laid him out. She felt so bad that she paid his hospital bills and bought his house for him and his wife. I personally found it absolutely hilarious. Big Boy has a tendency to think he is tougher than he actually is. This took him down a peg or two, at least for a little while. I bet he'll be back to shit talking in another month or so."

"Damn, that's some crazy shit."

"Yo, but we're serious—you need to keep this shit under wraps. If anybody starts coming here looking for her because one of us snitched, they will kick all our asses out of here. Harry feels like he's being patriotic, and I think he thinks he can somehow con her into competing, although she won't even hear of it. She knows she would kill the competition, and it wouldn't be fair."

"Shit, if I had her abilities, I'd do it and rake in the fucking dough."

"I'm pretty sure she has plenty of money."

As the guys talked, the door creaked open just slightly, and Gabriel, cloaked in the shadows, slipped through and stepped into the corner. No one saw him enter, and no one noticed him standing there watching Katie from afar. The hood of his cloak was pulled up over his head, and his eyes were fixed on her. It had been a while since he had come around, but he had to step it up.

Calvin stood in the living room of Sofia's San Diego bungalow, her hands in his. She was smiling comfortingly, but he was struggling to do what he needed to do. Work couldn't wait any longer. Things were getting crazy out there, and he knew it was time to get his ass back in the game. Still, the idea of leaving Sofia here was terrifying him. He had almost lost her twice already, and not being here to protect her was a struggle for him.

"I'm going to be fine," she told him for the hundredth time. "You have to continue fighting this war. I'm not going anywhere."

"I know. I'm just worried, that's all."

Korbin walked up and put his hand on Calvin's shoulder. "We got this. We won't let anything happen to her. We rented a small apartment one block over, top floor, and can even see her house from the living room window."

"You rented a place out here?" Calvin asked surprised.

Korbin shrugged. "The sea is a bit nicer than our home in the country, at least for a little while. It'll be like a working vacation for us, and we will keep our eyes on her all the time."

"I'm just going back to check for potential hits, and I'll only be gone for a little while. I want to make sure that no one is coming after you. We've got a great intelligence center at the base, and you know Timothy. He will be all over making sure you are safe."

Sofia smiled. "I trust all of you. I know that nothing is going to happen. And if it does, I'll just start kicking their asses. I learned a few moves by watching you guys."

Calvin chuckled and Stephanie stepped up beside her. "Actually, that's not a bad idea. I could teach her some martial arts while I'm here. Give her a little bit of self-defense so she can protect herself if anything ever happens; drug lords, or just some asshole in a bar."

"Yeah, that would be awesome." Sofia smiled. "Would have come in handy in Mexico."

"I really appreciate that." Calvin nodded at Stephanie. "And Sofia, I'm sorry you have to learn martial arts just to make sure you can protect yourself. You should be living a nice comfortable life with no worries. This is only going to make things harder for you."

Sofia shrugged. "The world is a scary place, and everyone is going to eventually need to know how to defend themselves, I might as well get a head start on it. Besides, it'll give me something to do to keep my mind off missing you."

"I'll miss you too." He smiled. "I promise I won't be gone too long."

"I know it won't do much good to say, but take your time searching. Make sure you know for sure, and you are satisfied. Stephanie and I can stay for at least a month if we need to."

"Thanks, Korbin. You always did have my back.

Korbin smiled. "I don't remember that, but knowing you now, I have a feeling that is more than true."

"It sure was." Calvin smiled. "And I truly appreciate this. A month should be more than enough time for me to do the intelligence work and then plan what to do next. I owe you."

Korbin smiled and shook his hand. "Nah, you don't owe us anything."

"I need to do some training, but not just hand-to-hand combat. I need to use weapons."

"We have those," Harry told her.

He was a short, stout guy, and wore long gym shorts and a zip-up track coat with dirty old gym shoes. No matter what the temperature was outside he had his stock cap on, the sides rolled up above his ears. His hair was cut really short, and you could only see the grey and silver stubble coming out the back. He was a private man and a hell of a coach, and he had worked with some of the greatest boxers out there. In retirement, he ran the gym where he was born and raised and spoke with a thick Brooklyn accent. His name wasn't really Harry, but that was what everyone had always called him. He couldn't even remember when it had started.

"I don't need guns or anything like that, obviously, but I do use a staff a lot and I want to work on my defensive moves. Offense comes naturally to me, but reading the demons, knowing where they're gonna strike next, leaves me rolling across the floor in an all-out brawl half the time. With as many demons as there were this last battle I was in, I don't want to be on the floor for any reason."

"Heard. Give me five, and I'll have two guys meet you in the ring."

"Thanks, Harry," Katie smiled.

She walked over to the ring and pulled herself up on the side, stepping through the ropes. She cracked her neck and rolled her head from side to side, getting ready to spar. The other guys in the place slowly stopped their workouts and took a seat to watch. That was the only time she didn't mind a crowd, she knew even if they weren't sitting there they would watch her, and so she might as well not distract them like that. They could get injured with the equipment if they weren't careful.

A couple of minutes later two of the guys walked out from the back, agreeing to use the staffs to work her out. They were two of the most accomplished guys with that kind of weapon, which was perfect. Harry took a stance next to the ring and crossed his arms. The guys climbed in and stood in front of her, staffs at the ready, ready for her signal.

She nodded and waved them forward, her hands up. They started in on her, not wasting any time, just blowing right into the hard stuff. She used her forearms and legs to protect herself, large welts building up on her skin. The guys moved fast, but she was doing well, only getting hit in the side or back a couple of times. She knew, though, that if that had been a demon's claw she would have been done for. She needed to be so good the staffs never touched her. That took quick footwork and reading their body movements, something she definitely needed to work on.

Ouch! What the fuck? This shit is crazy. Can we go back to living at the base and sparring with your teammates?

First of all, I don't have but two, and secondly, not to be cocky, I am better than them. It's not a workout, and I don't learn anything if I'm not challenged. These guys don't give a fuck who I am. They are here to train me, pain or not.

I didn't take all that time giving you beautiful skin just to watch it get all red and puffy. I'm going to have to work all night to get the damn swelling down in those arms.

It will make me tougher. Besides, it'll get numb after a while. Just got to give it time.

Katie narrowed her eyes and watched her opponents for any twitch that would give their next move away. The one to the right swung low, and the other high. She blocked the high strike with her forearm and jumped, tucking her knees to her chest to avoid the low blow. She landed back on the pad, and the guys clapped on the sidelines. The two fighters nodded, appreciating her skill. She looked at her forearm to see a nasty contusion forming, blood ran down her elbow where the skin had split at the point of impact. She walked over to the edge of the mat and Harry tossed her a clean towel. She wiped the blood away and stood there pressing on it for a second. By the time she lifted the towel off the wound had healed.

She dropped the towel over the side and moved forward again, wanting to keep going. She could tell from the way they were backing off that they were a little worried about making her bleed. She shook her head and waved her hands, keeping her feet moving.

"I'm practicing here, don't let up! I can heal from this stuff but I don't heal from bad timing, so fucking WORK IT!"

The guys shrugged and kept after her, using as many moves as they could pull out of their bags of tricks. After a while, she got nailed a couple of times; a couple of really *good* times. She didn't stop, though. She knew that was part of it, taking the pain, learning from the mistake, and pushing forward. The demons would have no mercy and take no time-outs. They were out for blood and Katie had to be in it that way too, no matter what cuts or bruises she might acquire. She patted each of her shoulders slapping away the sting from the constant jolts of the staff.

The guy on the left stepped forward, lifting the staff high over his head. Katie watched him move fast and swirled around, kicking his stomach. All the air in his chest blew out of his mouth, and he flew back into the ropes.

"Sorry, you okay?" she asked, realizing she had to tone it down or she would kick right through someone.

He nodded and waved her off as the other guy stepped forward. He twirled his staff all around, over his head to each side and near his knees. He stopped and snapped the staff straight up and down before going to town swinging at Katie over and over again, her body moving and twisting to miss as many blows as possible, the others blocked with her arm or upper thigh. The guy breathed heavily stepping back and putting up his hand for a break.

Katie smiled and slapped his hand, walking over and catching a bottle of water from a guy below. She had to give him a break, they didn't have the same kind of stamina that she did, and that was mainly because she was part demon and part angel, rewarding her with a higher tolerance than most.

Across the gym in the shadows Gabriel shut his eyes, searching the gym until he reached Katie's mind. He blocked her and reached inside, pushing into Pandora's consciousness. Neither of them even knew it until he started speaking. Pandora was shocked as hell.

Pandora.

What the ever-loving fuck? How are you in my mind? Where the hell are you, angel boy?

Close enough.

Why is Katie not responding?

She can't hear me. This conversation is for you and me alone.

Normally I would tell you to go fuck yourself, but since I don't particularly want you talking to Katie, I am going to make this exception. But get on with it. I don't like the feeling of you inside of my mind. It hurts.

You haven't given her the information I relayed.

I don't know what the fuck you are talking about. Some armor and weapon bullshit? If you haven't noticed, I'm a demon, not an angel. I ignore angels whenever possible. I did the research, but I couldn't find a thing about your sword and armor bullshit.

It seems I was wrong. I thought maybe you just hadn't told her out of spite, but you really have no clue.

No shit, Sherlock. Fuck, why does this hurt so much?

We are two very powerful beings with opposite powers. They are clashing, so I will get through this quickly.

Why don't you tell Katie yourself? I am not your messenger.

I can't tell her these things, not directly. It would cut too close to having too much involvement. I am not allowed to give her knowledge she doesn't already possess. If you remember, humans have free will, and it will decide the fate of man. I can only guide. This is the best way I know to give her insight into who she is without breaking the rules. They don't really like it when angels break the rules.

Fuck, so you really aren't *going to tell her the information. You really are going to let her figure it out unless I help her.*

Yes.

Pandora sighed and then groaned from the intense pressure building. *Fine, lay it on me, but hurry. I feel like I am about to explode into a thousand pieces. I won't promise I'll tell her. I'll be the one to make that choice.*

Of course. As with all beings, demons have always had free will as well. They just tend to point themselves to the darker side of things.

Thank you for the lesson on demons. Can you hurry the hell up? I knew this was going to be bullshit from the first time I saw you. The whole "God is on my side and will give me the answers" shit. No, they withhold the truth to preserve free will, because magical wings preserve free will.

She has the choice to use them or not, and when she chooses to use them for good, it increases the human ability to make wise choices.

Gross.

Gabriel started speaking fast and straight, giving Pandora the layout as fast as he possibly could. Halfway through, he had to stop and block out Pandora's screams of pain from Katie so she wouldn't know what was going on. His power was too pure, too light to connect with any mortal or dark creature for more than a few seconds. For Pandora it was different. She was feeding on Katie, which meant that unless he held her there for a long time, she wouldn't die. She would just be in one hell of a pain spot. If he had told Katie directly, she would have died. Even the strongest person on earth couldn't hold it together with the touch of pure angelic power.

You sick son of a bitch, this fucking pain is worse than the time Lucifer bound me to the volcano for a week to punish me for skipping the yearly ceremonies. He fucking hung me on the volcano using nails. Your boss knows what the fuck that shit feels like.

Concentrate. One last thing, and this is really important.

Pandora took a deep breath and focused her attention on what he was saying long enough for him to finish. When he was done, he moved out of their minds and released Pandora from the pain. She breathed deeply and cursed at him, screaming all kinds of things before she realized that he had already slunk away into the shadows. Pandora quieted and ducked down into Katie for a moment to think. She couldn't believe that Gabriel, a messenger of God, would treat her Katie like a mushroom. She deserved to be told the truth, not kept in the dark and fed a line of shit.

Pandora had always been a demon, but being so close to Katie, the way she looked at the world had changed drastically. Every fiber of her being fought against the compassion she'd developed for Katie and the other humans close to her. She didn't want to be evil, not anymore. The days of inflicting pain—the bad kind, at least—were over for her

Gabriel was right. No matter what her impulses tried to

dictate, she had the free will to choose differently. Now the knowledge was Pandora's, and the secrets were hers to divulge—or not.

It seemed so odd to her that the survival of the human race was in the hands of a creature from the other side. She didn't know why Gabriel had trusted her with the information, since she could easily give it to Lucifer. He couldn't know that she wouldn't do that.

If they won, then she'd lost. She could go to Lucifer that day and give him the ticket to win, and he would still throw her down in the pits of hell if he didn't just kill her outright. Besides, she had something else to contend with. Something that had been growing inside her steadily since her first day with Katie.

Her conscience.

18

Calvin's plane was on its descent into the airport in New York. He sat with his bag at his feet staring out the window of the plane, watching as they dropped over the outskirts of the city. His mind was locked on Sofia, and all the things that went along with that. She was this amazingly strong woman that had landed in his lap at a time he wasn't looking for anything other than a good summer vacation fling. He knew it wasn't the damsel in distress kind of attraction, he had saved beautiful women before. This was something more than that, something pure, something right, but at the same time, something that seemed almost impossible to hold onto.

The plane touched down on the runway, shaking Calvin from his thoughts. He sat patiently and waited for it to taxi to the gate. He was close to the front, so he grabbed his bags from the overhead bin and headed into the jetway, nodding to the flight attendant as he passed. He kept his sunglasses on, not feeling quite as brave about showing his eyes without Sofia there to remind him that he was still an amazing man.

Calvin hadn't packed much on his race to San Diego, so he didn't have any luggage to grab. He put his carry on over his shoulder and headed out of the airport to the curb where all the taxis were waiting. He jumped inside the first one he got to and gave him the address to the condos where Katie lived. The traffic was horrendous as usual, so he sat back in the seat and relaxed, watching the droves of people walking along the sidewalks as they passed by them. He was shocked, even with the world in peril, even with so many demons on the loose that people still went about their lives, vacationing, working, doing what they did without even a pause. Even in the city that had seen some of the worst terrorist activity in the states, they soldiered on, not willing to pause their lives for even a second.

The difference was that they had a future they were holding onto; something they were looking forward to. They had goals and plans, and up until Calvin had met Sofia, his goal each and every day was just to make it to the next day alive, and preferably in one piece. With Sofia, there was a possibility for a future that wasn't exactly compatible with the reality he was living in.

The problem was, he was struggling to grasp onto what that future looked like. He was in angst over it, trying to figure out what he had to offer this woman, what he had to give that would make a future with him worthwhile or even possible. He was a demon hunter, a mercenary, floating from city to city, living out of military bases. He never knew if he would come home that night alive or in a body bag.

What would a woman like that do with a man like him? Sit there every day, dreaming of his red eyes, waiting for the call that he didn't make it back? He knew better than most that the next day was never promised, especially not to people like him and Katie. He had buried and mourned so many amazing warriors, some even stronger than he was at the time. He had watched them run off into battle and then carried their broken bodies back out in the end. Calvin sighed and leaned his head against the window. He wasn't sure about anything in life at that moment. Not his future, not their future, not anything.

The only thing he felt was pain deep in his chest, as his traitorous heart tore itself to shreds at the necessity of leaving Sofia behind.

Moloch pulled open a medium-sized portal in his office and nodded at Baal. The two demons slid through to the other side. They emerged in a remote area southwest of Beirut, about a hundred miles from the ocean. Moloch looked down at his feet and kicked a body to the side, stepping through the rubble of the crushed town. The place was basic and had no defense against any kind of attack, especially not one that included more demons than there were people.

Moloch's lip curled in a satisfied sneer. "Ah, lucky location number eleven."

They looked around the town at the devastation that ranged from corner to corner. Half-eaten bodies lay in piles, fearful looks frozen on bloody faces. Some of the buildings still smoldered from fires, and the rest were reduced to rubble. The only ash on that property belonged to humans, not demons. They had taken off from there and headed toward Beirut before Moloch had called them back, not wanting to draw attention just yet to the major city. Kind of like in New York, devastation needed to occur. A warning, but nothing huge enough to create mass panic. Not yet, at least.

Both Moloch and Baal felt the power inside of them, the pleased surge of emotion at seeing all the death and destruction around them. They were from hell, a place filled with death and destruction, but to see the humans laid to waste was a special kind of high that floated through them. The two demons walked through the town, observing the heinous crimes that had occurred there. They passed a stone wall the demons had nailed several humans to and picked their entrails out while they were still alive.

As the demons passed with grins, several birds flew off the bodies, cawing as they felt the evil natures of Moloch and Baal. They stepped through a small area to the right that used to be a school for the children. There were pieces of paper with drawings in the dirt, splatters of blood soaked into them. As they rounded the corner a cat jumped out, hissing and growling. Baal snapped his hand out and grabbed it, hissing into its face before tossing it into his mouth and chomping down. Moloch laughed as Baal spat out the bones, wiping the fur from his mouth.

"I like ferals. They taste a bit gamey."

"Then you would love Lilith. I hear her human is a bit feral."

"There would be nothing more pleasing than to feast on the body of that meatsack while Lilith screamed in agony inside her. I would keep the human alive just to let Lilith writhe in the pain, let her know what she had done."

"Then we kill her."

Baal smiled an evil smile. "You don't mean..."

"Yes. We don't ever let that traitor come back. She will be in a world where nothing exists. None of her precious donuts, none of her shopping, or her men. And we would keep the human's soul as a trophy. Lock it away in my fire-place with the rest of those who created a mess for us over the years. I'm tired of playing fair, Baal. This display of chaos should show you that if you had doubts before, you no longer have to. I took care of this battle, I put these men and women in their graves, and I did it successfully in twelve places all at once, all over the world. If I can do that, I can do it anywhere, and the humans would never even stand a chance. I would come down and stand in the center and revel in the sounds of their whimpers and screams, the best sounds there are."

Just then a groan floated in on the wind. The demons turned, narrowing their eyes, taking in deep breaths, sniffing out the life they could feel still pulsing from the beaten and battered village. Moloch put out his hand and looked at Baal, both of them hearing screams and the growls of demons, but they didn't see anyone or anything around them. They followed the sounds through the rubble and found a tablet lying open next to a young male, dead on the ground. Moloch leaned over and picked it up, finding that he had been YouTubing the event. Moloch laughed as he pressed Play and watched the horror on the video. There were demons everywhere, people being ripped in half, and children being eaten like snacks.

When the video was done, he laughed and hit the upload button. Once it was finished, he posted it and tossed it back down beside the boy, his empty eye sockets staring into nothingness.

Brock and his team were at their base, sitting around in the gym. Two of the guys were working on their deadlifts, another was on the treadmill, and Brock was using hand weights, bending his arms up and down, watching himself in the mirror. One of the guys behind them looked at the other teammate and smacked him, nodding at Brock.

"Hey, saw you guys on TV in New York, you lucky bastards! Going out with Katie AND getting to work with her? The fuck? You guys are TV sluts if there ever were any!"

Brock chuckled. "Just doing our job, and looking damn good doing it."

The other guys shook their heads and went back to working out. Brock winked at his teammates in the mirror. No one but them knew Brock had gotten lucky with Katie, and he wanted to keep it that way. They didn't need to know his business, and they definitely didn't need to know hers. He was a little wistful, sure. He liked Katie and wished their lives were different, but they weren't, and he was okay with that. The best that he hoped for was maybe another date.

The guys finished their lifts and crowded around,

putting their stuff away. Brock looked up at them and rubbed his stomach. "Chow time?"

"Fuckin right, bro."

One of the guys groaned and threw his head back. "What I wouldn't give for another donut."

The guys laughed, and Brock patted him on the back. "Maybe another time. For now, we are back to routine, buddy. Ready to kick ass and take no fucking names."

"Hell, yeah!"

Outside one of the academies in London, a group of high school students was in the courtyard, watching the video of the of massacre outside of Beirut. The video had only been up for about twenty minutes and already had over a million views. As they watched, a couple of them put their hands over their mouths, shocked and disgusted by what they were seeing. The guys cheered every time a human lost a limb, being asinine teenagers. The video followed this kid through the streets of his village, dodging demons and hiding.

On the screen a man screamed at a demon in front of him, waving a broom at the beast. The demon grabbed the broomstick and broke it in half, sticking the pointed end through the man. The demon lurched forward and grabbed him, and just as he was about to rip the guy in half, the video went black.

"Noooooo," one of them yelled, shaking his fists in the air.

"They pulled it for security reasons. Damn shame."

"I bet they pulled it because no one was supposed to know about it. They probably are there right now bull-dozing the town, burning the bodies and starting construction of some resort over the top to act like it never happened."

"*They* probably sent the demons." They laughed.

Little did they know they were playing right into Moloch's hands.

19

Timothy sat in the dark intelligence room, bathed in the glow of the computers. There were microwave burrito wrappers, chip bags, and Mountain Dew cans all over the place, including a pile around the trash can by the door where he had thrown them over his shoulder and moved on to the next one. He hadn't left that office for more than a bathroom break since the general had given him the go ahead. He wanted it to be perfect. He wanted everything to go smoothly, but it was being a little more difficult than he had first thought.

He leaned back in his office chair and ran his hands over his face, groaning loudly. He had been stuck on this one thing for six hours, writing and rewriting the code, trying to get it to do what he wanted. He had spent an hour on the phone with the intelligence crew that worked for the general, trying to keep them from kicking him out of the satellite imaging every five minutes. It took the general himself coming down to lay into them before they left him alone. Once he was secure, he started all over again, fighting with his mind to get it right.

"If I change the directive here, I can input the coordinates here..."

He was trying to figure out how to make the system better, more efficient, and less specific. He wanted to be able to show a large area—even as large as the whole country—while still allowing the system to ping him when there was an intense burst of heat and energy. The whole process had to work seamlessly. It couldn't spend twenty minutes loading every time it zoomed in or out.

Timothy pulled the map out until it was showing the entirety of the East Coast. He moved to the other computer and simulated a "ping of pain" for a specific location in New York. He put his hand to his chin and waited for a couple of seconds, and *BAM*...there it was—the flashing yellow light. He put his hands in the air in victory, then rubbed them together.

"Okay, now it just has to automatically zoom in on the coordinates as well as sound an alert to tell people there is advanced activity in that quadrant."

He typed fast on the keyboard, switching between screens. He typed three more keystrokes and pulled back, letting the screen show the whole United States. He turned to the other keyboard and restarted the simulation, which would show enough energy to signify one small portal. To him, one small portal could quickly turn into a full-on gate, so it was important to know what was happening. Of course, with the final product, he would make sure the operator could adjust the sensitivity to show whatever size energy burst they wanted, from one infected to a full-on portal.

After about ten seconds the screen flashed yellow, and the map zoomed in to hover over a small shop on the outskirts of Little Italy. A soft buzzer dinged, and he toggled with the sounds, making it a blaring alarm. He clapped his hands together and laughed, proud of himself. He turned back toward the computer and started typing again.

"Okay, baby... What if I want to work this on England? What would I need to do to make the same process happen all over the world?"

He wasn't sure if the satellites he had access to would allow that, but he was going to give it his best shot. Whoever used the software would have to have direct access to their government's satellites, which made the product more federal than private, which was okay because they didn't want random citizens rolling out to try to kill demons or reporters getting to the scene before the authorities.

"Hey there, wizard," Joshua said from behind him, looking wildly around the room at all the cans. "Holy crap! You are going to give yourself a heart attack or diabetes or something."

Timothy laughed and leaned his head back looking at Joshua. He spun around in his chair and kicked the pizza box off the other one. Joshua chuckled and walked in, sitting down.

"You haven't left this room in forever."

"I know." Timothy groaned. "But seriously, I have this project, and I don't want to waste even five seconds. I am really getting it going. I think it is going to be pretty badass if it works in a real-world scenario."

"I don't know how your brain works that fast, seriously. I have to focus on metal, that's it, and now it pretty much runs itself. You are rolling code and math problems and all kinds of shit in that dome of yours. My brain wouldn't handle it, you'd find me drooling on myself crying in my bed."

Timothy laughed. "Nah, you could do it, it's just learning a language that's all. Once you know the language, you can apply it to just about anything you need to. There are specific rules you have to know, but if you put me in the armory, I would burn my arm off and set one of those grenades off in the building. It would be a serious shit show. Someone would probably lose an eye or something."

Joshua chuckled and pushed one of the cans off of the desk into the trashcan. "So, how is everything else? I heard Stephanie and Korbin were back."

"I don't know about *back*, but they are definitely helping Calvin right now, which is pretty cool. Neither of them is Damned anymore, so they are kind of vulnerable in my opinion, but they are apparently still badass."

"Of course, they are. Stephanie was always badass, even before her demon."

"She is a fierce queen for sure, and I hope they come back here before going home. I miss her manicures and girl talk."

Joshua chuckled. "I don't know about that part, but I definitely miss her. She gave me the courage to be some-one, to take charge, to not let things outside of my control define who I am. She is a big sister to me."

"She is a special lady for sure. Anyways, I gotta get back to this project, but come get me later we will do soaps and popcorn, promise."

"I'm gonna hold you to that."

Timothy smiled and turned back to the computer. He cracked his knuckles and placed his fingers over the keys. He opened the settings and started working on highlighting three countries—England, Thailand, and Japan— and trying the program for them. He worked and worked at it, letting his frustration slide away every time something pinged or became a little clearer. His motivation cleared his head and pushed him to be better at what he was doing. It was a circle of pain in some ways. He would get frustrated enough to take a break, and then all of a sudden something would work again.

When he finally got it where he wanted it, he decided to say screw it and give it a live test. He set up all the parameters and stood there nervously watching the screens. He nodded and turned, heading out to go have some fun with Joshua, leaving everything running on its own.

"Personally, I'd like to see an incursion in the heart of Russia. I know the demons don't like cold, but it would be fabulous to see what it looks like when the snow is painted red. I bet they could make a nice picture out of it for us." Baal laughed loudly, stepping over a body in the street.

Moloch and Baal were taking a stroll through one of the last successful incursion locations to tour. It was one of the larger villages in the China Provinces, but too far out for anyone to even know that there was an incursion going on, much less save them. It would take one of the merchants traveling there to find the village completely ripped apart, to know. It would come out though, and it would add to the mass hysteria that Moloch was aiming for.

Baal stopped and waited for one of the few remaining demons to run across the street in front of them, dragging half of a body with it like a wild lion after attacking a gazelle. The demons were still milling around, finding the last of the few remaining survivors and killing them in the background. To Baal and Moloch, it was music to their ears, to everyone else it was an untold horror of mass proportions.

"I think that this next time we should go after the Motherland, England." Moloch snarled with a grin. "Have tea with the Queen and then eat her."

"What about Germany?" Baal asked.

"No, no. Germany has already paid enough for now, what with the World Cup and all."

Baal laughed loudly, throwing his head back. "What? I can't help it if they didn't know a demon was on their team. What better way to upset a whole country than watching their teammates get demolished by a red-eyed soccer player? These humans and their international sports! They are just so damn easy to manipulate."

Moloch laughed. "They can never say we didn't allow the country to rebound before we attacked again, that's for damn sure. The PR about demons not having hearts is so one-sided and biased, it's a wonder anyone trusts the news these days."

"I've heard the humans don't trust the media at all, but they are such primal creatures that as soon as murder and mayhem show up, they can't turn the channel."

"We must be giving the news stations a fucking boost then, they should be paying me royalties for this shit."

The both laughed and shook their head, glancing at each other. Baal opened his mouth to ask, but Moloch shook his head.

"No, I am not in cahoots with the news, but that would be brilliant, wouldn't it? The humans found out that the news sold their lives for some commercial spots and extra footage? Not only would they be devastated by our entrance into their country, but they would also be heartbroken by the angst their own people left behind."

"Oh, boo hoo." Baal smirked, rubbing his eyes dramatically. "We could drink the tears of our enemies."

"I'd rather drink the blood of our enemies personally, but to each his own, I suppose."

"I don't know, there are so many unhealthy humans it's hard to get a proper pint anymore. I've turned to panda blood in recent days. They are vicious but cute, and they only eat greens. Their blood is organic or some shit like that. It's some fad the demons brought back from Earth. Some movement about eating healthy."

"That sounds miserable."

"I know." Baal laughed. "But it's honestly not bad. I don't mind it so much."

"Don't tell me you are on another one of those health kicks again? I don't want to see you huffing it around the office, jumping the lava pits to lose a few pounds. Most of your weight is in the scales anyway."

"That's probably true. I'm big scaled."

"*OH!*" Moloch yelled, slapping Baal on the back. "That reminds me, did you see the Swedish play in the World Cup?"

"I missed that one."

"There was a moment where the goalie just about jumped out of the ring. No one could figure out what the hell was going on, but he let the other team score twice before they took him out to replace him."

"What did you do?" Baal grinned.

Moloch pursed his lips and looked around. "Oh, nothing but put a demon soul into the lining of his gear. The damn thing was scratching through the plastic trying to get inside him and put his claws right through the man's back. By the end of it, the goalie was possessed, and they had to sew his back up. It was fucking hilarious. Damn Swedes, always thinking they are better than everyone. Even the souls that come to hell; they think they are proper demons or some shit like that."

"What the hell is a proper demon?" Baal chuckled.

"Who fucking knows? I like the Americans. Full of lust and greed; they always know exactly why they are there, and have no problem just rolling right into the torture."

"Hopefully, we will have a few more to feed our blood-lust soon."

"Mhmm, yes," Moloch replied, rubbing his hands together.

They walked to the edge of town and watched as the last of the humans was destroyed, ending the incursion. Baal put his hand to his chin and furrowed his brow.

"What about Stonehenge during the tourist season?"

Moloch shook his head. "Thought about that one, but there really aren't that many people and it's too obvious. It would be like setting Vatican City aflame. We need a place teeming with people, and I want it to have internet access. This right here does no one any good if the other humans can't see it. It's like that old human saying: 'If a tree falls in the forest, does it make a sound?' If the demons kill an entire village but no one witnesses it, did it even happen? I looked at that YouTube thing, and the guy's video had over a million views before they yanked it. By that point, though, it had gone viral."

Baal tried to hold back a laugh. "Too bad the kid couldn't see it."

Moloch laughed loudly and patted Baal on the back. "Good one. We need a good place to spread fear. Somewhere the information will spread wide and fast, and people will actually care that it happened. Hmm..."

They stood there watching the demons start to enter back into the portals and head back to hell. Moloch racked his brain trying to think of the perfect spot, wanting attention but not so much that they would call out the mercs. He put his finger in the air and smiled.

"I know just the place, I had fun there in 1461..."

Moloch opened the portal, and the two stepped out onto the battlefield that had hosted the Battle of Towton in 1461, where the Houses of York and Lancaster fought for the English throne. Henry VI had been overthrown, not that it made much difference since the two houses passed the crown between them for years after. Moloch thought human politics had been so much more entertaining back then. The town was near the village of Towton in Yorkshire, the perfect place for a deadly battle to the finish. This incursion, though, would be less of a battle and more of a bloody rampage through the town and off to other parts of England.

"This, Baal, is the site of probably the largest and bloodiest battle ever fought on English soil, and it will now be the site of the bloodiest massacre in the history of the world, videoed and shown live on the internet. What better way is there to sow fear into the hearts of millions?"

20

The alarm went off in Timothy's room, Mozart flowing over the airwaves to gently wake him up. He yawned and stretched his arms over his head before reaching over and turning it off. He pulled the covers off and shuffled into the bathroom. As he performed his morning ritual—applying moisturizer, flossing, and putting serum on his hair—he thought about the project and wondered how it did overnight. He didn't have high expectations, or really *any* expectations at all. It was the first test run, and those never turned out well.

He dressed carefully in a pair of khaki chinos, a collared black shirt, and black loafers, spritzing a bit of cologne on just for his own pleasure. He hated smelling bad, and he knew that with the office strewn with trash and leftovers, it wasn't going to smell good in there. He made his way down to the kitchen and started the coffeemaker, flipping on the television and watching the first few minutes of some stupid early morning infomercial while waiting for his coffee to be brewed. He giggled at the host as she swooned over some celebrity and switched it off when he heard the coffeemaker hissing.

Timothy hummed as he filled his tumbler and added just the right amount of milk and sugar. He twisted on the cap and took a small sip, letting out a deep breath. He smiled and flipped off the machine and headed to the IT room. When he walked inside, he flipped on the light and stopped, grimacing at the mess around him.

"Guess I know what I'm doing today." He picked a pizza box up from the floor and took it over to the pile of cans around the empty trashcan. "I'm not playing in the NBA anytime soon."

He sat down at his computer and set the coffee on the table, pressing a couple of buttons and rolling his chair over to grab the reports out of the printer's tray. He leaned back and crossed his legs, going over the numbers and activity from the night before. He flipped to the page for England and scanned down, his finger stopping midway. He furrowed his brow and looked up at the screen, which was hovering over Russia. He looked back down at the paper and shook his head in surprise.

"That can't be right. There is no way this thing was accurate the first time around. The IT gods are messing with me."

He slid over to his computer and started bringing up the different reports from the past night. He read through them several times, checking the system to make sure all the settings were correct. He took a deep breath and shook his head, pushing back with his eyes wide with alarm. The reports all said the same thing, and the screen was showing the bright yellow spot, flashing the alarm he had silenced the night before.

"Holy shit, it can't be!"

He grabbed the office phone and dialed Katie's number while at the same time grabbing his cell and sending a text message.

"This is earlier than even *I* get up." Katie groaned. "And I literally have an alarm clock from hell."

"Girl, prepare to get your ass to England. Not joking. This is not a test. Call you soon with more details."

"Wait, wha—"

Timothy hung up the phone and finished his urgent text, panting with excitement. He put the cell down and rolled up to the screen, scanning out and then back in over and over. He couldn't get the exact location, but he knew something big was definitely going down. His heart was beating wildly. Although a threat like this was a bad thing, he was kind of excited that his program had worked the first time around. He had figured it would take months to even calibrate for New York accurately. He just hoped the general wasn't too pissed. England wasn't really in his jurisdiction.

Just then the landline rang, and he rolled over to pick it up. "Timothy speaking."

"This is General Brushwood, and I would like you to know I am not even in the office yet, even though I get there insanely early. You texted me. What is it?"

"Man, you people are grumpy." Timothy sniffed. "Look, I know we have things to talk about, and you'll understand after I tell you, but you are going to want to stay focused here. There is something huge, and I mean MASSIVE, happening near the top part of England."

"Can we be a little more specific in like *all* of that?"

"There is a massive surge of energy, bigger than the one here in Brooklyn, and coming from the top quarter of England. Before you ask, I can't tell you exactly where. This thing wasn't even supposed to be working yet. And no, I don't know off the top of my head. It's not like we take England's geography in tenth grade or something."

"No, even I don't know where that could be. Okay, I'll have my people start looking at it, though nobody has called me about it so far, so either your work is flawed or my people are slacking big time over there. Then again, it *was* the night crew, and I worry about them at times."

"Night is when it all happens. You should have the good people work then."

"Office politics, Timothy. Those who are more valuable don't want the graveyard shift."

"Well, hell I need to work there. I have the all-the-time shift."

"There's only one of you."

"Yeah, well, maybe we should hire some people here. I am only one lady, and I can only get so much done."

He could almost hear the general rolling his eyes. "Hold on, I am going to connect us with command. I want you to explain to them what you are seeing and where in that vicinity to look. It's quicker than sending them to hunt for a needle in a haystack."

"Okay."

The general put him on hold for a moment and clicked back over with the supervisor on the phone. Timothy went through the list of results on the readout, letting her know exactly what they were looking at. The numbers were up and then down, and then *boom*...they hit the roof and hadn't come down since then. Not to mention that the images were showing a gate that spanned a pretty good distance.

The woman took down all the information; he could hear her typing on the other end. The general stayed quiet, letting them do their thing until they were finished. "Ellen, how long until we have those results?"

"I don't know, sir. We are working on it now."

"All right, keep me abreast of the situation. Timothy, I'll call you as soon as I know anything. You might want to put Katie on notice."

"Already did, while I was sending you a text."

"Good."

They hung up and Timothy sat there for a moment staring at the pulsing yellows and reds on the large screen in front of him. He put his hand to his mouth and destroyed his manicure. He hated to wait. He hated that technology hadn't come up to speed with everything else, and that in dire situations all they could do was wait. He could have gone into his system to see if he could tweak it for a better location, but if he did that he might ruin the whole thing and not be able to get it back. His only option was to sit there feeling helpless.

He picked up his phone and fidgeted with it, looking up at the time and then the screen about every five minutes. He tapped his foot and then got up, crossing his arms and pacing the room. He knew it might be hours, but that was a damn shame, especially since if it were in the US he could already have picked up the exact location. Hours could mean the difference between mass casualties and none.

After about forty minutes of him going crazy, he threw his arms in the air. "Fuck it. If this is going down, we are going to be ready. If not, then we just did a lot of work for no reason, but no harm, no foul."

Joshua stood in the armory looking down his checklist for the day. They had a ton of weapons to get through, and twice as much ammunition than in previous months. The recent surge of demons had pushed them to their limits and they were again struggling to keep up with the demand, not to mention the house stash that had to be kept full at all times in case of a call.

"Where am I today?" Chelsea asked Joshua.

"Oh, um....you are on ammunition packaging."

"Oh, good. I love that area."

Joshua smiled as she bounced away to start work. The women had just gotten there about an hour before, and were going through the shift change lists for the day. They worked like a well-oiled machine, which Joshua was thankful for. He wasn't sure he was ready to handle a huge business and a troubled staff at the same time. All the women gathered at the front for the normal morning discussion where Joshua went over any must-knows and upcoming special orders. Everything was in its place, and all was right with the world.

Well, not all. But for Joshua, this was as good as it got.

He cleared his throat and put his hands in the air,

quieting the women. "Morning, ladies. So, today is just like yesterday. No new orders, but the ones we have are stacked to the brim. As usual, priority lies with federal orders, and once those are packaged and shipped we move on to retail orders. The retailers know there can sometimes be a delay, but let's not get behind if we don't have to. We don't want a snowball effect to occur. We may be the only company out there with the product, but that doesn't mean we should have shitty service. I will be in the lab putting the finishing touches on the newest batch of metals before they go through the system. If you need me, you know where to find me. And as always, be safe and be quick."

The women nodded and talked loudly and excitedly to each other. The rumor of Stephanie's return had run through the factory like wildfire. Joshua looked at the desk in the corner, hearing the phone ring. He sighed and walked over to answer.

"I'm assuming that since it was the house ring, this is Timothy."

"Well, aren't you the smart one. Here's the deal... I need you to ship everything we have in the house stash out the doors. Katie is going to need it, and need it fast. Put it out on the airfield, and when the time comes, we will have someone pick it up. Sound good?"

Joshua fumbled with his clipboard as Timothy dropped the bombshell on him. "Yeah. All hands, got it." His heart hammered and his head swam as he tried to process the unexpected interruption to his morning.

He hung up the phone with a shaky hand, and just about remembered to breathe. He sucked in another breath, then another until the dark spots in his vision faded. He clenched his jaw, angry at his loss of control. "Get it together," he hissed. "Katie needs you." He grabbed the receiver to the intercom and mashed the button as he brought it to his mouth. "Attention. All hands. All hands. This is not a drill. All house items are to be moved to the airfield immediately. I repeat, all house ammunition and weapons are to be moved to the airfield immediately."

He hung up the receiver and ran over to the area that housed the supplies. He fumbled with the keys for a moment, then slid the flat key into the slot and typed in his code. The door clicked, and he groaned as he pulled it open, the adrenaline dump his body was dealing with robbing him of his strength temporarily.

He stepped to the side as the women filed in and out of the room, then went in after them and grabbed a pallet with the pallet jack and moved it through the factory toward the airfield. They moved fast, unsure what was going on, but if all of it was called for then there was something really big about to go down.

Part of Joshua was jealous. He wished he could be part of the action, but then again, he still had nightmares about Incursion Day. And from the sound of it, this was building up to be even worse.

They worked hard, first stacking all the pallets in the pick-up area and then going back and pulling out the stack of duffel bags stowed in the locker and stacking the cases of bullets inside. The women had practiced it many times, so they were strong enough to carry the duffels without help even though Joshua was struggling to get one out there. They ran back and picked the locker dry before Joshua grabbed the checklist from the vault's wall and went out there to go through each piece and make sure they had everything. Not only was it a good to know, but if it were a military operation, they would be able to invoice the government for everything.

Joshua spent the next hour going over the inventory of each duffel, pallet, and case to pass the time and quiet his tumultuous thoughts. He already knew exactly what was there, since he did inventory once a week. It just gave him something to do while he waited the endless hour until Chelsea stuck her head out the door and yelled for him, shaking the phone in her hand.

"Joshua! The general is on the phone for you."

Joshua nodded and checked the last box on his list, a feeling of relief coming over him. He took off across the sandy base and snatched the phone from her as he reached the door. He held his hand over the speaker as he stepped inside, breathing heavily. He sucked air in through his mouth and out his nose several times before putting the phone to his ear.

"General, what can I do for you?"

"I need you to get busy packing everything that you can and place it on the airfield."

Joshua raised an eyebrow and looked at the clock. "Yes sir. It's done."

"Timothy got you to move, didn't he?"

"Yes, sir, about three hours ago. I just finished the final count of everything."

"Good. The plane will hit there in about thirty minutes.

I don't need any help loading. There will be plenty of guys. Just make sure you are there to give us the invoice. These things are easier done all at once instead of billing later."

"Yes, sir," Joshua replied. "Anything else?"

"No, son. Thank you for rushing."

"Not a problem, sir."

Joshua hung the phone up and looked at the women, who were waiting for his instruction. "All right, ladies, you did a fantastic job. The plane will be here in thirty minutes. I will handle the rest of it, so go back to work. We now have to add replenishing the house stock to our list. Chelsea?"

"Yes?"

"I want you to take this house list, and you and two of the girls pull from our stock and get the vault filled. Make sure to mark off what you take so we can account for it. Eliza, I need you to go through once they are done and redo our daily task list. Prioritize according to what we have and what our goals are. I need to know what has to be manufactured daily to meet our orders."

"Sounds good." She nodded, taking the clipboard from him.

"The rest of you, continue to pack and organize the new materials coming out of production."

They all nodded and headed off in different directions. Joshua leaned back against the post and shook his head. His initial reaction aside, there was something satisfying about moving at full speed, knowing you were the driving force behind the ability of an army to kill demons.

They were part of something bigger, and that was what Joshua had wanted all his life. He wanted to know he'd made a difference when he went to bed at night. With his metals, countless lives would be saved out there on the battlefield.

He just hoped it didn't cost too many mercenary lives in the process.

K atie stuck the last of her guns in the holsters and adjusted the belt on her hips. It felt a little tight, but she wasn't in the mood to argue with Pandora over it. The general had just called and confirmed that Timothy's information had been correct. They had to get moving if they wanted to get there before the entirety of England descended into a complete shitshow. She walked out of her room and almost bumped into Calvin. She looked him over. He looked so...*Calvin* in his tight green t-shirt, army pants, and boots, with his weapons strapped to him. She couldn't help but smile at having him back where he belonged.

Calvin made a face. "What?"

"Nothing. It's just nice to have you back."

"Yeah, well, I'm sure Pandora has other thoughts on the matter."

Nope, damn glad to have Long-Schlong Silver back with us.

Katie choked and covered her mouth to hold back her laughter.

"She called me some weird name, didn't she?"

Katie couldn't talk through her tears. "Long… Schlong…Silver."

Calvin grinned. "I think she just wants me to shiver her timbers. Not happening, P."

That's because Calvin's in looooove. Pandora snickered.

Katie looked at Calvin. He did seem different; more assured in some way. "I concur."

"With what?" Calvin asked.

Katie winked. "Come on, we gotta get to the airport. The car should be downstairs."

Calvin nodded and slung his duffel over his shoulder. Angie came in and hugged Katie silently, too full of emotion for words. They hurried down to the elevator and out the front doors of the building.

As soon as they stepped out, bulbs flashed and the paparazzi went wild.

"Katie, Calvin, are you on your way to an incursion? Are you going to fight in England?"

"Katie, can you confirm that the United States is converging on a massive portal in England?"

"Katie, are you dating the leader of the Damned Military Unit? Former rock and roll star Brock?"

Calvin looked at Katie. She rolled her eyes and climbed into the Humvee that was waiting for them. She slammed the door and stared out at the reporters, wishing they would just disappear. Every time she saw them, it was another reminder to her that her life was not her own. She was tired of feeling that way, but short of disappearing and hiding out there really wasn't anything she could do about it. The public was curious, and the reporters were vicious.

Calvin and Pandora could immediately tell that the reporters had gotten to her. Her mood had sunk and fast, which was not what they wanted when she was headed into battle, a battle that sounded bigger than anything before. Calvin cleared his throat and looked at her.

"Long-Schlong Silver would like to know if you let Brock swab your decks?"

Katie giggled.

He grinned and pointed at her. "*That's* why Pandora is being so nice. You two got some!"

Okay, fun's over. He's going to get some in a minute.

Katie started laughing.

What happened to the innocent young woman who blushed at so much as the mention of a penis? You've changed, Katie. I was totally threatening violence.

Calvin held up his hands. "Hey, I'm just glad your dry spell is over. You two deserve some fun. Pandora still isn't getting her claws on me, though."

Pandora and Calvin went back and forth, doing everything they could to make Katie laugh. Calvin shrugged and put up his hand.

"High five! It is about time you smiled, dammit—though I don't know how much fun it was. I totally picture Pandora in your head shouting orders like a drill sergeant."

Damn straight. You gotta twissst those hips, lady. None of this...two wet seals slapping it together. There's an art to it.

Katie laughed. "Okay, you two, enough."

Oh, oh! Holy shit! You have to tell him about the magazine.

Katie giggled. "So, there was a magazine in the train station that was an *authentic reproduction* of what I would look like as a pin-up doll. It was mortifying. Seriously, it looked like they took a tire pump and just inflated my tits to a G, left my waist where it was and did the same to my hips. My head was soooo tiny on my body. I looked like a tick about to explode. If that was real and I popped a tit, someone would die."

Calvin laughed loudly. "'Popped a tit.' I'm gonna start saying that every time I get hurt. Dagnabbit, Katie, I popped a tit."

"Oh, my God!" Katie gasped. "You sound like my grandpa Joe."

"Oh, so now I'm *another* old white dude." He laughed. "You're really hitting those comparisons today."

They pulled up to the private entrance at the airport and got out of the Humvee. They went around back and grabbed their bags and pushed through the five or so news reporters trying to get footage of them heading out. This time it didn't bother Katie as much, remembering that whatever they thought they knew about her life, they had no idea. She had her secrets, ones that even they would never get their hands on.

"Katie just one question..."

"I'm sorry," she said going inside. "We are in a hurry."

They raced through the airport and out onto the airfield, stopping and watching as the military planes landed and moved toward them. They were fast—hella fast —but luckily this time not as tiny as the ones when they went to France. Calvin nodded and let out a deep breath.

"Thank God. I was thinking I would have to close myself up in that plane again like a fucking can of tuna. The guy had to tell me three times to take my hand off the red lever."

"Was it on the red lever?"

"Fuck yeah, it was. If we were going down, I was pulling that shit and floating off with my parachute. I am too young to be going down like Hollywood stars in some tragic plane crash in the ocean."

"I always think about Goose from *Top Gun*. I'd pull the handle, and my ass would slam right into the lid of the plane. I know it."

"Yeah, but you are made of demon ash and angel dust. That fucking plane top would crack into a million pieces, and your wings would come bursting out and you would make a fucking dive right into the water and come out looking like a supermodel. The whole time I would be holding on and screaming my ass off. I can take a big-ass demon, but don't drop me from heights. Nope. I was made for the ground, thank you."

Exactly what I have been saying about your damn wings.

Katie rolled her eyes. "Great, you just got her going on the damn wings again. She is *not* a fan."

"Me either, Pandora," Calvin yelled.

Katie laughed and rubbed her ear. "She can hear you just fine with inside voices."

"Not as dramatic."

The planes taxied to a stop and the crew started toward them, bags in their hands to load onto the planes. Katie lifted her eyebrows thinking about how fast-paced her life was. She rarely had time to think about anything before she made a move.

"I'm starting to think I should have probably negotiated a higher rate for this shit. We are flying into possibly one of the largest incursions in history, and I let them lowball me because I was in a hurry. Those bastards are good at that. They know exactly when to hit you with it, too. When you are panicking, trying to get your shit together, and just want to get moving."

Calvin chuckled and patted her on the back. "Yeah, but sometimes it ain't all about the money."

Katie thought about Brock's team and how they pushed through any demon situation, any time, on military pay. They had been given a small increase on the regular military rate because of what they faced, but didn't get even a tenth of what Katie and Calvin charged to go out on incursions. She nodded at Calvin, acknowledging that he was right. Sometimes, and actually even more than not, it wasn't all about the money. It was about securing freedom, killing demons, and keeping their world a safe place. It was about using the tools and gifts she had been given to do something more meaningful than a game of volleyball or getting the right degree in college. Becoming a Damned hadn't just changed her outward life, it had changed the woman she was at the core.

An eldritch air hung over the sleepy English night. The moon was hidden by the clouds, and deep rumbles rolled through an uncharacteristically dry sky. The heat from the massive portal had filled the atmosphere with heat and gasses, and the unearthly pressure change sent random streaks of lightning that went from the ground to the sky.

The mood among the military and police surrounding the field was tight.

They'd set a wide perimeter around the field, and watched the portal from that safe distance. There hadn't been an incursion on British soil previously, so the only ones who had seen anything like this had been present at an incursion overseas.

The police were barely armed, and even the firearms units were only equipped to deal with humans. The British military didn't have access to the special bullets that the U.S. Military had been using for months. They didn't have mercenary teams like the U.S. had, and hadn't made the most of the intel that had been shared.

They were now realizing what a serious situation they were facing.

As the police and military moved from their vehicles and checked their weapons to ensure they were loaded the gate pulsed, sending out a wave of heat and energy. The people surrounding the field could barely breathe, the heat was so bad, and it only increased as the portal became more and more active.

One of the army officers was on the phone with his commanding officer, trying to figure out what the hell to do. "I don't know what to tell you, Smythe. Hold the perimeter until the Americans turn up. The mercenary Katie and her partner Calvin are heading this way as we speak. I had a call from one of the US generals. Their intel picked up the portal before we knew what was happening."

"Sir, what if those things come out of there?"

"Then shoot them in the head and stay alive as long as you can."

"That's hardly a plan, sir."

"It is what it is, Smythe. I only wish I could be there

with you instead of dealing with the logistics of transferring Her Majesty and the rest of the royal family to the safe house. It's been testing, to say the least."

"I can only imagine, sir. What does this Katie do that we can't?"

"What does she *not* do? I've only seen footage, but I promise you it's nothing your body is capable of—not unless you've grown wings since the last time we saw each other."

"Wings? No, I don't have any of those, but if *she* does, I sure as hell hope that I make it long enough to see that. First demons, and now angels. What else is on the way, Bigfoot?"

"Don't be ridiculous, man. Bigfoot isn't real."

"Of course. All right, sir, keep safe. We'll do what we can to hold it down here until the backup arrives. If I don't make it through this, it's been a pleasure serving with you, sir."

"Today is not the day you die, Smythe."

Smythe hung up the phone and looked at the gate, swallowing hard. He grabbed his comm, reaching out to the others preparing for whatever was about to happen next.

He steadied his breathing and gave the order a little less bluntly than he'd received it. "Attention all units. We have backup incoming. Until the mercenaries arrive we will defend that gate to a man. Our orders are to shoot anything that comes through in the head. Make every shot count."

One of the officers cut in over the comm. "So just point and shoot until the cavalry arrives? Sounds simple enough. You'd think they'd give us a challenge of some sort."

Smythe's smile reflected in his voice as he replied, "Sorry, ladies and gentlemen. No challenges today, I'm afraid.."

"I signed up for the stellar dining experiences, sir," one of the squaddies shouted.

The mood lifted, but only for a second.

Suddenly the portal began to vibrate.

Smythe dropped the comm and grabbed his rifle. He braced the stock in the hollow of his shoulder and took aim at the center of the rippling. It was so huge that no one really knew where to look or where to aim. Tongues of flame shot out from the gate, heralding the demons. They erupted from the portal and spilled out onto the burnt grass. They hissed and barked as the police officers stared wide-eyed. They weren't trained for *this*.

The soldiers jumped into the back of their armored vehicles and spun the gun turret around.

With the drop of the sergeant's hand, they unleashed a hail of bullets at the demons. Several of the demons were taken out in the first barrage. However, they weren't deterred, and new limbs grew to replace the ones the soldiers had shot off even as they dragged themselves toward the humans

"All right, then. Take *this*, fucker," he whispered as he pulled the trigger.

The bullet whizzed through the air and struck the demon right between the eyes, dropping him to the ground. Everyone stopped shooting and watched that one demon until finally it exploded into ash. Cheers went up around the perimeter and the guy shook his head, raising his weapon for the next shot.

"One down, infinity to go. I can do this."

The gunfire began again. This time all of the firearms officers aimed for the heads while the military sprayed the demons with higher-caliber bullets. They watched the hordes of demons spilling out, realizing that none of them were attacking the perimeter. Instead, they were running forward and diving down, digging through the ground, trying to unearth something. They looked like a bunch of rabid hairless dogs, scratching and crawling through the dirt.

One of the police officers turned to his partner. "What in God's name are they looking for?"

His partner shrugged with wide eyes. "I have no id..."

Just then a demon jumped across the car and sank its teeth into his partner's neck. The officer brought up his recently-issued service weapon, and as soon as the demon looked up with a mouthful of flesh, he shot it right between the eyes. The cop backed up, shaking his head and still pointing his gun. The other demons were busy digging, but he had never experienced anything like it. His fight-or-flight response was engaged and he wasn't sure whether to jump ship or stay put.

"Rodgers," another officer called with his hand up. "It's okay, mate. Just aim and shoot. Keep doing it until we tell you to stop. You're gonna be okay."

Rodgers shook his head. He started firing over and over, hitting demons right and left. He wasn't sure if he was killing them, but he was trying to make the best dent he could in the situation. He knew one thing: that backup better get there, and it better get there fast or all they would find would be a big hole in the ground and a bunch of dead coppers. He didn't want to be one of those dead coppers.

His gun clicked and he looked down, realizing he was out of ammo. He reached in his pocket to pull out more, but instead, he pulled out a picture of his wife and brand-new baby girl. He ran his finger over their faces and closed his eyes for just a moment. He had to protect them no matter what it cost, even his life. He couldn't help his partner, but he could avenge his death. What two better reasons to fight were there? He grabbed more ammo out of the car and gritted his teeth.

"Okay, you sodding bastards, you want action? I'll give you some damn action."

22

Katie and Calvin held tightly to their seats as the plane made its descent into the base in England. The thing moved fast, both in the air and as it headed toward the runway. The wheels hit the ground hard and Calvin looked at Katie, shaking his head.

"I'm telling you, just pull the red handle and freedom is mine."

"No red handle in this one, big guy."

"No, but you have wings, which is the next best thing."

"Very true, though Pandora might disagree."

The plane came to a stop outside of the hangar bay, and the doors opened. Several English soldiers stood by, waiting to show Katie and Calvin to the helicopter. There was no time to waste. The trip there had taken long enough.

The officer running alongside them shouted as they ran. "The portal has continued to grow. We had men on the scene, but they have slowly been chipped away by the demons. The demons are digging into the ground. We don't really know what they are doing. All we know is we need you guys there."

They stopped at the edge of the helipad, and the officer saluted Katie and Calvin. "Good luck out there, and may God be with you."

He means Pandora. May Pandora be with you.

Of course.

Katie and Calvin threw their bags into the chopper and climbed inside, nodding as they slid the door shut. They situated their bags and put on their headphones since the pilot was wasting no time. Three other choppers lifted off at the same time, and they all took off through the air in formation. The pilot clicked the button on his mic and looked back in the mirror hanging above him.

"I am Sergeant Hudson, and I'll be getting you to the scene. It's about a twenty-minute flight, so hold tight."

"Thank you, Sergeant," Calvin replied, nodding.

"Oh, and Sergeant?" Katie added. "When you start to get close, definitely take it up a notch, and by that I mean get us higher into the air. Those fuckers can take out helicopters. I've seen it over and over, and I'd rather make it to the ground in one piece than die in a giant flaming ball of metal."

"Me too, ma'am. I'll make sure we are above their line of sight and far enough away to dodge any incoming projectile."

Katie nodded, then glanced at Calvin and shrugged. "Korbin would have said the same thing."

Calvin smiled. "He still would."

I have a strange feeling about this. Pandora sighed. *I don't know what it is, but there is something different about this incursion.*

Yeah, it's fucking massive. We'll find out just how big in about fifteen minutes.

No, there's something more, but I can't pinpoint it.

Well, let me know when you figure it out. All I feel is the angel burn in my chest, and it's like heartburn times a thousand. You would think early warning signals wouldn't make you distracted, but sheesh.

Sorry, I can't help you with that one. My powers do nothing on their magic.

It's the thought that counts.

Really?

Katie chuckled. *No, but it sounded nice didn't it?*

Touché, my friend, touché.

They flew over the quiet English countryside. Katie would never have guessed there was something so massive ahead of them. After about ten minutes, the pilot switched on his microphone again. "Um, ma'am? You might want to look straight ahead. I've never seen anything like this."

Katie gave Calvin a side glance of worry and sat forward, looking out the front of the chopper. Ahead in the distance was a massive rip in reality, a gate that was more than just a portal. It was a grand entrance, big enough for anything in hell to use to join the fight. Even Pandora was impressed by the sheer size of the thing.

Holy shit, that's fucking huge. That is the work of at least two of those fuckers. There is no way either Moloch or Baal did that themselves. They aren't that powerful.

What about Lucifer?

He could make it, sure, but he wouldn't. If he did, he would get a serious Godly foot right up his ass, and I'm pretty sure this time God wouldn't keep him around to guard hell. Nothing those dickwads up top in heaven have done allows him any special privileges. If nothing else, it keeps him trapped in the slums of the underworld, just trying to get by.

I'm sorry, P, but I don't feel bad for Satan.

He hates that name. He prefers Lucifer, but a word of warning—don't ever call him Luke. He will rip your innards out and fry them up for dinner. I've seen it, and it's not a pretty sight. In fact, I think he kept the guy alive and made him eat his own intestines. It was very Hannibal Lecter of him.

That is not helpful in the least.

Pandora stopped talking and watched through Katie's eyes as the choppers flew closer to the rip. She blocked her thoughts from Katie and thought about the knowledge she held. She didn't know where she got the full details from, but it felt like they had been there all along. Either Katie had it, or Gabriel was setting her up for a really bad situation. He had been very forthcoming with the knowledge, and had done everything he could to keep Katie safe. Still, that didn't mean that anything Gabriel had told her was true.

Pandora hated to be played. In fact, she hated it so much she had once killed twenty-five people in one sitting because they had messed her up so bad. She was a demon, but she didn't tolerate devious behavior or lying. She would take them out really fast.

She decided that until it was a life or death scenario, she wasn't going to inform Katie of anything; not yet at least. She wasn't going to set Katie and herself up for total failure, and if that kind of secret were to be used, it just might kill them both. She didn't trust the angel. They were known for being tricksters; the mercenaries of the high courts. They weren't known for pure unbridled truth, and took their jobs way more seriously than they actually were.

"Holy fucking shit, look at the number of demons down there." Calvin gawked out his window. "They are all scratching and pawing at each other, digging into the ground. What the fuck are they looking for?"

"They heard we were coming and thought it would be easier to dig back to hell." Katie snickered. "But seriously, they're probably looking for whatever Moloch sent them there for."

"Whatever it is has got them in a frenzy. A smoke bomb would be perfect right about now. Just drop it right down the center."

"Unfortunately, there are still too many men and women down there, and we don't know what their demon status is. We don't want to come to England and kill their guardsmen. It would be an international clusterfuck."

Calvin chuckled. "Too true. This is why I keep you around."

Katie smiled. "For a while, at least."

She unbuckled her belt and looked at Calvin, who reached up and patted her on the back. "Have a good fall!"

She slid the door open, and the air whooshed into the chopper and whipped her hair wildly. She looked back at Calvin and laughed. This was what she lived for; what she was made for. Nothing was going to stand in her way, and she definitely wasn't going to let those bastards down there fuck with anyone else.

The residents of Towton were stuck right in the middle of the chaos, and had no idea what to do or what was even going on. They ran wildly to escape the town the portal sat next to, screaming and trying to beat off the demons with anything they could get their hands on. One had a rake, another a shovel. A couple of others brandished knives from their kitchens and were attempting to slash their way through the demons before they were ripped to shreds.

A few of the local hunt club members had pulled their rifles from their safes and were striding through the town blowing demons to bits, at least until a demon got them from behind. On the other side of things, there were more than a few hiding in the shadows or running through the crowds with their phones out, streaming it live on Facebook and Instagram and posting sections to YouTube. The world watched in horror as people were eaten right out from underneath their phones.

The carnage was worse than any incursion thus far, but that stemmed more from the idiots than from the number of people close by. It was like they hadn't any paid attention to the incursion that just occurred in France, or all the battles raging across the Pond. They were running through the streets, staring into their phones and yelling at the top of their lungs like it was a joke.

"I'm going to die, but you will be able to watch the whole thing live here on my phone. Make sure you share so my dying wish goes viral!"

To make matters worse, the people watching were egging them on, laughing, and finding the entire situation more humorous than tragic. Some of those reading the comments were starting to think that demon selection might just be a good thing for some of the more idiotic members of society. Of course, no one thought *they* were among the terminally stupid, even those with phones streaming in their hands.

One guy, a college student home on holiday, ran across the cemetery at the front of the church looking into his phone whispering.

"I just saw a demon take out Ms. Beasley's house, so if you are in her science class you'll probably get away with a late assignment, you get me? The rest of the town is going wild. It's a proper mob situation. I've managed to escape a load of demons. The wankers were laughing as they ran off in the other direction."

He turned the phone around and showed the chaos on the streets. A demon jumped off a roof, taking a middle-aged woman down and knocking the garden trowel from her hand. She screamed as the demon grabbed her by the hair and began to drag her back toward her house. The guy turned his phone back around and grimaced.

"Not a good day for Mrs. Alberts. Looks like that demon is on the hunt. Look, people, I don't know how long I am going to survive. I don't know if I *will* survive. Make sure you share this video and hit the Like button. If I make it through I'll make sure to upload it to YouTube, but if I don't, well, it was a bloody good ride."

Just then he looked up to the side and put his hands up. The footage tumbled about as the phone hit the ground. The viewers could see the boy fall to the ground dead, his eyes wide and blood coming from his neck and mouth.

Slowly he slid off-camera, although the muffled sounds of groaning and crunching could still be heard. There was a slight pause, and a demon picked up the phone. It looked right into the camera lens and shook the phone, not sure what to do with it. It bit down on it but realized it wasn't edible.

The demon snarled and tossed the phone over its shoulder, no longer interested. Those viewers watching were left staring straight into the bloodied and half-eaten face of their formerly-humorous host. Slowly the viewers dropped out and his video was lost, lumped together with the victims of England's first major incursion.

All across the town and out into the countryside, the screams echoed loudly. People fought with everything they had, but there was just no hope for most of them. The mercs were there, but there weren't enough of them to go around. It was just Katie and Calvin, and though they wanted desperately to help the people, their focus had to stay on shutting down the gate and getting rid of the demons who had already crossed over. All anyone could do at that point was run, hide, or fight.

The people of that small-town England village weren't backing down.

"Is it bad?" the teenage girl huddled in the corner asked. She held her ten-year-old brother in her arms, hugging him tightly.

Her mother walked over to the small window in the attic wall and looked out. She watched as people ran screaming through the streets, some still with weapons and others hobbling while clutching injured limbs. No matter who she looked at, there was at least one demon close behind them. She turned back to her children, glancing down at the boy and back at her daughter. She nodded just once and crossed her arms, pacing back and forth.

"Sit down, Mam," her daughter chided. "If any get in the house they'll be able to hear your footsteps. We'll sit here and wait. They won't leave us here without help forever. It's stupid to think that people are running. So stupid. The best thing to do is hide and wait."

The boy leaned back and wiped tears from his eyes. "When's Daddy coming home?"

The girl looked at her brother and forced a smile, pulling him toward her and kissing his forehead. "Soon, sweetie. He just went down the street to get some milk, remember?"

She hugged the boy close to her and looked up worriedly at her mother. She had always been the strong one, dealing with her mother's crazy nerves and her father's inability to handle anything. She was the only one there for her brother, and she would be damned if she let anything happen to him.

Her mother made for the door. "We should try to call for help, but I left the phone downstairs. I could go get it."

"No." The daughter shook her head. "Sit down here with us and hug your son. We are going to be okay up here. I told you, just wait it out and someone will come for us. I swear it. I saw the footage in France and in America. They never just leave the people for... for.... Well, you know. They come to help."

He mother nodded and walked over, then sat down on the floor and pulled her son into her lap, wrapping the blanket around them both. The daughter stood up and walked over to peer outside. Suddenly she could hear the clacking of a helicopter. She smiled and turned quickly back.

"I told you they would come. Any second help will fly over. Just watch."

She stared out as a chopper crested the hill and came toward them. She furrowed her brow and sighed. "What's one helicopter going to do with about a million demons?"

Her brother jumped up and ran over, looking through the window on his tiptoes. They watched the chopper get closer, and they both gasped when a woman swan-dived from the chopper, her wings gracefully unfolding as she swooped down and skimmed the ground. She flew through the people, taking the heads off several demons with slashes of her sword. The demons screamed and hissed at their angelic assailant as she swooped again.

All three watched open-mouthed. "I think they're following her," the mother gasped.

Katie blew past the church and the cemetery and back toward where the portal had initially appeared. The demons all dropped what they were doing or who they were eating, and took off after her. They swarmed through the streets, blood and saliva dripping from their jowls, ready to attack the new enemy. None of them had any clue that they were rushing to their doom.

The girl turned around and happily looked at her mother. "They are here—the Killers. We are going to be okay."

Just then there was a loud bang on the attic door, and everyone jumped. The boy slid around behind his sister, and the mother clenched the blanket close to her face. They stepped forward quietly, wondering who was below.

"Open up. It's your father."

The girl sighed in relief and ran over, opening the thick wooden doors. Her dad was standing outside, battered and bruised but okay. He kissed his daughter's forehead and handed her the carton of milk. He locked the door behind him and dusted off his clothing.

"We should stay up here. Right now it is the safest place for us to be. The demons all ran off chasing that winged woman, and I have no idea why that whole sentence isn't absolutely absurd. Anyway, whoever that is, she is leading the demons back toward that portal thing that opened. Hopefully, they will be able to keep them there and destroy them. For right now, though, I want us to stay here and stick together."

"I know who she is," the girl exclaimed excitedly. "That's Katie from Katie's Killers. She is pretty much the biggest badass on the whole planet."

23

Katie rode a low air current through the streets, letting her wings take her just low enough to swipe through the demons who were attacking the locals. She took several heads, then grabbed a demon from its perch on a roof and flung it away with one hand. It hit the side of a pale stone building and smashed into the ground below. She dove again and knocked another few demons for a loop.

For some reason, the demons abandoned their food and chased after her. It was the perfect moment to get them the hell out of the populated area and back to the dirt mound they were digging in.

She flew up and over the rift and landed on the ground. The demons attacked as soon as her feet hit the ground. She pulled the halves of her staff out of their sheaths and launched into her kata. She hit two demons in the neck and then pressed the buttons, slicing them with the special metal blades on the downswing. She yanked them both back out and twirled them around, sticking them back into their spots. She pulled out Tom and Harry and blasted the demons in front of her.

A demon jumped on her back, and she twisted and shot it over her shoulder. Luckily for her, the beast flew backward, only lightly drenching her in demon blood. She turned to the right and pulled the trigger until she had cleared a circle around her. The demons hissed and screeched and she pulled the triggers again, but her big guns were empty. She slammed them into their holsters and drew her small pistols. She turned in a circle as she emptied them into the approaching horde.

She released the magazines from the weapons and slammed them down on her belt to reload. She tore through the crowd of demons, firing left and right as she ran. A demon launched itself at Katie, and she sidestepped and pulled the triggers of her pistols until they clicked empty a second time. She snapped back up and holstered those, realizing that she was completely out of bullets.

"Looks like it's time for a little swordplay." She smiled and reached back for the two swords that were crisscrossed on her back.

She whirled around and brought her swords up to slice through the necks of the five demons closest to her. Their heads fell from their shoulders, and she held her backstance as their bodies turned to dust at her feet one by one, like dominos,. She looked to her left to watch a cop, probably the last one standing, surrounded by demons, his gun useful only as a club.

She ran toward him in a storm of flashing metal. She turned right and then left, stabbing the demons in the stomach and ripping her swords up through their bellies. Finally, the two stood together, the demons stalking them.

Katie reached down and picked up a picture of a woman with a small baby and handed it to the guy. "You dropped this."

"Thank you." He smiled. "And damn, am I glad to see *you*!"

Katie patted his arm. "Get to safety. Reload or whatever you need to do, but don't stay here," she yelled, taking out another demon with an upward slice.

He nodded and took off through the perimeter, which was just a pile of beat-up cars and empty tanks at that point. Katie sighed and turned back, ready to take down some demon ass. She stomped through the crowd, killing every demon she could get her hands on. She swung around to strike a taller demon, and it grabbed her wrist and glared at her with bulging red eyes.

She growled as it pried the sword from her hand and threw it away. "Hey, fucker! That was fucking expensive."

She jammed the other sword into the demon's side, and it winced and hissed in pain. She pulled the sword out and took a step backward, straightening her shirt and cracking her back. When the demon looked at her again, it only caught a quick, bright flash before its head was cut clean off its shoulders. She kicked its body to the ground and ran over the resulting dust pile.

She jumped onto the armored vehicle and got behind the turret, blasting the crowds of demons with bullets. Hundreds of shells fell from the large gun, bouncing off the metal of the vehicle onto the ground. When she had run out of bullets there, she jumped back down, looking out across the field. She felt like she hadn't even made a dent.

Damn, that's a lot of red eyes and black scales.

No shit. I didn't even know we had that many low-level demons down there. They are stepping up their game.

Just then Katie felt herself being lifted off the ground and she yelled as she was thrown into a pack of demons, knocking them down. She landed hard, and her hand hit the ground. Her sword flew across the grass and into the hole the demons were digging.

"Well, fuck." She was running dangerously low on weapons, and things were starting to look bleak.

Calvin rappelled from the chopper on the west side of the incursion. All he could see was a sea of demons in front of him. Katie was fighting her heart out, a small speck in the distance. He saw her sword fly out of her hand into the hole. He wanted to get to her, to help her, but the field of demons was too thick to push through. He growled and pulled his automatic rifle around from its place on his back.

"Compliments of humanity, bitches," he yelled as he pulled the trigger and sprayed the demons with bullets.

The special bullets tore into the demons, taking down five or six at a time. Calvin braced his feet and turned his spray right and left, destroying every demon in front of him. However, as soon as he was done with one line of the bastards they were replaced by another. He blasted the gun until it was out of bullets and threw it around his body onto his back.

He drew his pistols and fired with precision. Several of the demons flew back as they turned to dust, showering the other demons with ash. They didn't react, just continued to claw ever downward. The sound of a scream to his left made Calvin turn to find several people in the small town behind the rift fighting for their lives.

Without thought he took off into the yard, delivering a bullet to the back of each demon's heads as he got there.

"Thank you so much," the woman cried.

"Go inside, lock yourself away, don't come back out."

She nodded and backed into her house, shutting the door behind her. He figured if he couldn't help Pandora then he could do the next best thing, kill demons that were trying to kill the humans.

He marched through the town still loaded with weapons, shooting every demon he came across. Most of them seemed distracted, but that was not enough to get them away from the rage that was flowing through Calvin.

Through windows and half-cracked doors people stood with their phones out, filming Calvin fighting off the demons. Even away from the main area, a few angry demons were charging him. He pulled out his short sword and faced off against two of them with a growl. He didn't want to miss and kill an innocent by mistake, and he had more than enough experience fighting with the other weapons.

The first demon charged, and Calvin brought his sword up to cut the beast across the chest. The demon screeched, feeling the burn of the metal. Calvin didn't flinch. He ran straight at it, cutting off its head just as the beast sank his claws into Calvin's arm. He growled, the beast turning to ash, the claws falling out of Calvin's arm. He breathed heavily, his eyes bright red with anger as he swung around behind him, taking the head off the second demon as it charged him.

Calvin glanced at high school kid with wide eyes filming from under a small crack in his garage door. He shook his head slowly at the kid who slammed the door shut and locked it tight. Calvin had no idea how people could be filming shit like that when demons were tearing their neighbor's limbs off. His attention was pulled to the middle of the street when a young girl ran out screaming and swinging a cricket bat. Calvin ran over and put his hands up, trying to calm her.

"Hey, hey, calm down. What's going on?"

"My dad—he's in there with the demons."

Calvin looked at the house and then across the street. The neighbor had the door open, the woman calling to the girl. Calvin pushed her in that direction and pointed.

"Go hide. I'll take care of this."

Calvin took off into the house, not slowing down as he pulled a knife from his belt and jumped onto the back of the demon standing over her father. He slit the demon's throat and threw it to the side, looking around wildly. The man groaned, holding his arm, blood seeping from his leg.

"That's it. I killed the other one. He turned to dust."

Calvin nodded and reached down, easily helping the man to his feet. "Your daughter is quite the powerhouse with that bat."

"Yeah." The guy chuckled and grimaced at the pain. "She's a brill batter."

Calvin helped the man to the neighbor's house and let her take him in. He walked down the steps and stopped as the girl opened the door and ran out to him. She put her arms around him and hugged him tightly.

"Thank you so much. You are the angel we have been waiting for."

With that, she ran back into the house and locked the door. Calvin looked at the hordes of demons, Katie still fighting them off.

"No, that angel is still trying to get through."

F *uck, they just keep coming,* Pandora panted from inside. She was giving Katie everything she had, pushing her through the exhaustion, even swinging her sword for her at times. Pandora was switching back and forth with her, their minds twining. Neither knew at any moment who was on the outside and who was inside. The armies of beasts continued to march from the portal. Sweat dried on Katie's forehead as the heat poured over her. She grabbed her canteen from her belt and took a long swig, Pandora moving her other arm as she drank, jabbing at the beasts with her knife.

Katie swallowed and poured some of it over her head, steam rising off her shoulders. *I don't know what to do. we need to get the portal closed, but it's so huge that I'm not sure where to even start.*

To be honest, I don't know either. Even with my advantage, these bastards are way outnumbering us.

Katie dropped the canteen and slashed another demon's neck with her knife. Its blood splurted briefly, and it turned to dust. She was irritated by the situation and had few weapons left to fight with. Bloodied and bruised, her eyes flashed bright red, and the demons around her started to back up, hissing and whispering.

"*Daemon Ignis...*"

For fuck's sake, Pandora growled.

What now?

Apparently, my order for a guy with rock-hard abs and a big dick got confused with a request for big abs and a rock for a dick.

Uh...what?

Katie turned and watched as a stone creature emerged from the portal. Its eyes smoldered like lava, and so much heat radiated from it that the ground and all the dead bodies around the portal burst into flames. The thing was huge, fiery, and fucking *pissed*. She started to back up, her eyes wide, never having seen anything like it before.

That is one big hot motherfucker, and I don't mean attractive.

Yeah, he doesn't do so well with the ladies.

Katie watched as just the wave of his hand set a row of demons ablaze. He was like the sun, melting everything in his path. Katie scratched her forehead and continued to back up, not really wanting to be turned into a puddle of flesh.

How in the fuck are we supposed to fight something if we can't get near it?

We can't, that's the fucked-up part of it, Pandora replied. *Even in hell, even as Queen, this beast was dangerous. It has no fear or understanding of moral concepts. It is hot, angry because it's hot, and fucking hard to be around, mostly because he's fucking hot.*

So what the hell do we do?

Is it perhaps time that we make a strategic retreat?

You know I won't do that. There are people's lives on the line out here, and Calvin and I are the only ones fighting. We have to stick by these people and figure out how to take these bastards down. Come on, P, think! *There has to be something we can do with this guy. It's a possibility that we will go down out here, but I will go down fighting, I will* not *run away. We both knew that might be the only option we had one day, and we are going to face it with dignity and honor.*

Pandora sighed. *That's what I figured.*

Katie could feel Pandora gathering energy inside her, but she had no idea what she was doing. The tingling in her chest and the rush of power in her body made her almost woozy. She stumbled back and shook her head, blinking.

What the hell are you doing in there? I didn't mean kill me so this could be over.

Relax.

Right, because this is exactly the atmosphere conducive to relaxation.

Pay attention, little one. Focus.

Katie focused on the beast, but she had no idea why she was doing it. Pandora was acting weirder than normal, and the way her head was spinning, she was almost afraid that she was going to go down hard. She blinked her eyes several times as heat enveloped her. She felt like she needed to get away, but there was nowhere to go. She was stuck fighting something she didn't know how to fight while her demon was acting all kinds of strange. She was just about to come to the conclusion that things may not end the way they had in the past.

I told you to focus!

Katie shut her eyes and looked within, sensing the motions and feelings that Pandora was sending out. She switched back to the inside, giving Pandora the reins while she prepared for whatever she was about to do. Katie could hear Pandora reaching out, calling on the power inside her.

Mail Demones, Deorum et Angeli mihi exaudi preces. Scientia et undique intus. Angelus non incolunt in extrema rectae. De antecessoribus eius meditari fecissemus eget magicae, et cum alis Dei: et ut det telum quod auxilium sibi se in armis, hanc cladem malo, et mitte hoc daemon uidet inferos. Exaudi preces tabulae conectatur atque in manu de sancti Gabriel ego voco super te sentire ad eam vires ad eius interiorem fortitudinem.

Suddenly Katie was pulled back into her body, and a flash of light burst around her. Just the little bit of movement from body to soul caused Pandora to black out in pain. Katie opened her eyes and looked down, finding a long golden sword in her hand and armor on her body that looked like it belonged to a time period thousands of years before. At the same time, it could also have come from a thousand years in the future. She turned the sword over in her hands, and although it was solid and strong, it weighed nothing. Her armor had two chest plates, and on the back, a pair of golden wings.

On her head was a golden crown, the delicate filigree gracing her forehead and entwined with her hair. She furrowed her brow, unsure what had happened, when the beast behind her let out a high-pitched scream of frustration and fear. It turned to retreat through the portal, but the rift slammed shut, sensing Katie's angel. The rest of the demons were left to fend for themselves. She looked at the demons, who had stopped digging and were backing away from Katie. They knew what she was, and apparently, the fire demon knew as well.

Katie could only assume that the spell Pandora had performed was a simple push, and the armor and weapon she carried were sent from above.

Look at this shit! Pandora? Hey, are you okay?

Katie felt an immediate sense of panic. She couldn't contact Pandora, which had never happened before. She had always been in there, even if she was deep down inside hiding in the quiet of her soul. This time there was nothing; not a peep or a sound.

Katie looked down at the shimmering sword, and suddenly realized that calling the armor and the weapon must have messed the demon up. What had she done? Had she sacrificed her life? Her health? And all to keep Katie from dying in that field amongst the fire demon and the horde.

Katie shook her head, knowing that Pandora wasn't gone for good. All of the questions she had would have to wait to be answered. There was a huge demon stomping around setting shit on fire, and that bastard had forced Pandora to make a choice that hurt her badly. Katie's anger and resentment overflowed. She gripped the handle of the sword tightly and her whole body glowed with the energy whipping around her.

She opened her mouth and screamed her battle cry, lifting her sword to the sky as she sprinted into the fight.

She ran past the demon and swung, bashing a huge chunk of molten stone from its leg. The demon stumbled but kept moving. It tried to crush her as she raced around it, going faster than she had ever gone before. With every pass she swung the sword, carving larger and larger pieces from the demon's body. With every step she took, she felt the energy building in her chest.

"That is for all the fucking hell you are putting me through." Katie screamed her fury as she hacked a chunk out of its back and swung again at its leg. "And that—that one is for Pandora, because you caused her to fucking disappear, you fiery ball of lava shit!"

She screamed again and slashed at the demon's legs and thighs. She lashed out at its chest and arms, watching as the pieces crumbled away to smolder in the dirt. She crouched low and pushed off, jumping high into the air. She pulled the sword back behind her head, but before she could make the fatal blow the demon pounded Katie in the chest with its fist and sent her a good forty yards through the air. She hit the ground and rolled to a stop, sliding on her back. The demons took their chance and piled on.

Katie heaved under the weight of so many demons. The whole time she fought, the energy built until she felt like she would be torn apart by it if she didn't release it soon.

The Angelic Sonic Boom radiated outward, knocking all the demons around her into the air and sending them crashing into the others. She breathed heavily, unclenching her fists and opening one eye to peer down at herself. She half-expected to see her armor torn from the blow she took, but to her surprise, there wasn't even a scratch or a speck of dirt on it.

She raised her swirling blue and green eyes and began to swing her sword at every demon that was anywhere close to her. They screamed, but only until the blade met their scales and passed through like a knife through butter. Whatever that blade was made of, it was almost better than what Joshua had created. As soon as the sword hit their flesh, they exploded into a pile of ash. All around her there were dust clouds from the demons she was killing.

She looked at the fire demon and smirked. She darted across the cleared area and leapt, slamming her armored body into the beast. They traded blows, Katie taking them with ease. She opened the demon's belly with her sword and knocked it to the ground. It grumbled and stood back up, pushing the heat of its body outward. Katie put up her arm and covered her face with her vambraces.

She opened her eyes as the fire and heat streamed around and over her, almost as if she were encased in a protective bubble, the grass burning except around her feet. The demon looked over, expecting to see her charred remains, but Katie stood there stronger than ever.

She stared the demon down, ready to end the war she was fighting. She shifted her sword back and forth in her hands and took her stance, everything she had practiced in the gym coming back to her.

She leapt through the air, bringing the sword down into the demon's shoulder and nearly taking off its arm. The beast screamed. Everywhere the sword touched, it left burnt flesh and stone. She chuckled, watching the big lug follow her around him with his eyes. Pandora was waking up, and she backed up slowly, clearing a path, then sprinted straight at the beast.

She dove at it with her sword at the ready and Pandora added even more power to the sword as it swung. The blade connected with the demon's neck and sliced its head off its shoulders. The head rolled across the grass and the body broke apart like a crumbling building. Katie landed in a crouch and watched as the huge fire demon disintegrated.

Pandora, on the other hand, was done. She had used the last little bit of her power to help the sword cut through the demon's neck. She had sacrificed her strength, not just to save Katie from damnation, but also to help the rest of the innocent people hiding in attics and cellars all over the English countryside. It was the biggest sacrifice Pandora had ever made.

That's all I got, Pandora wheezed. *I'm sorry. I'll chat with you later. Right now I've got to sl...*

Katie chuckled, relieved that Pandora was okay. *Night, sister.*

She turned to the rest of the beasts still milling around. She concentrated and began the killing dance again. With each step Katie took, demons turned to dust.

In the background, the military were starting to land as she battled the demons around her. The sword made all the difference, sending the beasts plummeting back to hell, caught so deep in the depths they wouldn't see another battle for a very long time.

The military exited their choppers and planes and started setting up on the hill. Katie huffed and puffed as she cut through necks and bashed in skulls, but she could hear the rattle of semi-automatic weapons firing into the village behind her. They had finally arrived and were ready to help, only to find that the battle was pretty much done.

Baal and Moloch sat in large overstuffed chairs wrapped in silk robes, watching the action happening live. They both had munchies in bowls in their laps, Moloch's being his favorite deep-fried hamsters, and Baal opting for organic turtle heads. They laughed and pointed at the different battles and deaths flashing across the screen. The soldiers apparently couldn't figure out why the demons were digging, and Moloch remarked, "Humans. Give them something and they will make up all sorts of stories. I love fucking with them."

When the video of Katie came up they both leaned forward, watching as a bright light flashed around her and she was suddenly cloaked in angelic armor. Their mouths dropped open and Baal cringed, hoping Moloch wasn't about to flip his lid.

"We...might have been played," Baal hissed.

The two demons put their snacks down on the floor and closed their eyes, focusing on the battle in England where they knew Katie was fighting. That was supposed to be the easy one, Moloch having sent almost all of the troops in to get a different kind of education—the kind where they turned and burned, taking out anything in their way. They focused harder, searching for their demons, and realizing the entire portal had clapped shut.

"It's bad there," Moloch replied. "But no, I don't think we were played for fools. This is bad, though. The last time, we burnt our problem at the stake. I remember the smell of flesh rolling off it, the golden armor sparkling and hissing until the life was dragged out of everyone involved. Of course, burning Lilith at the stake would be a nearly impossible feat, so that probably won't be the direction we go. Again, these two show up out of nowhere and thwart my plans. England was supposed to be my crowning moment, but no! This bitch rolls in like she owns the place, and now we are watching the rest of the soldiers go down hard. I should have sent higher-level demons through to fight. Now I have these morons who don't know their ass from their elbow and would die within the first three seconds if they didn't have something to focus on. We need a solution to this issue right now."

Baal, a frown on his face, leaned in. "Got an Angel? Get a Leviathan."

Moloch let out a deep sigh and shook his head, picking up his bowl and sitting back. "Like it's that easy? If that were the case, we would have taken care of this long before, don't you think? This isn't 1-800 Get a Monster or something like that, Baal."

Baal shrugged. "I really don't think it is that bad. I think she hurt your pride, but she can't be everywhere. We deal and cut our losses on incursions like this one, but revel in the bloody battles at the other places. How many have we destroyed so far?"

Moloch smirked and rubbed his hands together. "Thousands. I should show you my new screaming souls collection. They sound so delicious. I designed the entire thing so that my office is always filled with the songs of my lost souls. I can mute them if I don't want to listen.

It's fabulous background music while I'm working; very tranquil, and it helps me focus. You should really start one for yourself. I know it would bring you all sorts of joy."

"I'd rather start 1-800 Monsters." Baal laughed. "At least then I could make some money and provide a valuable service for demons like you and me. Katie or Lilith or Pandora, whatever they are calling themselves, would be out of mind right now if we had known the truth."

"Yes, but that is not how it went, and I am determined to set my sights on the realistic. We could call the biggest, most powerful demon in the area, and Lilith would out-fight, out-sass, and outdo herself every single time. We will take care of her in due time, but for now, you are right—let them have one of many incursions every time we send out portals. It will make them think she is taking down crime, but in reality, we are using decoys and distractions while creating the perfect plan and collecting the souls left behind."

"I believe you have just become a guru." Baal laughed. "But that plan is perfect. Keep them guessing and chasing. Eventually, they will figure it out. They always do. Until then, we will run them in circles. One of the blows ahead will be the fatal one, leaving Earth ripe for the picking."

———

Calvin swiped his sword through the demon's neck and kicked him hard in the chest. He panted heavily, going through the motions of trying to clear the fields. He could hear screeches of pain around him. When the screeches ceased he chuckled, hearing Katie bitching as she cut through the beasts.

"I finally get to fucking come to England, and I have to deal with you bastards," she yelled as she decapitated another demon. "On top of that, you bring Uncle Freddy, the fat guy with the hot breath who ended up knocking my demon the fuck out. I am so sick and tired of dealing with you bastards. Will you all just fucking die and get this over with? Please!"

After about an hour of turning demons to dust, they finished out the section they were so diligently hacking away at. It happened to be the largest section, the one with the pile of demons trying to dig their way to China or whatever it was they were doing. Calvin walked up to Katie, who was standing with her sword resting on her shoulder, wiping the sweat from her brow.

Calvin lifted an eyebrow and looked her up and down. "Nice armor. You kind of look like She-Ra or the original Wonder Woman. You holding out on me?"

Katie shrugged and stabbed the last demon in the chest. It was lying on the ground taking far too long to die, and Katie had lost all patience. "It seems Gabriel wasn't shitting around about the sword and armor. The problem is, it almost killed Pandora to make it happen."

Calvin shook his head and stuck his knife back into his belt. "Not a good exchange. She is pretty much the most important one out of all of us, no offense."

"None taken. She kicks major fucking ass. She's a pain in the ass, but worth it."

"Yeah, life wouldn't be so annoying without her." Calvin

grinned. "Though I'm not sure she would say the same about me."

Katie laughed. "I think she would. She just plays hard to get at everything, including friendships. She's a demon, so it's a slow progression for her. She's advanced by leaps and bounds since the beginning."

"I agree, but I would be sad if she was gone."

Pandora started to wake up just as they were praising her, saying things that, even though she wouldn't ever admit, touched her cold, dark, black heart. On the inside she was ashamed for not telling Katie earlier about the armor and weapon when they could have saved her a lot of grief and stress. She had almost been killed that day, standing in the field with no idea how to take out a fire demon. She had said she would fight to the death, and Pandora knew that if she hadn't been so stubborn, if she hadn't fought angel things so hard, Katie would never have gotten to the point where she would accept defeat. However, no matter how bad she felt, she couldn't bring herself to express those feelings to Katie—at least not yet. Calvin, on the other hand, was a little bit easier to handle.

Pandora jumped into the conversation, taking over Katie's voice for just a moment.

"I heard that, big man. Keep it up, and I'll make you so long Sofia will have a screaming orgasm yelling your name in San Diego while you are still in Las Vegas."

Calvin looked at Katie for a moment, who shrugged and pointed at her chest, letting him know that was all Pandora. The three of them let out a deep bellowing laugh, enjoying the relief it brought them. The last of the demons were wiped out by the military who were sweeping the area, helping survivors and making sure no more of the beasts were hiding in closets or basements.

Calvin walked over and put his arm around her shoulder. "You know, the three of us will never just go down in a ball of flames."

Hell, no. I'd definitely pee on you if you were on fire, buddy.

Katie chuckled. "Pandora said if you are ever aflame, she will be more than happy to pee on you."

Calvin grimaced, trying not to picture that. "Oh, so Pandora is into the super-weird freaky shit. I bet she likes feet, too."

Now he's going a little too far. I can reverse that earlier promise; don't let him forget that. This girl has got game.

A ngie and Katie walked through the doors of the police department, Katie nodding at the front desk clerk as he pressed the button to let the two of them walk back. This time neither of them were dressed for battles or clubs, but were instead decked out in business attire. Angie was wearing her brand-new black rimmed glasses. Katie thought they made her look smart, but Pandora thought the two of them looked like the beginning of some skanky porno in a police station. The sight of Jim, the twenty-year veteran with a belly bigger than Buddha, shook that thought immediately from Pandora's mind as they walked in.

Katie was in a great mood, knowing that she was going to make Angie run the show. If she was going to be the go-to for the new business, Katie wanted to know that she could command the attention of a group of men watching and waiting for her to screw up. She had to get tougher skin, and in their line of work, she had to be able to stand up to a bunch of assholes.

They walked through the precinct, all eyes on them, and nodded at Travers, who held the door to the conference room and walked in behind them. These cops were hard-nosed but respectful, and waited patiently as they set out the information and demonstrated the new product. Angie handed the notes to Katie, but she shook her head, pushing them back toward her.

"This one is all you, girl. You did the work, you understand the system, you sell it."

She looked a little nervous, but very excited. She turned to the group and clapped her hands to get their attention.

"Good morning! My name is Angie, and for those of you that don't know me, I work with your favorite neighborhood merc, Katie. I know your time is precious, so we are just going to cut straight to the chase, no fillers and no bullshit."

"I like this woman already," one of the guys told his partner, leaning back and crossing his arms.

Angie winked and turned to the display board on the easel beside her. "We are offering the opportunity to have twenty-four hour service providing potential demon incursion information. This service is not only superior in quality, but it is also faster than the service provided by the government at this time. Now, if you remember the incursion in Brooklyn at the complex over the historical cemetery, you have already worked with our main guy. Timothy is a computer genius, and he is in the intel center at all hours of the day. He has created a system that can track excess energy and heat the second it develops. He then can zoom in and pinpoint the exact coordinates where that portal, gate, person, or demon is located."

She flipped the board and pointed at the picture of the building in Brooklyn.

"For example, during the Brooklyn incursion, he was able to give the exact location, potential size of the gate, and floor that the gate opened on in five minutes on the phone with the so-called experts. Hours before the military could pinpoint the English incursion, and long before they even recognized the heat signature, Timothy had called General Brushwood and let him know where to search. He delivered two large incursions into the government's hands within minutes and never set foot outside his office."

She smiled and flipped the board to more specific information.

"Right now the system is in the trial stages, but don't let the word 'trial' fool you. This is the same system that detected the English incursion the very first night it was tested. These things usually take months or sometimes years to get working, and then they go through tests, more tests, and then trials. This system is so good that the word trial is just a formality. Those who wish to sign up for this program will be a part of a research group to prove how much faster Timothy's information is than the government's, and possibly how much *better* it is as well. Everyone knows that in these situations that accuracy is paramount."

"Sounds fantastic, like something the entire world would want," one of the guys remarked. "But the big question is, how much does it cost?"

Angie smiled and leaned against the desk. "For you and the rest of the officers here, the price is $100k per month."

Several of the cops whistled and fanned themselves.

"Okay, what's the reduced price, since this is a trial and everything."

Angie smiled and stood back up, tapping her pen in her palm. "That *is* the reduced price, down from $250k per month. That's over fifty percent off."

"I don't know, that's a lot of fucking money for someone to do something just a little faster than a service we get for free. Why would we pay that much more for it?"

"Yeah, we already use our tax dollars. How much faster could this possibly be."

Angie put up her hands to calm the masses. "Let me ask you something… If it was your house the demons were porting in next to, how many minutes' head start would you want the support teams to have? Do you want them to show up when the demons are already hanging out with your wife and kids, or do you want them there, guns drawn, blasting them away as soon as that portal opens? Personally, I would want them already there so I don't have to put down my bonbons and miss my shows."

The guys chuckled, talking back and forth with each other. Katie smiled and nodded at Angie before stepping forward.

"How about this? If we don't give you a fifty percent better timeframe, we will do the service for $10k a month instead? That means you are still getting the service, but you are paying way less, and with the possibility of us still being faster than the government. On top of that, you get to deal with Angie instead of the general. I would argue that Angie is a little easier to deal with than Brushwood, but then again, she can be a tyrant."

"Tyrants turn Thomas on. He can't get enough of them."

"Ha-ha." Thomas laughed and threw a piece of paper at the guy.

Everyone chuckled and talked about the product a little more. They were interested, there was no doubt about it, but the price was damn steep even if it was coming from the budget and not their own pockets. They already had a hard time collecting overtime, much less asking for a system that would cost a million dollars a year to run.

"Are you letting the price get in the way of personal safety, safety for your families, and safety for your loved ones and the community?" Katie asked, lifting an eyebrow.

"Okay, okay," the chief called. "Everyone settle down. Just to make this crystal clear so that I understand, if we give the contract to you and you give it to us in eight minutes, then they give it to us in four?"

Katie held back a chuckle. "No. It means if we give it to you in eight, they take twelve or more."

"So, that means if the government takes forty-five minutes to tell us, you guys would have to let us know within thirty minutes," the chief said, trying to make sure he fully understood.

"Yep, that's the deal. If that doesn't happen, we give it to you for $10k a month instead of a $100k. We are sure of this system, and even surer of the guy who not only created it but monitors everything twenty-four hours a day. He created an app that does the same thing on a smaller scale, to use along with this program. It will allow him to step away from the office, to sleep, shower, shop, or whatever, and still be able to monitor what is going on from the comfort of his cell phone. He is pretty much a genius."

The chief nodded and looked at his officers. "Would you two mind stepping out for just a second? I just want to go over it with the others."

"Sure thing." Katie nodded as she and Angie left the room and closed the door behind them.

"Well, that was terrifying."

Katie smiled at Angie. "No one would have ever known you were scared. You were assertive, funny, and interactive with those guys. That is how I want you to continue to work. There will hopefully be a lot more appointments in the future."

"I like this part of things. I never thought I would. I guess living in that apartment barely getting by, squashed by the troll of a man, I never took the time to picture myself as a businesswoman or personal assistant or jack-of-all-trades. I didn't want to daydream about things that I never in a million years thought could be true. I stuck with reality, and knew the best thing I could do was just go one day at a time."

"I can understand that. When I was first Damned, I didn't think there would be anything else in my life. I thought fighting demons, training, and more training were what I would spend my days doing until I was gone. I tried not to think about futures I couldn't achieve, but then something happened. I started to feel more confident about myself."

"Me too." Angie smiled. "The moment you carried me away, I started to feel more confident. Then you gave me the chance to show you that I could be the woman I think you saw in me before I even saw her in myself. The opportunities seem to be limitless, and if I haven't said it before, thank you for that. I never really had anyone in my life who believed in me, or felt that I could be more than what I was. It's a good feeling waking up in the morning knowing there is so much more for me out there, and all I have to do is work hard and grab the opportunities."

"Good." Katie smiled as the door to the conference room opened. "I want you to feel like you can do anything. This project—it's just a start, but it was your brainchild. You and Timothy came up with something I would have never thought of. I'm just the money in this situation."

"That's not true." She chuckled. "You were the motivator and the person who said, 'Yes this can be done, and I want you to do it.' Otherwise, it would have just been some silly pipe dream. It still feels like a dream, and Timothy even said that on the phone yesterday. He couldn't seem to wrap his head around the fact that he created something this big, this helpful, and this important. It's a double whammy. You make money, and you help people."

The women were ushered back in and they stood at the front of the room, watching the others mumbling under their breaths about the new program. The chief stood up and waved his hand for them to sit.

"We love your inspiration, we love your enthusiasm, and we especially love the idea of heading off demon incursions, lessening the casualties, and keeping us on our toes. So, we have decided that you have your first buyer. Congratulations. We will get everything set up with Procurement, and then you can go over the exact details of how everything works."

Katie and Angie nodded excitedly, shocked that it had actually worked in such a short timeframe.

"We are so happy to work with you, and you will see. You will be the groundbreakers for a new, faster way of finding demons before any more precious lives are lost. Thank you, people."

Angie was starting to come into her own, and it looked as though she was going to be a force to be reckoned with. She had made her first corporate grand slam, a million-dollar-a-year contract, and a product that she was proud to have been part of. Looking back just months before, if she would have been told she would be there signing those contracts she would have laughed and walked away. Once she was there, though, there wasn't anything in the world that was going to hold her back—and Katie was right there beside her.

Katie leaned back against the seat of the jet and yawned, pulling her arms up over her head and stretching. She was exhausted, and had fallen asleep almost immediately after takeoff. She looked out the window, realizing they were making their descent. She saw Las Vegas in the distance, and sand everywhere else.

Calvin looked at her and smiled. "Good morning there, rockstar." He smiled. "Have a good nap?"

"Mmm, I did, and I didn't even dream. It was just good, solid, no-frills sleep. How about you? Too excited to see your lady to get any shut-eye?"

Calvin chuckled. "Something like that. I'm just happy to be home, I missed Vegas, the base, the people...everything.

When Sofia said she was going to meet me here instead of San Diego it was like music to my ears."

"I know Timothy is going to be happy to see us. He is waiting for me to tell him how our first sales pitch went."

"It made him rich, that's how it went." Calvin cackled. "I wonder how many pairs of alligator dress shoes he will own after he starts getting paid?"

Katie shrugged. "I don't know, but it is up to him. He can wear whatever he likes."

Calvin nodded out the window. "Home Sweet Home."

Katie smiled at how little contrast the base was to the luxury condo she had been spending all her time in recently. It wasn't about the fashion or the art, it was the fact that both places, no matter what was going on, felt like home. A place where she could walk in, kick off her shoes, have a glass of wine, and no one was going to question her about anything.

After the plane touched down, they climbed down the steps and out onto the runway. Waiting there was Sofia. She bobbed up and down excitely, then raced over to throw herself into Calvin's arms. He dropped his suitcase on the ground and wrapped his arms around her, picking her up and squeezing her tightly. She kissed him on the lips and smiled, feeling like she had been away from him forever.

"Hi there," she gushed as he set her down. "How was England? I heard it was quite the party."

"Oh yeah." Calvin laughed. "Me and about a thousand of my closest friends. We had some real good conversations. Did the electric slide a couple times, got drunk. You know, the normal..."

Sofia laughed. "Well, you are back, and I am still in one piece."

"I see that, and I am really glad. The whole you is much easier to handle then if I had to lug around pieces."

She giggled and kissed him again, looking back at Korbin and Stephanie. Calvin looked up at them and smiled, walking over and putting his hand out.

"Thank you again for watching out for her."

"Easiest assignment of our lives." Korbin laughed. "We got to chill on the beach and didn't have to fight a single person."

"And Stephanie came and had sleepovers to make sure I was safe at night."

"Uh oh, watch out. She will steal your girl."

"Not quite." Stephanie laughed, putting her arm around Korbin. "I already got a stubborn one to call my own."

Calvin chuckled. "You noticed she was stubborn."

"Hey, I'm just strong-minded," Sofia bit back. "You coming inside, or do I have to drag you?"

"I'm coming." Calvin laughed, looking at Korbin and Stephanie. "You guys coming in?"

Stephanie shook her head. "Just give us a couple of minutes, and we will be right there."

Calvin winked and nodded, seeing Katie walking down the steps of the airplane. "We'll see you inside."

Katie walked over to the luggage area and hooked her bag onto her shoulder.

Uh oh, looks like the gang's all here. Do you want to take bets on whether you will get punched or hugged?

Even when Korbin was my hard-headed boss, he wouldn't have punched me.

I'm talking about the Madam, Miss Stephanie.

Katie chuckled to herself. *She's too good for that.*

She started toward Korbin and Stephanie, butterflies fluttering around in her stomach. She stopped in front of them and looked each of them in the eyes, first Korbin, then Stephanie. She could feel the tears welling up in her eyes, and she dropped her bag and ran forward to hug them both tightly.

They hugged her back, not a bit of animosity in their hearts. They didn't remember Katie, that was true, but they could feel the love between them and they could sense the familiarity, something that didn't happen very often.

"I suppose you both need to catch up on the soaps?"

"What, you mean the angels and demons one?" Stephanie asked. "I watch that every day. Was so strange—I woke up one morning in my new house with my new husband sleeping beside me, and I just couldn't get them out of my mind. I binge-watched the first half of the season and then pulled Korbin into it."

"You would be surprised to know he used to watch them with us."

"I'm actually not surprised at all. He gives that face, but I know deep down he really enjoys them."

Korbin rolled his eyes and looked at the two of them, Stephanie's arm around Katie's waist. "Were you two like this when we were here with you?"

"Of course." Katie smiled. "Besties to the end. We kicked some major demon ass together, made a bunch of money, and worried the hell out of you at every turn."

"Why does that not surprise me? I can see the two of you getting into trouble that would make my eyes rattle."

"That was why we didn't tell you. Only the good parts."

Stephanie grinned at Korbin, and he looked at her fondly. "You too? Am I going to have to separate the two of you?"

"I think Timothy will be trying to do that before you can. He is really your biggest competition."

Korbin sighed. "Come on, show me this base I designed. I need to see how amazing I really am."

They laughed, and Katie slung her bag over her shoulder again, put her arms around both of them, and walked them all toward the elevator. The sun was setting in the background, cascading oranges and reds across the sky. Everything was exactly how it was supposed to be, and the base never felt more familiar to Katie. She was home, and she had most of her family by her side. Now all she had to do was figure out how to get her badass armor back without killing Pandora.

Hey, don't get too wild, Pandora teased. *I don't know if I like that angel warrior look on you. I'm sure there's something else out there that would suit our personality just a little better.*

Are you already trying to change my new gear? It makes me look like a Roman goddess. You should like the idea of looking like a goddess.

Hey, gold is out, and badass is totally in.

First, THANK YOU for not only reading this story, but our *Author Notes* as well!

If you are part of the Protected by the Damned Facebook group, you probably already know this. If not, why not join us? You get to see lots of Dessert Porn (the fun to eat stuff, not the sandy place.)

With that kind of marketing, how could you not join? It's right here:

http://www.facebook.com/groups/320172985053521/

I put the cover from this book into the group to get a couple of opinions, and #@@%#% did we get a few opinions! However, the results that I found out included:

1) Awesome!
2) Don't you dare be telling us someone major died.
3) Where is the staff?
4) We need some smudges!

All of these (and others) were read and reviewed. We did change it up some (see staff, smudges) but the main question I wanted to resolve was, "Did it look right?"

Did we have a powerful cover to convey the series, when most of our stuff has been "focus on looking badass... Not beaten."

So, I want to THANK the fans who are in the group for giving me my answer so quickly, and then continuing (not everyone was "hooray!" – but there was a good discussion amongst many. In the end, I have to choose as I think best, but the input was considered.)

In this book, we have accomplished what MANY (mainly the ladies) wanted. Katie was able to open her heart a bit again.

I won't even go into what Pandora thought of it.

Next book, Katie has to fight a 'new' player...and no one, not even ancient historians, thought she was real.

See you next book!

Ad Aeternitatem,
Michael Anderle

AUTHOR NOTES - LAURIE STARKEY

AUGUST 2, 2018

Hey there! Thanks so much for picking up another *Damned* book. That's just a little too fun to say. It's like a running joke around here. Everything feels *Damned*, but in a good way.

You don't hear that often, do you?

This series is just getting better and better. I love that we've taken something with a negative connotation and given it a different spin within the realm of fiction. That's what a good book does, though. It gives us a safe place to visit, to play, to retreat to.

Hopefully, you're finding that in this series. I know Michael and I are.

In other news... We've been to Minnesota, Chicago, Lake Michigan, St. Louis, Toronto, and finally we're in New York state now. We did a few days here, a week there, a day trip here, and now a month in NY.

I'm wishing like hell it was a little cooler, but it's beautiful up here. We're looking forward to a month of downtime. It's been a crazy few years, and not that this month won't be nutty, but I *promised* myself and hubs that I would try to step back and relax some this month.

We're in a small town with a few shops, a shitty little grocery store, and too many houses for one block. It's ninety minutes to the big city, which we plan on visiting a few times, but I'm thrilled to be tucked away.

I'm going to read some good books, write a few myself, and try to figure out this meditation thing. My brain revolts the minute I get in downward dog or sit Indian-style. Go figure...

I hope your summer has been full of memories. I feel like June and July raced by without even blinking an eye, but so have the last forty years. Anyone else? Ha!

Enjoy the series. There's more to come, and we're moving deeper and deeper into our side stories that are coming your way this fall. I appreciate you picking this book up. My hope is that it gave you a *Damned* good ride for your dollar.

What? I couldn't help it...

Slave to Many Stories,

Laurie Starkey

BOOKS WRITTEN AS MICHAEL ANDERLE

For a complete list of books by Michael Anderle, please visit:

www.lmbpn.com/ma-books/

All LMBPN Audiobooks are Available at Audible.com and iTunes

To see all LMBPN audiobooks, including those written by
Michael Anderle please visit:

www.lmbpn.com/audible

www.ingramcontent.com/pod-product-compliance
Lightning Source LLC
Chambersburg PA
CBHW031624100726
47898CB00006B/1944